Find the author:
E-mail: troy@chaoswords.com
Twitter: @chaoswords
Facebook: Chaoswords
Website: www.Chaoswords.com

Copyright © 2017 by Troy Kirby
Cover design: Valdas Miskinis

Library of Congress Control Number: 2017910900

ISBN 0-9835184-0-8

ISBN 978-0-9835184-0-2

Printed in The United States of America

This book is dedicated to the memory of a true friend
Scott Marion Sawyer (1972-2009).
I miss you, pal.

"Jefferson!"

1 Sugar was the drug of choice for Sideville State
Correctional inmates. Seven hundred residents
of *The Sides* valued sucrose higher than cocaine,
heroin or cigarettes. South American contraband in
prison had profit. But coke did not earn as much revenue as sugar
packets. General population had inmates stabbed for it. *Slinging cane*
had respect in the Rathdrum, Idaho prison. And minimum security
inmate Frank Gryzbowsky handled the trade as an art form.

Lifer Brian Tuttle owned the sugar racket and Frank was his best
earner. *You gotta know people. Empathize with customers, expect
their needs; the rules of business.* Frank and his partner Vic Ramsey
increased sales. Narcotics added years to an inmate's sentence or
good time taken away. But sucrose deals were not illicit. *Wonderful
shades of gray that people keep telling me about.*

Each corrections officer took a *taste* from the action. Worst among
the guards was Chief Corrections Officer Steve Powers. When the
man questioned a con, either the inmate answered or received a
thumped skull.

Powers spotted Frank dealing at the far end of the corridor. Shark
eyes, focused, glaring. The man running *The Sides* approached as
inmates moved apart, silent with respect. Powers blocked Frank's
movement. Offered him a stare down. *Man wants my money, what
the locals call 'paper.'* Powers rested his nightstick against Frank's

head. *Gonna sock me one for saying no.*

"How much you make today, Gryzbowsky?"

"In paper or trade?"

Powers said, "What's the difference?"

"Credit lines change the game," Frank said. "Tack on ten percent juice pushes to fifteen in twenty-four if they haven't paid up."

"How much on you?" Powers said. Snatched Frank's money roll. Let his nightstick tap Frank's temple light. A silent warning for Frank to *be cool.* Checked the roll with his thumb, then waved Frank free to continue dealing down the corridor. "Glad you see the big picture, Frank."

Deals at *The Sides* offered treks through long corridors. Sections where the heating did not work. Cold blasts of air down the hallways made Frank's arms chill. Each end meant staring into a security camera eye, then buzzed into the section. Vic Ramsey waited a few doors down. Vic eyed Powers suspicious, tailing Frank.

"What did he take?" Vic said.

"All of what he thought I had," Frank said. His palm touched his pants where a larger money roll hid in the pocket. "You got to see the big picture."

When they strolled through *The Sides* minimum security dormitory, Vic walked stiff. *Fella can't help it.* Vic was from the Virgin Islands. Man's dealing skills were fine, his company made sales easier for Frank. *Vic speaks his English as jazz lyrics. The notes go in different places than you expect.*

"I got cold bones," Vic said. "I should have done the job in Miami without guys dropping pleas on me. Ninety-seven and dry when I did the bank."

"The thermo goes upside down for Christmas."

"I need to earn," Vic said, nodding. "Money is money, man."

He knows the business. Sugar at *The Sides* rivaled the New York Stock Exchange. A packet went for ten dollars. But when the prison staff was late with fresh supply, the price jumped. An endless customer base devoured supplies, pushed demand. *Adam Smith, I see you smiling.* Any con could read *The Wealth of Nations* through *The Sides* extension course in the prison library. The state required inmates to take correspondence courses to improve themselves. *I got a business background on the state's dime.*

The prison housed the country's largest population of methamphetamine convicts. Created the market for sugar deals and superseded street drug sales. Sucrose produced comparative body chemistry highs as *amp* or *white crunch*. Inmates used it to withdraw from meth while serving out a sentence. What the locals called *"sucrose doping"* offered a heavy crash similar to using out on the street.

Transferred from county in early October, Frank had dismissed dealing. *Then the money rolled past my eyes.* The local grocery sold a four-thirty-six packet box. For five and a quarter, a guard would sell to Frank for half their weekly salary. A box sold out in twenty minutes at the medium security wing. In the minimum security dormitory, the inventory liquidated in ten minutes. On rare occasions, Frank sold sugar cubes. Buyers dropped to their knees, let him provide each with an open mouth communion. A kitchen staff member tossed Frank a box of C & H Brown Sugar Cane for baking cookies. Sold it in two minutes for three hundred bucks.

The Sides Administration became aware of sugar dealing as sales increased. The overall sucrose market was depressed. The kitchen dealt five free packets to each inmate at dinner daily. Budget cutbacks at the kitchen limited packet distribution to one per inmate for each meal. The price of a packet jumped to fifty-two bucks. Two weeks later, the kitchen switched from sugar to inexpensive artificial sweetener. The switch did not provide the meth-addled inmates with the same sucrose high. *The Sides* increased screening protocols and limited the traffic of new boxes to Brian Tuttle's dealers. The decision caused two inmate suicides and a small riot. The outcome forced the kitchen to return to a five packets per inmate policy. New inmate admission processes were reduced and the asking rate for a packet returned to ten dollars.

"Be thankful you don't sell purol," Frank said to Vic. "Dealer has to test it on someone."

Purol stench was strongest at the end of the medium security wing. Eye-watering odors of hooch hung where cons did twenty-five year stretches. Hardcore alcoholics favored the dank liquid. None of those group therapy sessions offered any illusion of recovery for those men. They downed three-hundred-eighty proof swill of mixed orange peels, corn mash and mold. *Cut with tap water it tastes worse.*

Frank's eyes zeroed in on purol hiding places. Laundry nooks with nasty humidity. To Vic: "You remember what I told you about not getting caught out on the open, right?"

Vic nodded, eyes bugged, serious. "Yeah, man, they want me to drink their shit, test it out. No go, man."

"You're damned right," he said. *Some poor lifer complaining of dimmed vision and a new heart condition.*

"They got two newbies last week," Vic said; thumb gesturing back to the medium security wing. "Four guys, they hold them down. Make 'em drink."

"Someone's got to be the guinea pig and gasp if they taste the foreshot," Frank said.

Vic shook his head. "Can't be me, man. I like my eyes. My ticker be fine."

"The shakes come down on you from a lifetime of drinking and you don't have a choice," Frank said.

"You didn't look so hot, I remember."

"That bad?"

"Not so well, I guess," Vic said.

Frank's *Sides* arrival culminated blowing point-one-fifty-two on a white stick. Got a cold turkey detox in the Kootenai County Jail after a state patrolman flashed a pullover of Howie Sims' Escalade. *The police noticed the invisible ink on the SUV saying it was D.W.B: "Driving While Black."* Speedometer hitting ninety-three, down the middle of the yellow line to escape the gangsta's party. Frank was at Howie's party to fix a clogged basement toilet. Had a tool box and nursed a fifth of vodka. *Didn't know Howie was on the "down-low." Found out by opening the bathroom door. Howie looking up from his man at me, pissed.* Sims wouldn't allow his fellow thugs to discover his secret life. Frank panicked at what Sims might do. He stole Howie's SUV and sped away.

The state patrolman put the cuffs on Frank. Tossed him into a cruiser. Frank tried to remember bus bench advertisements of ambulance chasing lawyer or bail bondsman's phone numbers. Eyes on the patrolman as he searched the SUV. Frank figured the heat might find a little weed in the backseat. Maybe some pills. The officer produced a nine millimeter. Displayed it for Frank. *Stone-cold sobriety when my eyes caught the gun.* The legal hammer fell on Frank's head for the unregistered weapon. The judge's gavel came down for a felony. Moved Frank from a county stay into hard time at *The Sides*.

Frank's thoughts floated around booze. *The last beer I drank.* He dreamt of *Grey Goose* bottles opened. *The charcoal flavor of Jack poured from the heavens into my mouth.* Subconscious images of shot glasses lined along a bar counter. *Shots of Wild Turkey* hugging the yellow line of the glass enough to be sipped before being picked up between a finger and thumb. *I understand my sugar buyers because of my own demons. We're slaves to different vices.*

February afternoons sat cold; this Sunday no exception. Frank's supply ran low after seventeen minutes in the minimum security dormitory. Three boxes of packets sold to people withdrawing from *Speed Racer* or *Smurf Dope*. Each hid evidence of meth mouth smile. *Beast is a hard one to kick even on the streets. Harder still in lockup.* Frank listened to the circular talk of the prison. *Every con speaks in those ghetto plurals. Plans to visit their 'moms' after they're paroled.*

Vic to Frank: "Should we resupply?"

Frank eyed convict stragglers in the dorm. They eyed the dealing suspicious. Worried about entrapment by the guards or a beatdown by fellow inmates while they were preoccupied in the sugar sale. *Once they trust the situation, they'll come.* "Take mine. I'll do re-up. Meet back with you in ten, get some of that lifer chow."

Vic took the supply. Sold packets to an inmate serving time for arson. *A trusted con is rare.* Criminals serving time told of being burned by the cops or a witness at trial. None of them accepted their prison arrival to be of their own accord. *People make shitty choices; Convicts magnify theirs'.* Frank felt he was no different. But he had his moments. Personality covered his imperfections of small shoulders, a weak mustache and ruined hair. *My charm changes people's expectations of me.*

His face bore acne scars. Frank's tenure at paratrooper school in Louisiana produced his only morning exercise routine. Hangover severity never eliminated fifty sit-ups, pull-ups and a variation of Hindu yoga picked up from a Las Vegas Ashram. He displayed a hunch when his walk was considered unimportant. Frank figured life was a pain in the ass with no illusions of being less than a miserable failure at the pursuit.

Frank's livelihood in the outside world had been as a journeyman plumber but he was canned for constant absenteeism. It forced him to become self-employed as an unlicensed independent. Picked up jobs by low-balling the competition with quick-fix alternatives. *Never would have witnessed Howie Sims' alternative lifestyle if the man had only asked to see my non-existent license.* Frank shook off regret and chance. *No use thinking that way at The Sides. Doesn't help me at all.*

The dreams of alcohol subsided once Frank was recruited into Brian Tuttle's sugar organization. *I'm supplied with the stuff.* The alternative made him shudder. *Glasses filled with purol that would dim my vision. Or waiting for a heart attack to end this miserable life.* Every inmate had choices how to survive in prison. *I'm a con of two institutions; the state and Tuttle. Gotta always make good choices. Otherwise I'll regret it for the rest of my life in here.*

Brian's last dealer, Eric, made the wrong choice. A strong sugar supply needed Tuttle's dealers to serve as prison kitchen trustees. Eric fashioned himself as an unpaid comedian. *Man tosses detergent into the food at chow time. Several inmates start puking. Every con investigating what trustee caused a bleeding assholes epidemic. The Sides* had an unwritten rule: Do not mess with another inmate's food. Five inmates went to the infirmary, each heard Eric laughing and claiming responsibility. Man's humor didn't get a large fan base. A gang took turns beating Eric with a can of jack mackerel in a sock. *Man's jaw wired shut.* Eric got diesel therapy down to Boise Correctional as a reward. Word spread to Boise's inmate population. Eric received 57 stab wounds as a show of convict solidarity. *No one messes with another inmate's food.*

Top earner status in the sugar trade offered privileges. *I go where I need.* The kitchen and dining hall separated the medium and minimum wings. No prisoners crossed wings except Frank and

Vic. *I got juice with the staff.* The staff generated revenue from his sales. *They won't bark unless the paper stops coming in.* His mailroom journey went unobstructed. The prison mail trustee was palmed twenty dollars when Frank arrived. Fresh supply of three brown boxes full of packets for the sugar trade went into Frank's possession. He accepted the boxes with a grin, then turned to locate Vic.

"Hold on. Give me your John Hancock," the mail trustee said.

"Huh?" Frank said.

The trustee held up a sheet. Thumb pressed against the signature line. Frank raised an eyebrow, scrawled his name using a little pen on a chain. The trustee passed him an envelope.

Frank: "What's this?"

"You tell me."

"No one writes me here," Frank said. "My wife ain't doing it."

"Different source of dependence for you," The trustee said. His forefinger directed Frank's eyes across the envelope's landscape to the return address. "Gryzbowsky, when the state writes, you read it."

The Sides' second major industry was information. The penal system's largest economic producer was knowledge. Convicts had two choices for legal counsel; either a public defender or a jailhouse lawyer. The Public Defender Office's backlog on appeal requests was a year wait. *They may never read an inmate's appeal request at all.* Convicts solved this bureaucracy by turning to an inmate with a prison library law degree. Legal action and advice from a fellow prisoner was made available for money or sexual favors. Jailhouse lawyers helped inmates sue cops for brutality. File appeals because their public defender slept during their trials.

Coronado Garrett was a valuable convict at *The Sides* because of his legal expertise. Frank sought him out before opening the state's correspondence. Garrett's medium security cell sat amid thick purol odors. Frank coughed as his lungs sucked in heavy fumes. Garrett was a notorious state treasure and legend at *The Sides.* Garrett and fellow inmate Jarvis Whitlock had served as a legal dream team for every Boise Correctional convict. Against the state, the convict legal pair won seventy percent of the time. One of Idaho's U.S. Senators declared both *Public Enemies.* Their trouble, both received *diesel therapy* to split them up after they sued the state of Idaho more than anyone in history. Garrett was transferred to *The Sides,* Whitlock got sent to Pocatello. The governor refused to comment to the local press on Garrett or Whitlock. *Man didn't want them kicking his ass in court for slander.*

Garrett had lost his family home to the bank. Had a mental breakdown while holding a gas station attendant hostage. Garrett divorced his wife and finished law school distance learning on the state's dime at Boise Correctional. The *prison wolf* sued the state healthcare provider to cover his sexual reassignment surgeries. Garrett sat in the shadows of his cell when Frank arrived at the open door. Light shined off Garrett's skull while he examined a legal brief. Frank gasped as purol fumes went into his lungs. He covered his mouth, eyes watering.

Garrett looked from his papers to Frank: "Hard to sneak around with that cough."

Frank gestured to Garrett's papers, saying he could come back later. Eyes unintentionally on the jailhouse lawyer's lap, wishing they weren't. *Please don't let me catch sight of his lady parts.*

Garrett grinned, tapping his thumb against the legal brief. "This represents my latest legal action against the state. Kitchen serves crunchy peanut butter. No creamy for those without teeth. Fifty-two convicts are part of the biggest class action prisoner lawsuit in state history over this issue."

"Sounds important."

Garrett shrugged. "Who decides importance? Keeps me busy, state defends it in court. When they spend money, it keeps them on their toes. Fun to piss them off."

"You have a point."

Garrett gestured to the envelope in Frank's hand. "I trust this friendly visit has some use of my legal expertise."

Frank handed Garrett the envelope, who read the contents, smiled as if hearing an invisible joke, then tapped his forefinger on the letter.

"You got a H-540, kid," Garrett said. "These aren't issued anymore."

"What the hell is that?"

"State bureaucracy. The state's attorney avoids putting plea bargain convictions in his success rate by issuing one."

Frank said, "Still a conviction, right?"

"Election years change everything. If state's attorney doesn't get a full sentence on a conviction, opponents challenge his record," Garrett said. "If you beat them on appeal, hurts his rate, he gets crucified at the polls. So the state's attorney plays politics. Refuses to sign the plea agreement you had with him. The state laws go to work. Causes a H-540 penalty to be issued after three months. Conviction stays on your record, but you walk like you did the whole time."

"They do that?" Frank said, snapping his fingers. "Like that?"

"Politicians are the dirtiest crooks. They could teach us about screwing someone over. County jail is overflowing all the time, so they can't put you in there. And you haven't tried to escape to tack on an extra five years to your sentence. You're a nobody so they don't have a problem letting you out."

"Glad I could be so insignificant."

Garrett returned the letter. "Tuttle needs to know. Word runs quick."

"How should I approach it?"

"Fast," Garrett said, eyes giving Frank a once-over. The jailhouse lawyer frowned. "What's the matter, kid? You're getting fourteen months off your stretch."

Frank shrugged. "Guess I'm starting to like what I do."

Garrett stood, body in the light. *Oh, shit.* Frank's eyes focused on Garrett's enhanced bust. A tight lime green khaki shirt held it tight. The seventy-two-year-old *Cheetah* underwent nineteen sexual reassignment surgeries. Sued all the way to the state supreme court. Advocated to lop off his manhood on the taxpayer's dime. *Hold it together, Frank.*

"Don't put yourself back in here," Garrett said. "You're reformed."

"I ain't been reformed." Frank said.

Garrett laughed, shook his head. Frank palmed fifty dollars or what the inmates referred to as *half a yard* to the jailhouse lawyer. Frank's eyes drifted down with the fifty dollars as it went into Garrett's cleavage. Frank exited the cell to locate Brian. *Tell him before someone else.*

Catcalls addressed Frank passing along the medium cellblock corridor. Inmates excited, admiring Frank. Saying everything they would like to do to him. The fear of rape held after his arrival at *The Sides*. Rape was uncommon in certain respects. Plenty of prison friendly cons sold personal services for ten bucks. Rape still occurred but in limited episodes. *Never ask where the money comes from when they buy packets. I don't know and I don't want to know.*

The kitchen staff greeted Frank with handshakes and nods. The majority of staff made money off packet sales. Those staff not in the game shut their mouth, pretending not to notice him. Frank headed through the facility, figuring Brian Tuttle was easy to find. Tuttle refused the standard prison garb of green khaki shirts, pants and slip-on shoes called "*bo-bos.*" Tuttle wore a canary polo shirt and plaid pants separating him from every other convict.

Tuttle gave the impression of a golfer at a country club ready to hit the back nine after brunch. Calm, his reading glasses stuck out of his shirt pocket. Tuttle was serving out twenty-two for armed robbery. But his demeanor showed different. Brown haired tufts covered his ears. Gray brows hovered over small black eyes. Tuttle licked his spork as if he savored the prison chow.

Convicts were quiet around Tuttle. His outside connections scared the convicts enough he ate in peace. Lowlife cons, scumbags filled the room but did not tempt fate. *Type of guys who take you down with them in a bust for a reduced sentence.* Frank spotted a crook caught after leaving his wallet behind in a grocery store hold up. His eyes drifted to the M.M.A. reject who smashed a beer bottle on his friend's head. The cons were docile around Brian and knew not to mess with him.

"You eating, man?"

Vic offered a metal tray, gestured to the food line. Frank wasn't hungry. Medium security boys ate superior food than what the minimum security dormitory offered. Frank's eyes returned to Tuttle. Frank considered his approach to give news of his pending release. *Let him finish eating first.*

Frank to Vic: "We out of packets?"

"People write down their names after I ran out," Vic said. "Tomorrow, we sell out on a waiting list."

"Keep setting those records. They'll talk about us after we're dead in the ground."

The two men shared a smile. Frank's eyes casually floated back to Tuttle, then down a few tables behind Tuttle, fixating on inmate Robert Nash. A six-five white gorilla with stained ink who was not eating his chow. Man was giving Tuttle the red eye. Frank noticed Tuttle paid no attention to Nash behind him. Nash hunched over a tray of mystery meat and gray potatoes, displaying jail muscles. Twelve years remaining on a *tease and squeeze* sentence. Nash had that *big boy* attitude staring at Tuttle. Planning how to aim a shank in Brian's *pudding cup. He's prepping it right now, ready to be a crash test dummy.*

Nash sported a blonde mane that cascaded down the front of his huge shoulders. Mouth gnarled three bottom yellow teeth tombstones over his lip. He displayed Gypsy Knight biker membership on each elbow: A tattooed black spade. The G.K.'s biker chapter resided in abandoned homes throughout Spokane Valley. The G.K. controlled prison populations in five states. It was common for G.K. members to break parole after being stupid and violent. Chain-dragging an artist for drawing weak ink or shooting their best friend for an insult. Nash had been different. He tortured a college co-ed with a blade after her boyfriend cut him off in traffic.

Vic spoke to Frank but it went unheard. *Too focused on Nash to hear it.*

Frank to Vic: "Sorry, what's up?"

"You got fan mail?"

Frank: "Sort of."

"They deny you parole?"

Changing the subject, Frank gestured to the chow line and said, "They're about to stop serving."

His eyes stayed on Nash. Gave the food line a glance, waiting until there was an opening. Eyes ran up the guards as Frank moved toward the line. Two guard stations were in the dining hall for meals. The catwalk above the food area held a guard named Trent. Below him, on the floor, was another guard, Christopher. Frank caught the floor guard Christopher motioning at Trent on the catwalk. *A signal?* The catwalk guard Trent returned back a nod to Christopher. Both guards exited into the shadows, slow. Inmates unaware they were alone. *Three hundred cons with no hacks guarding us.*

Guard payoffs took heavy influence. The G.K. were one of the few organizations who could pull it off. While Nash did his thing on Tuttle and the guards counted their take for ignoring it, the prison wouldn't burn to the ground. The G.K. usually kept that promise. Nash would be sentenced to a straight eight years in addition to the time he would have instead of fighting the matter at trial. Frank's eyes darted to the dining hall security cameras. A little red light on each camera went off, meaning the place was dark. The guards' way of ensuring no incriminating video existed of their complicity.

In the distance, Nash rose. Frank's focus locked on the 3-1-1 clown edging around the table. Man grinned at Tuttle, who was oblivious to the shark coming for him. Nash moved in, thirty feet from his target. *Nash doesn't notice me eying him, recognizing what he's about to do.* Man's focus was tunneled on his prey unobstructed.

Vic waved his hand in front of Frank's face, gaining his attention. Vic smiled saying that Frank wasn't focused, man. Vic didn't recognize the guard payoff. Frank observed the room; none of the cons acted as if they knew of Nash's attack. *Place is prime for this.* Nash glared at Tuttle's back while creeping closer.

"We doing this, or what?" Vic said, gesturing to the chow line.

"Yeah," Frank said. "I'm hungry."

"I hear you."

Frank moved around Vic in the chow line. Snatched a metal tray off the rack. Glided along the buffet row. Glanced over the dirty sneeze screen at kitchen trustee servers willing to increase Frank's portions in exchange for packets. Frank sped through the line, taking none of the servings. Each trustee wore confusion on their faces, holding ladles of slop; instant mashed potatoes and gray sauce. Frank kept his attention on Nash. Frank snatched a white roll out of a basket. Vic clutched Frank's wrist, held his arm in the air, drawing Frank's concentration.

"Ain't no way to eat, man," Vic said, concerned.

Frank: "There's room for seconds."

Frank freed himself from Vic's grip. Turned to the dining hall, weaved himself through inmates. Ethnics grouped tables; Latinos chatted Spanish; Blacks played dominoes; Russians laughed & mocked doing time in America's penal system in comparison to their own country's version. Tuttle sat alone at the hall's epicenter. Nash and Frank closed in on Tuttle from opposite ends. Frank caught Nash removing an object that the biker had used his ass cheeks to *suitcase* into the hall. Nash's prison weapon was a *trazor*: A melted bristle toothbrush holding a disposal razor. Nash's eyes turned from Tuttle and caught Frank coming at him. *He sees a challenge.* Frank took the roll off the tray. Underhand tossed it at Nash's chest.

"Have mine."

Nash snatched the roll out of the air with his gritty paw. Man displayed confusion to why it was thrown at him. Frank gripped his tray with both hands. Swung from his waist upward. The metal surface smashed hard against the biker's jaw. The impact vibrated through the tray. Lightning ran down Frank's arms, his fingernails were ready to leap off his digits. Sound reverberated through the dining hall. Every inmate focused on the noise. Frank held tight to the bent tray, holding his ground. Nash stood solid but rocked in a mental vacancy.

Frank swung the damaged tray again with an uppercut. Caught Nash's chin. The shot catapulted the biker off his feet. Man hit the floor, eyes rolled into his skull, blood from his nostrils, mouth. Face was cut deep. Frank surveyed the room. No con rushed to Nash's aid. None of the guards charged in dressed in ninja turtle gear. The lockdown alarm was not sounded. Inmates in the dining hall returned to their meals, in unison. Conversations restarted. *Acting as if Nash ain't out cold on the ground.*

Frank heaved the damaged tray into a plastic trashcan. His hands ached from the strike against Nash. Frank's focus went to Tuttle. The man in the canary polo sat at his table, frozen and confused, eying Frank. Tuttle's plastic spork handle stuck out of his mouth, unable to swallow the last bite of food. *I've got his undivided attention.*

"By the way, I'm getting out this week."

2 "You hurt me, baby."

Sully Brooks closed his lids while on his cell phone. Trying to keep his patience with his girl, Angel. Talking her into returning to his South Hill Apartment. Angel saying she didn't dig his strange vibe. No longer trusted him. Sully remained calm, talking smooth. *She has to come back.* Sully scratched the five o'clock shadow on his chin, and checked his reflection in his refrigerator mirror. Looked fine in his black t-shirt, white Armani sport jacket. Admired his new slip-on sockless loafers while coaxing Angel saying, *baby, please come back to me.*

"Let me make it up to you."

Sully lost his words but not his style. Angel's end of the line offered silence. Sully figured Angel was thinking of what else to say. His mind drifted to all of their naked talks. Both revealed history no one else knew. Issues never told to anyone else. *What makes us who we are.* By sharing with Angel, the conversations meant something to Sully. *Made our time together intimate. Real.*

Angel said to him, "Leave me alone for a while."

"Don't talk that way."

"You hurt me. I thought you broke my arm."

Sully: "You gotta come home."

Silence again from her end of the line. Sully listened for a minute, then two, before Angel finally broke through and said, "I thought I was special to you. Thought we clicked."

"We do," he said.

"You sent me to see him. Told me to do what he likes. You don't treat someone you care about that way," Angel said.

Sully admitted nothing. Irish Pete's call had been important. The old man saying to send him a girl, so he gets a girl. Sully's options for Irish Pete's female companionship were limited; Tina left to find religion; Ericka overdosed two weeks before in *The Blacklight* alley. Angel was the only one available for Sully to send to Irish Pete.

Angel returned with an unexpected story. It changed everything for Sully. Angel overheard Irish Pete give orders to ice Brian Tuttle at *The Sides*. The street hadn't heard Tuttle's name in a while. Sully was skeptical, put his fists into Angel. Threw her out of the house. Had the idea her story would get back to Irish Pete, make the old man think that Sully was trying to spy on him. Irish Pete killed people for doing less. *Then, Junior texts me. Saying he's been tasked by Irish Pete to locate Tuttle's diamond score.* Everything made sense.

"Come back," Sully said. "We can talk about us."

"Do you love me?"

He lied. "You're my girl."

She hung up. Sully redialed, but came up empty. Angel's cell was a *burner*, a pay-as-you-go cell phone model. It meant Sully had no idea where Angel was hiding. His partner, Rahn, wanted Angel back, to prevent her Irish Pete story from spreading back to the old man. Sully had never killed anyone. *That's Rahn's skill set, not mine. I'm the smooth-talking machine.*

Sully exited the kitchen and spotted Junior sitting in the living room. Sully tossed his cell onto the coffee table, frustrated. Sulked on the couch, surrounded by 1980s art deco style.

"She ain't coming back," he said to Junior.

Junior Perry sat across from Sully. Man was fixated on his own cell. Reading a friend's text. *He should be paying attention. It's important.* Sully stretched his arm, waved his palm in Junior's face. The kid's eyes fixated on Sully, unconcerned.

"Huh?"

Sully: "How bad does the old man want her?"

"He thinks she's going to talk," Junior said. "Top priority. Next to Jonas."

She's been talking. Rahn was saying they needed Angel. Keep her from blabbing to Irish Pete. *The old man can't be tipped off about what we're about to pull. Otherwise, he'll kill us all.* Irish Pete was legendary at reckonings. Every business rival was dead. His challengers destroyed without mercy. Irish Pete settled scores over insults as much as money.

"So, the green light goes on Tuttle. Did Nash do him?"

"No," Junior said. "Betcha Carcetti will make the next attempt on Tuttle."

Sully disagreed. "Carcetti rides the needle. Nash took a hard sentence to ice Tuttle. Carcetti ain't got that level of commitment in him."

Nash held a college co-ed hostage during rush hour. Marked her face with his blade in front of her boyfriend while cars passed by. Tossed the boyfriend a cell phone. Said for the kid to call the cops. Second the heat arrived, Nash released the girl without any trouble. *Nash wanted to go back in The Sides for violating his parole.* No one on the street believed Carcetti to possess the same skill set. *He's a low-rent junkie who doesn't have the plums.*

"Irish Pete is pulling out all the stops," Junior said. "Doesn't trust Tuttle's word."

The stones' location remained Brian Tuttle's secret for two years. *Waited until the old man took the gloves off before deciding to give the diamonds up.* Irish Pete had sat through two criminal trials and waited until the heat simmered. *Never trust a guy going inside to bend to the will of time.*

"You going after Jonas?"

Junior sent another text on his cell. The kid's eyes showed boredom as he looked from his cell phone to Sully. "If Freeway can move the ice, I want twenty large. Nice pay for tailing a guy."

"That's why you came to me," Sully said. "Glad to help."

"I could have gotten Freeway if I'd wanted to."

Junior smirked and Sully took the expression as insulting. *I've got a reckoning of my own for you, Junior. Soon.* Sully imagined that Junior's family found the kid to be a disappointment in their lives. *An adult child suffering from this generation's affliction: Social Asperger's.* The *tap, tap, tap* of Junior typing on his cell phone covered the living room's silence. *Sending stupid messages to other myopic idiots.* Sully combed his flop of brown hair, adjusted his pinkie ring. Watched Junior but noticed the kid was indifferent to who stared at him. *Rahn wants him dead after we get the stones.* Sully desired to kick Junior in the face. *Gotta cocky bullshit attitude.*

"Are you laying down bodies for the stones?"

"Naw," Junior said. "The old man has no interest."

Irish Pete had sound logic. *Why kill people?* Media attention forced the heat to act. People asked questions. The old man's place was hidden in the outskirts west of Spokane. *Hell, I couldn't find the place with G.P.S.* Junior's *tap, tap, tap* typing interrupted Sully's thoughts. Eyes locked on the kid before Sully shook off the urge to hurt him. *No, Rahn kept saying to entertain him until he has no use.* Sully grinned at the prospect of having Junior disappear. *I'll order Paco at the Boneyard to put Junior in a Turkish roll. Drive Junior's body up north. Let the kid rot forever in a rusted Buick trunk.*

If Junior detected Sully's plans, the kid pretended to be oblivious. Mired in his cell phone, Junior typed another text message. Junior was a maniac with his thumbs. *Reminds me of taking Angel to the movies. Tried to concentrate on the flick. Kept hearing that tap, tap, tap sound of some kid texting on his cell phone. The sound of locusts attacking a wheat field.* Sully broke some texter's nose in the theater. *I told him to stop and the texter acted offended.* Junior acted as callous as the movie theater texter. Junior acted as if he was an expert at everything. *Bullet in head says he don't know shit.*

"What's with that stuff?" Sully said, pointing to Junior's cell.

"Keeps me informed."

"Informed? You want informed, pick up a paper."

"This is the future, Sully."

Sully said, "The future ain't too bright, is it?"

He left Junior in the living room, letting the kid text his friends. Sully entered his apartment kitchen, sick to witness Junior removing himself from society. *These kids miss the finer things in life.* Sully shook his head, disgusted, then stopped at the photograph of the *RMS Queen Mary* in Miami. The photograph taken in Miami was crooked, so he adjusted the frame. *Junior wouldn't know what to do with a pad like this.* Tina and Ericka never had Sully tell them to bring out a mirror and chalk. It was part of the deal of staying at his place. *Angel wasn't into coke at first, but we got her snorting her fair share*, being part of the group. After the girls each took a *bump*, Sully would do his thing with them. *Gotta have style to pull that off.*

Sully took a lite beer from his fridge, popped the cap. Took a pull but his eyes zeroed in on a small mirror on the kitchen counter. *Some chalk is left on that mirror.* Sully resisted temptation, wiped his mouth with his arm. The mirror was supposed to be Angel's welcome home present. *But I could have a taste.* He had a little straw in his pocket. *Wait until everyone's gone. Show I have control to this thing.* Junkies like Jimmy Carcetti didn't have self-control. *But I do.*

Another pull from his beer, but Sully was unfocused. It was an effort to shake off a *bump* from the mirror. *Rahn makes the rules. I set the tone.* Sully brought Rahn in on the diamonds score. Rahn was an idea man. Made the plan Sully and Rahn were going with. *The fat man eyes nine moves ahead on a chessboard. Every crook except for Rahn said the ice was lost after Nash, Carcetti and Tuttle busted up that jewelry store two years back. Man kept telling me that, someday, that amount of ice is going to turn up somewhere.*

No fence ever pushed the score. *The street lit up like a Christmas tree when major ice moved.* Time passed, few jobs went down. *Tuttle was sent up to prison; the location of the ice stayed with him.* When Irish Pete asked Sully to find Angel, he was giving off a vibe. Old man was worried she had overheard his orders and wasn't taking chances. Sully felt unsure about letting Rahn kill Angel. *I gotta find out what's going on between me and Angel first.*

Rahn dumped Junior at Sully's apartment around noon. *Said he would be back soon. Left me to watch a babydoll who uses a sawed-off shotgun as a scare tactic.* Sully wasn't impressed with Junior. *Kid treats this like a video game. Doesn't realize what's at stake.* Rahn viewed the kid different, saying the kid's got drive, knows what to do, who to talk to. Sully didn't see anything in Junior except sloth. Rahn ignored Sully's feelings, brought Junior into the mix, then departed to grab Freeway Phil Asone. Freeway was the only city fence able to move the stones. *See what he knew.*

Sully eyed the mirror again. Grain sat off the reflective surface. *Put my nose against the glass and breathe. Let the world go by at warp speed. Forget about Angel.* Sully was distracted by Angel's absence. *Maybe I love her.* Sully shook off his need for chalk. The grain could sit until Rahn returned. Sully closed his lids, rubbing his eyes with his finger and thumb. *I can have any girl to love me like Angel. Anytime I want a girl in my club, she's mine. Angel's as good as dead. I need to move on.* Sully wondered how he would feel after Rahn got ahold of her and did his thing.

The front door opened. Sully leaned around the kitchen, eyes catching the living room. Looking around the corner at Freeway Phil Asone entering his apartment. Sully set his beer on a coaster, returned to the living room to greet Freeway. Sully caught a glimpse of Freeway first coming through the door, then Dan Rahn following. *I smelled Rahn first.* The fat man's skin had an embedded odor which made Sully wince. Rahn had a tough hombre look. Eyes hid underneath the brim of a tan fedora, large frame covered by a trench coat. *Rahn has attitude. You're in trouble before he says a word.* Sully worried for Angel. *I don't want to know what Rahn does when he finds her.* Rahn gestured for Freeway to sit on the couch. Junior set aside his cell phone, stared at Freeway. Everyone paid attention.

Freeway Phil was a strange character. *And I've seen Paco.* Freeway sat on the wrong end of the three-twenty-seven scale. Wore bland XXXXXXXXL T-shirts with no design on the front. Pants hemmed together, clothes with no class. Flipped-back baseball cap covering a shaven head. Bottle-bottom glasses magnified Freeway's squinting eyes. The Garland fence smiled a set of rotten teeth at Sully, who stared at tiny bare ridges of socket stems poking out of diseased gums. Freeway plopped his girth onto the couch without preparation. The man's weight shift caused the springs to protest, the wooden base to buckle.

"Who are you guys?"

Sully said, "We're the ones who talk. You listen. Otherwise my associate gets nasty."

Rahn opened his trench coat, showing a sheath inside. Drew out a curved knife, long and nasty. *A Damascus blade.* Sully eyed Freeway with sympathy. *Man wants you to listen, pal, you need to listen.* Rahn displayed the wicked blade for Freeway. The fence's eyes soaked in the Arabic writing engravings. *Reading evil biblical shit down the middle of the knife.* Sully noted Junior's reaction. *Scary potential.*

Sully to Junior: "You sure this is him?"

Junior nodded. "The old man said a bagman was delivering the stones to him."

Rahn leaned in. "Whose suppose to drop off the ice to you?"

Freeway tried to show tough. Didn't work on Rahn, who pointed the blade's tip south. *Man wants Freeway's attention. Convince him that anything can happen.* Sully shuddered at the idea of killing Freeway in his apartment living room. *Rahn will destroy the rugs.* Sully also worried about his own back trying to get rid of Freeway's body. *Does Rahn understand how heavy a dead body is?* Sully decided to lean in to Freeway. Caught the fence's mix of energy drink, chocolate breath.

Sully gestured at Rahn while eying Freeway. "My friend here can do a lot with the blade."

Rahn said, "Slice you in two."

"Make a mess," Sully said. "This place turns red in two minutes."

"Do you with a thin slice, drops your guts into your lap," Rahn said.

"Then he does your throat."

Freeway couldn't hide the fear on his face. Man was scared. Freeway attempted twice to straighten himself, show tough again, but Sully saw through it. Freeway said, "You can't do that. The heat will come down on you hard."

Rahn and Sully shared a smile. Rahn yanked out his badge, tossed it on the coffee table. The detective's shield spun 780 degrees before stopping upside down in front of Freeway. *The fence gets the message.* Sully grinned. *No, Freeway, the cavalry ain't charging up the hill to find you. Start talking before Rahn becomes nasty.*

"He ain't convinced," Rahn said to Sully.

Sully agreed. "Then convince him."

Rahn latched his hand onto Freeway's wrist. Pulled the fat palm over the coffee table's center. Slammed Freeway's mitt against the glass surface. The force bounced Rahn's badge off the table. Freeway struggled, but Rahn held tight. Rahn ran the blade against the back of Freeway's hand, but prevented himself from slicing through the flesh. *Enough to make Freeway understand that Rahn means business.* Freeway whimpered, shutting his lids tight. Sully noted Junior's disinterest; the kid's focus returned to his cell phone. Junior began typing away another text message. *Junior gets his turn when we take the score. We'll see how he acts then.*

Sully refocused on Freeway, pointing his finger in the fence's face. "Who's the bagman for Tuttle's ice?"

Freeway shook him off. Eyes remained shut, but tears forced through the cracks in the cracked lids. Sully dropped his finger, stood straight, ashamed of Freeway. *How did this guy come into the life if he can't stand tall? I'd do it different. No running away, crying. I would pull out my nine and make sure I emptied it.* Sully gave Rahn a curious eyebrow. Noticing that Rahn was ready to do his thing. *So do your thing, Rahn.*

Rahn stabbed into the center of Freeway's hand, causing the fence to scream. Then, Rahn pushed deeper. Rahn placed his free hand over Freeway's mouth to muffle the sound. Blood spurted out of Freeway's mitt as the blade burrowed down. Sully's eyes expanded. *Jesus, Rahn's going to mess up my coffee table.* Rich red fluid flowed from the hand onto the table's glass surface. Sully got upset. *Shit, my carpet.*

Sully ran into the kitchen, yanked a hand towel out of the sink. Tossed it across the living room to Rahn. Freeway blubbered as the curved knife stuck out his hand. *Freeway's scared of what happens next. A large amount of ice, we'll do anything to get it.* Sully smiled at the prospect of the score paying off his debts at *The Blacklight. No more living off credit cards or drug scores.*

Rahn to Freeway: "Well?"

"Jonas…" Freeway said, exhausted. "…Jonas is doing the drop sometime this week."

Sully to Rahn: "Jonas? He's being trusted with this?"

"Must be desperate," Rahn said to Sully. "He ain't a thief."

Rahn gripped the knife's handle. Sully waved his hands, stopping the fat man. "Wait. Blood don't come out of white carpet well."

Rahn shrugged. Tossed the towel at Freeway, hitting the fence in the face. Rahn released the knife's handle, waiting. Sully headed into his bedroom, past the Lussorian bed with satin sheets. Opened the closet sliding door. Found two beach towels that the late Ericka had left at his place. Sully returned to the living room. Found Rahn eying Freeway as the fence cried. Rahn held the knife's handle, calm.

Rahn to Freeway: "You ready?"

Freeway: "No."

Freeway squeezed his lids shut as Rahn yanked the blade free of Freeway's hand. A geyser erupted from the wound, splatting down red fluid on the glass coffee table surface. Sully bandaged Freeway's hand with the beach towels, wiped up the mess. None of the blood splatter hit the couch or carpet. Sully glanced at Freeway's bloodshot eyes. Man was terrified, cheeks caked with salty tears. *Some people need that type of convincing.*

Rahn turned to Junior. "Off the phone before I stomp it."

Junior's eyes instantly shot to Rahn. Sully grinned at the exchange.

Junior's never been given an order in his life. Kid needs structure. Junior hid his cell phone in his pants pocket. Gave Rahn his full attention. *The kid doesn't need convincing. Not after what happened to Freeway.* Rahn cleaned Freeway's blood off the blade, using a beach towel, then returned the knife to its sheath. *The blade does enough convincing of its own to grab my attention.*

Sully to Junior: "Find Jonas, tail him until he picks up the ice."

Junior said, "What about the old man?"

"After you snatch the ice, tell him you don't have it," Sully said. "Drop Jonas, bring the score back to us, we do the split. Then, go collect from Irish Pete. This means two paydays for you out of this, kid."

"Drop Jonas?" Junior said. "You ever dropped even one guy, Sully?"

"I've done my fair share," he said, trying to be convincing. It didn't work. Sully noticed Rahn smiling, knowing a lie when he heard one.

Rahn to Freeway: "You up for unloading a score?"

Freeway nodded. "Sure."

Junior pulled his cell phone out of his pocket. Freeway was eying the front door, as if it were an option to escape. *Too late for that, isn't it, Freeway?* Sully pulled out his money roll. Flipped about five hundred dollars. Made it rain in Junior's lap, regaining the kid's attention from his cell phone.

"Our friend needs a ride to Moreland's place. Make sure that kook stitches Freeway up."

"Ah, man," Junior said, frustrated. To Freeway: "Don't bleed all over my ride."

Junior and Freeway exited the apartment. Sully waited until Junior had loaded Freeway in the kid's ride. Watched the fence depress the vehicle's shocks, making the frame sit low to the ground. Sully turned to Rahn, hands on hips.

"You got that briefcase yet?" Sully said. Spokane Metro had busted some diploma mill three months ago. The take was eighty thousand in bills. Rahn had been saying he could snatch the money out of evidence control to buy-in on the Gypsy Knights' valley meth trade. Irish Pete was distasteful of the methamphetamine racket but neither Sully or Rahn had similar discriminations on the drug industry. *The old man looks down on the revenue brought in by the smurf set.*

"Middle of the week, maybe," Rahn said. "Has Angel called yet?"

Sully lied. "Not a peep. She will, though."

Rahn's eyes focused on Sully, who felt them burrow into his heart. Rahn said, "You can't protect her, Sully."

"Look, if she came by, I would cut her throat," Sully said, trying to be convincing. Wanting to sell Rahn on the idea that Sully wouldn't hand Angel a bunch of cash to leave town, never to be heard from again. *Maybe I would, because I don't want to see what Rahn will do to Angel when they meet.*

Rahn said, "You want me to believe that?"

"You saying I can't go through with it?"

Rahn smiled, nodding. "Okay. When the time comes, we'll see how willing you are."

3

"Breathe in… Come on… you can do it. Now… breathe out."

Shay Baxter eyed his son, Tyler, and resisted tears. *Tyler needs me to be strong.* Tyler laid still in his hospital bed with a dialysis machine running. Little beeps chirped off seconds. Whirls of blood churned through tubes, cleaned by the machine. Shay was unnerved by the room's antiseptic smell. Tyler remained strong through the process. *My sweet little boy with baby blue eyes.* Shay toughened, checked his emotions. Refused to show fear in front of his sick son. *No child should have to go through all of this adult stuff.* Shay cupped Tyler's cheek, rubbed with his thumb. Shay edged closer to the hospital bed while the machine spun Tyler's blood and it exchanged out.

"You're a champ," Shay said.

"Thanks."

Tyler's voice croaked. The machine drained the boy's strength, grayed his skin. *A boy his age should have stronger muscles and bigger limbs but he doesn't complain.* Shay adjusted his son's baseball cap, kissed his forehead. Tyler remained happy throughout all of the surgeries, the kidney transplant procedures, and the dialysis. *My son is stronger than me with everything he's been through.* Shay held Tyler's hand tight while the dialysis procedure continued.

Shay brushed Tyler's hair away from his forehead. Kissed his son, then stayed a few inches from the boy's face. Their eyes met, stayed locked. Shay said to Tyler, "Where are we going when all of this is over?"

Tyler grinned. "Anywhere we want."

"Disneyland or Six Flags, your pick," Shay said.

"Dad, Disneyland is little kid's stuff."

Shay laughed. "Sorry, I keep forgetting."

Tyler closed his lids. Shay clamped his teeth, squinted his lids to hold back tears. He wiped his eyes with his fingers to prevent his son from witnessing. Tyler opened his lids, released Shay. Tyler reached out, touched the St. Benedict medal hanging around Shay's neck. The boy pulled it close, rubbing the pendant between his fingers. Shay smiled.

"Your mother tells me not to take it off," Shay said. "Says it keeps me safe at work."

"I wish she would come with you," Tyler said, hurt.

Shay: "She makes her own visits. Says you are always sleeping. I keep telling her to wake you up. But she wants you well so you can come home again."

"I wish she would wake me up," Tyler said. "I miss her kisses."

"I know you do, pal."

Shay's eyes drifted up, seeing outside the hospital room. Tyler's doctor, John Estrellado, waited in the hall. *Doctor wants to tell me how dire things are.* Shay to Tyler: "I am going out to talk to your doctor. Find out when you can come home."

"Okay. Tell mom to wake me up next time she comes," Tyler said.

"Sure thing, pal," Shay said.

Shay exited into the hall, down a few feet from the room to keep Tyler from hearing their conversation. Dr. Estrellado stood patient. The young doctor was a positive for Tyler. Fought with the insurance company to ensure Tyler received treatments. The kidney transplant's impending failure had caused Shay's insurance to reject future procedures the company classified as "risks." Shay offered Estrellado a smile which the doctor did not return.

"When can he come home?"

Estrellado said, "Presently, I don't know. His condition is worsening. The dialysis holds off the inevitable for only so long."

"What are the alternatives?"

"The pancreatic transplant is a last option. It's our Hail Mary pass," Estrellado said. "I spent two hours on the phone with your insurance representative. They are going to refuse. I can tell from the questions they asked. Mr. Baxter, I've dealt with these people for a while. They won't authorize expensive procedures after the kidney transplant."

"But he's rejecting the kidney you gave him. That's something, right?"

"It means he stays on daily dialysis and we keep him here," Estrellado said.

Shay: "How much does that transplant run?"

"One-to-two hundred thousand," Estrellado said.

"I don't have that kind of money."

"And we both know your insurance won't provide authorization."

"We can't cut him off," Shay said.

Estrellado: "That means he stays here."

A chorus of alerts wailed from Tyler's hospital room. Shay turned back to see that his son was having a seizure. Tyler's little body erupted in the hospital bed. Estrellado rushed to attend. Several nurses and doctors ran by Shay to stabilize Tyler. Each person shouted medical language Shay did not understand. The tears broke free of Shay's eyes. He grabbed at his hair, held his arms. Watched his little boy crash and have to be restarted. *I've been through this too many times before to stay and watch them keep him alive.* Shay hurried down the hall to let the emergency noise dissipate. His head began to ache, so Shay stopped at the front desk. Talked to a nurse named Grace who sat behind the counter, asking for some aspirin.

The hospital staff knew Shay after the past three weeks of Tyler's dialysis. Shay spent close to eight hours at work, then another ten at the hospital with Tyler. Shay remained thankful that his work cell phone did not ring during those visits with his son. *Means no one did anything stupid today*. Grace searched for aspirin around her desk. Shay's eyes locked on the guest sign-in sheets, hooked on a clipboard on the counter. He let his fingers run down the guest names of patients. Shay's name was listed several times under Tyler Baxter. His finger scrolled further, seeking his wife's name on one of the sheets. The absence on the sign-in sheet remained. His wife, Mariah, had not signed into the hospital in a few weeks. That revelation alarmed Shay. *How could you not visit your own son, Mariah?*

Estrellado headed down the hall, hurried. The doctor stopped in front of Shay, shaking his head. "His body reacted negatively to the insulin. We calmed it, but a boy his age is uncharted territory."

Shay said, "Is he okay?"

"Not unless he gets a transplant. I'm sorry, but we've done everything we can," Estrellado said.

Shay called his ex-partner from the Tactical team, Steve Powers. Needed someone to talk to. Someone Shay could trust. Powers was a good man, Shay's best friend. *He listens to me more than he talks.* Shay didn't know who else he could talk to. *Tyler's getting worse and there's nothing that I can do to change that. Where am I going to find two hundred thousand dollars to pay for another transplant?* Shay didn't enjoy the prospect of Tyler dying in the hospital without options.

The two met across the street from Lake Coeur d'Alene. Both sat on the hood of Powers' blue Chevy Caprice, drinking bottle Buds. Shay's eyes sat on the house across the street from the Caprice and he wished he could do something for Powers. *Steve wants that place back.* Shay remembered the barbecues that Powers held at the lake house for all of the team members when Powers ran Tactical. *His father built that place and now someone else owns it.* Powers spent evenings parked across the street from the house. Acted as if he still owned the place. *Man criticizes those new owners. Wants to be consulted if the carport is rebuilt or the house gets painted.*

"How are you holding up?" Powers said to Shay, eyes watching the house.

"Fine," Shay said. "Coll wants a meeting next week. Talk about my absenteeism. How it isn't good for the station's morale."

"He isn't blue."

Shay drank his beer. "I got time in and some of the boys have donated shared leave as well."

"Drag that asshole Coll to your kid's hospital room," Powers said, clinking his beer bottle against Shay's. "Let Coll sit while that machine runs. See if he doesn't understand where your absenteeism comes from."

"What am I going to do, man?" Shay said. "Tyler is so young."

"We'll think of something."

"I hope so," Shay said. "I hope so."

4 The ability to tune out the Blacklight club's house music began to erode for Christine Gryzbowski. Her skills favored making five Mojitos, seven Margaritas and two Lemon Drops in succession while the DJ offered Lady Gaga's latest hit on the dance floor. But Christine's talents slipped over the past few weeks. Club bartending was not for amateurs, though the club kept hiring inexperienced staff.

Christine had attempted community college courses, but studying disinterested her. *I'm good at pouring, not much else.* Other bars offered quieter settings, but The Blacklight paid best on customer tips. *In the end, it is about the money.* Christine put long hours on her feet. Men offered to take her home regardless of her wedding ring or club management booking her for too many shifts. *It comes with the territory. Someone's always trying to screw you.*

A retro-Elvis tune was lodged in her head. Musical style was not the issue; the loud volume beat her down. *My hearing is shot.* Nights lying in bed meant hearing speaker feedback. None of the music, just the feedback. Inner ear humming vibrations, hours after completing her shift. The heavy high-pumping bass had a reputation for cracking parked car windshields outside the club.

She savored her breaks from work. The club had few opportunities for Christine to take breaks. When those chances came, it meant that an inexperienced waitress, Diane, filled in behind the bar for

Christine. *Management needs to hire workers who can pour not just some girl who wants to flirt with the customers.* The waitresses were ignorant on mixing, angering customers. *Reading a mixed drink book is too complicated for women looking to make extra on their tips.* Christine's mind focused on Diane. The woman lived with a mother who babysat Diane's infant while she worked. A husband in Afghanistan, but Diane acted single around the club's muscular bouncers.

Smoking a cigarette on break was a precious exercise that Christine treasured. *I'm supposed to be using the patch.* Standing in the club alley, she felt the bass bump against the walls. Puffed out her stress underneath the light of a street lamp. *Small things I can be thankful for.* She wanted to quit her job at *The Blacklight Club. Shit economy doesn't make it easier. Not when you have a mortgage to pay for on your own.*

Frank came to her mind for a moment, Christine curious what her estranged husband was up to. No word from him after being sent up to *The Sides. My mother would say divorce his ass.* Christine's thoughts focused on her mother, wondering if the two would ever talk again. *She doesn't return my calls. The shit between us started off small. Then it festered.* Christine took another drag of her cigarette, then blew out the smoke. She touched her long, wavy hair, thinking about chopping it off. *No life to my bangs.*

Christine eyed several puffs float into the clutches of the lamp. The night sat at forty-five degrees. Walking around February without a jacket was disturbing. Spokane was never this warm in the winter. *When it snows, it dumps on us.* Christine shrugged. *Maybe God forgot about us.* Christine flicked her cigarette onto the ground, stamping it out with her heel. Prepped herself to return to the club. Five more hours of a constant beat before her shift ended. *Such is the life of a bartender, huh?*

"You work here?"

Two men approached Christine from the street. They were dressed in cheap suits so she pinned them as police. The two men closed in on Christine, preventing an escape. The first cop was black, put his hand against the alley wall. Other Blacklight staff members had relayed similar tactics by the police. Christine had never experienced a shakedown herself. The black cop stunk of Brut, but had welcoming eyes. Even winked at her.

The second cop was white. Wore glasses, sporting a goatee with a small mullet growing beyond his neckline. *He'd be cute if he lost ten pounds.* Christine guessed both men were in their late thirties. *The white cop thinks he's hot shit. I know the type.* Frank immediately came to mind. *He runs his mouth and charges up everyone else's bar tab.* The two cops flashed their laminates.

"Detective Tom Hammond, Major Crimes," he said. He pointed to his partner. "This fine gentleman is Detective Ben Dereks."

"My break is over."

Christine tried to worm out from under Dereks' arm. He pulled closer, blocked her exit. *Jesus, I hope Sully doesn't see me with them.* Christine eyed Hammond. "Am I in trouble?"

"Just a meet and greet."

Dereks said, "Yeah, talk about things."

"Get to know your owner," Hammond said.

"Shoot the shit," Dereks said. "No biggie."

"I don't want any trouble."

Dereks said, "We know. We want to chat."

"That's a fair assessment," Hammond said to Dereks.

She said, "Chat about what?"

The two cops shared a smile. Hammond to his partner: "She's cute. Thinks we'll go away."

"We need to come around more. Flash our I.D. Make sure everyone knows we're chatting with her," Dereks said.

Hammond turned to Christine, glared at her. "That work better for you? Or we go up to your boss and clear our conversation with him first?"

They'll come back too. They'll have me fired or worse. She smiled false at both men, then said sweet, "What can I do for you two officers?"

The two detectives shared a look of surprise. "Now, that was nice. All I want to do is help," Hammond said.

"Yeah, we want to help."

Hammond handed Christine a business card. "Want to find Angel before anyone else does."

"Before Sully uses her as a punching bag again," Dereks said.

"No one cares about a strawberry," Hammond said. To Dereks: "What was that one's name we found overdosed in an alley at the Blacklight?"

"Ericka Banks."

Hammond turned to Christine, leaning in. "See, Ericka used some hot stuff. But with Angel, we're thinking she might be in worse shape."

"She's got the interest of Irish Pete," Dereks said. "You know which one we're talking about."

"Pete runs the tables, numbers. Even down to the fifty-cent pull tabs on every dive along Sprague. If he wants Angel, she needs life insurance," Hammond said.

"We've heard from others that you and Angel were close. You want to help her, we need to find her first," Dereks said.

"I'll see what I can do," she said.

Hammond: "Give me a call."

Christine kept Hammond's card as they turned, leaving her alone in the club alley. She eyed the exiting detectives, suspicious. Knowing Angel could be found. *Place you went last time, when she needed money.* Christine recalled the condemned apartment complex on East Third where Angel and other friends smoked meth. Remembered how emaciated Angel was when Christine saw her. *Angel convinced herself that Sully loved her.*

Christine didn't trust Sully. She was worried about what to do about Angel. *Hammond can help her more than I can.* Christine decided to return to work. The club's loud music didn't bother her anymore.

5

Masterful thieves always forgot something big in the details. *Time to hang it up if you believe you've covered every base.* That was Jonas Reed's motto.

Skills were necessary, but a thief's worst trait was being unprepared for the unexpected. *Means you're about to be pinched.* Some guys had horrible prep skills. Found themselves in the can by midnight. Jonas loved prep work. Thinking through different scenarios. *I love getting into it. My profession allows me to see the playing field. It allows me to take advantage of errors other thieves ignore.* Jonas studied his craft, always learning.

Assholes cobbled together tools, pulled jobs without thinking. Access to a blowtorch, a few screwdrivers and a lock pick didn't take much knowledge. *When a hood does that, he leaves the situation to chance.* The alarm system he didn't know about would wail the second he broke in. Thieves left tools behind on the job to be used as evidence against them at trial. *Too many guys spend good years in prison because they don't prepare.*

Studying alarms was an art. Most crooks never had patience for homework. *The majority of art forms are unappreciated by the laymen. Burglary is no different as a craft.* Jonas respected artists of any kind. He once cased a Seattle gallery, eying a few limited edition paintings by a local artist. Asking price was five-hundred-fifty-two per piece at auction. Jonas attended the show out of respect for a fellow artist. Met some guy in blue coveralls. *Guy kept talking like he could do the same painting for free. Dismissed the artist's effort, saying it wasn't worth much.* Jonas resisted the urge to clock the guy as the show ended.

An artist should be afforded a level of respect from laymen. Jonas felt everyone should give any artist a nudge of approval as recognition over the time spent creating what no one could. *Laymen act as if art is created in ten minutes instead of hours.* Jonas became emotionally connected with other artists. The process of his jobs developed over a period of time, same as an artist. He didn't break into places on a junkie rage to tear out copper wiring from abandoned buildings. Jonas sat in his garage for hours. Eyed city planning blue prints, jotted down notes on a pad. Accounted for every type of alarm and each entry lock before accepting work. *That's why I'm not at The Sides with Brian Tuttle right now.*

Jonas did recon on his prospective jobs. Jewelry stores were where he played dad. Pretended to buy graduation presents for his kid at Gonzaga. Those trips let him notice the store's security camera positions, pinpoint blind spots. *If you're lazy at recon, you deserve to get arrested.* Prior to playing the role of dad, Jonas made one mistake: He used to play the role of fiancée, ask jewelry store workers about engagement rings. The con worked. The clerks would head into the back for their best stones. Gave Jonas time to stop the cameras, get his prep down. Everything appeared to be working while using the fiancée story. Except that one Pullman store became his downfall.

Jonas fashioned a story about proposing to his girlfriend to a jewelry store clerk. A book club member of Jonas' wife overheard the details. One phone call back to Spokane burned him before Jonas stepped through the front door that night. His wife, Gloria, came at Jonas, swinging a crowbar. She wanted an explanation. Busted out his car's back window when Jonas' pulled into the driveway. Gloria was the most confident woman Jonas had ever known. Not a woman to be trifled with. Jonas' brother Greg told Jonas over shots of *Maker's Mark* what Greg thought of his sister-in-law: 'Gloria's the scariest white woman I know.'

Gloria stood up five, hit two-fifty-one on the scale. An attitude of a wet cat. People asked Jonas why he belonged with her. Jonas loved Gloria. *If they mess with me, they have to deal with her.* Gloria was Jonas' polar opposite in demeanor. Jonas came from a tight-knit family down in Anaheim. *Gloria's family were born fighters.* Each of Gloria's kin argued, kicked or bit someone to win a fight. Including at Jonas' wedding. Jonas' new brother-in-law and his father-in-law threw haymakers at each other over an argument about the cost of the nuptials. The next day, both men sat in Jonas' bar, making nice with each other amid black eyes and broken teeth.

Jonas had been unsure about his expectations of Gloria until they were married. When the ring went on Gloria's finger, her dominance increased and items around her got damaged when she was angry. Gloria once kicked Jonas' car with enough force to damage the frame. Jonas sported a broken wrist requiring ten stitches after Gloria thought Jonas had called her "fat." Gloria was tough enough to moonlight at their bar, *The Sin Bin*. Woman enjoyed her work, cracking skulls if drunks got out of line. *She tossed a Wellpinit lumberjack on his ass after breaking the jukebox*. The man ran away on a busted ankle. Gloria was protective of her assets, including Jonas. *Hell, I fear for the man who hurts me. He's going to have to deal with her. And she'll be pissed.*

Gloria understood Jonas' art. That's why he pulled jobs with care. *She never pressures me for a check. Let's me go at my careful pace.* Jonas stood in the Central District clothing store with a measured delivery. The place happened to be a lower end shop. Jonas possessed a different reason for lurking in the shadows of the store tonight. The Central District had Spokane's finest doing random street patrols. Meaning the payouts for protection went higher.

Jonas stood to make forty-five percent off a cut with Brian Tuttle. The mastermind sounded scared when he dialed up Jonas on the phone. Speaking in a tone to convey friendliness, as if the two spoke regularly. Neither had spoken since Tuttle was sent up. *But the score was urgent.*

I need the package moved now, Brian told Jonas, *not tomorrow, not in a couple of days. Right now.*

Jonas sensed that the Central District clothing store was an illegal front. He noted the cameras were non-functioning aesthetics. Little black bulbs built into the ceiling gave the impression of security. A dumpster dive fished out the store's last three electric bills. The place did not have the power required for high-grade security. The working alarm was a 1980s relic. Complete with a red beam covering each door. *They want to stop a born loser on a stupidity streak. Prevent a half-assed break-in with a pair of pliers.*

Jonas breached the alarms, then headed to the back of the store. He picked a side office door lock in twenty seconds. His eyes focused on the room's ceiling tiles. *That's where Tuttle says it is.* Jonas grabbed an office chair, positioned underneath the spot, and stood on its seat. *Whoosh!* The chair's wheels shot the chair out from under Jonas. The chair hit the drywall and created a dent. Jonas fell, landed with a thud on the carpet. The air went out of Jonas. Took him a few minutes to recover, coughing hard. Jonas picked himself up and shook off the daze.

Jonas eyed a stationary chair with no wheels. He grabbed the stationary chair, stood on the seat, but was still careful. *You live and you learn.* Jonas punched at the ceiling tile. Popped it free. Jonas reached inside the crawl space. Felt around until his hand latched onto an object. Smiling, Jonas came down with a small satchel. Opened the mouth of the bag. Let three-hundred-five in diamonds shine soft light in his eyes. *Tuttle wasn't lying this time. This score will pay off. Run to Freeway Phil to fence the stones, then head to The Sin Bin, to celebrate.* Closing the satchel, Jonas jumped off the chair and exited the office.

"One of us is in trouble, pal."

Jonas froze with the flashlight beam in his eyes. Mind searched out the voice's owner. Figured the person for a cop, but didn't hear a police radio. *Man's waited for you to nab the score so he could steal it from you.* Jonas heard confidence in how the man spoke. *You should have brought a piece.* Jonas dismissed the thought because it violated Jonas' main rule. *If you bring a piece, you end up using it.* He desired to remain a middle-age thief instead of a street punk.

"Toss the bag over."

Jonas did as he was told. The flashlight's beam lowered. Jonas recognized Junior Perry at the other end of the flashlight. The kid had a reputation around the city as one who didn't work well with others. Wore a pencil-thin mustache on a muscular frame, bushels of black hair, and a thick jaw. Junior was a known stick-up artist. Jonas had heard stories of the kid. Holding a sawed-off against a guy's skull. Threatening to sneeze, pull the trigger on accident.

"This ain't your score, kid."

Junior said, "I decide what's mine and what isn't."

"Tuttle's got friends."

"No, he doesn't," Junior said. "He lost them when he went inside."

"He's trying to do right by the old man."

"The old man hired me too. Guess he's hedging his bets."

Junior opened the satchel. Checked the merchandise that illuminated his face from its shine. Junior nodded, impressed. Jonas received the gesture as a compliment. He grabbed a nearby chair and sat. Pulled out his brass lighter with a pack of Camels. Held the lighter in the soft light, examining it. *Gloria gave this to me for our thirteenth wedding anniversary.* Jonas stuck a nail in his mouth, snapped a flame, and took a drag. Blew out white death, squinted at Junior while Jonas' scratched his forehead with his thumb.

"Guess it takes a real person to be honest these days."

Junior looked at him. "No one tells the truth in this line of work."

"Sure, kid."

Jonas caught two blasts from Junior's sawed-off. Sound exploded off the store's walls. The shotgun pellets hit Jonas in the chest and face. Breathed out his bloody last while Junior exited the store with the satchel. Jonas felt his body thrown off the chair. Hit the ground in a heap. Vision dimmed as Jonas eyed the little black hole abyss in the white ceiling tiles. A vengeful smile curled on his lips. *Man,*

Gloria's gonna be pissed.

6

This how we respond in the 208 when an inmate throws a milkshake. Chief Corrections Officer Steve Powers smiled as *The Sides'* Administrative Control Unit opened. Light invaded the room from the hall. Steve's face caught a blast of cold air from the room's open vents. The A.C.U.'s room temperature sat at ten degrees. No sympathy was paid for Fruit Loop Johnson. Man laid naked on the dry concrete floor, Steve towering over him. *Checkmate, Fruit Loop, checkmate.*

Johnson's rectum was damaged, violated by a nightstick. The blood pooled, frozen on the floor behind him. The naked nineteen-year-old shivered with skin puffed over his right eye. Black holes buoyed his lip, a memory of teeth removed by a pair of pliers. The side of Johnson's head displayed a groove from a guard's nightstick. His left foot shattered, turned awkward. *Yeah, this is how we do shit in the 208. No one throws a milkshake at a guard at The Sides.* Powers lowered to his haunches, Johnson raised his head slow. Both were at eye level.

"I have you down as a stat in my sheet," he said. "That sweater vest butterball warden will not ask questions."

Johnson vomited shattered tooth fragments. They swam in bile and blood. Powers caught the stench but refused to turn. *Your homeboys won't be too impressed, will they?* Powers pointed at Johnson to gain the young man's attention.

"Throwing milkshakes is not recommended," Powers said. "My guard gets the bug and I'll have you buried alive."

Johnson was a member of the Bonner Loco, a rival gang of "the La979 Latinos" in the Spokane Valley. *The Sides* guards segregated gang members in A.C.U. to prevent further bloodshed. Johnson used his sole available weapon to retaliate. Made a milkshake from piss, shit and cum. The A.C.U. slot was opened for two minutes during chow time when Johnson made his move. Tossed the mixture into the face of Ryan McPherson, one of the newest guards. *We don't put up with that shit in the 208. You pull that here, we make you pay.*

"Guys who toss milkshakes are transferred to live with the Copperheads near Hauser," Powers said. "They make sure our nightstick routine never gets healed."

Fear covered Johnson's face. Sexual predators in the Idaho state penal system garnered the nickname "Copperheads." Two hundred and fifty-five inmates called a special housing facility home. It sat on Hauser Lake next to a copper mine. *The strongest violate the weakest there.* Steve's ex-Tactical Team partner Shay Baxter took pleasure in beating Copperheads who were caught in raids. *It's his way of setting the world back in order.*

"In your case, this is special," Powers said. "We'll call a 'hell-two-four' tomorrow. Spread word around here that you are the reason."

Johnson received a swift kick in the stomach from Steve. Johnson had been busted ramming a stash house with a stolen truck. Trying to steal drug money. Johnson's young age surprised no one in the penal system. The Bonner Loco recruited eleven-year-olds known as "pee-wees." Initiated by a twenty-two second group beating, they joined the family industry. Graduation to *The Sides* meant the crew fought over territory they haven't seen in ten years. Powers exited to the hall as the door sealed away the light.

"Checkmate," Powers said. "Checkmate."

Powers headed to the infirmary. Passed by hospital beds with restrained inmates. None made catcalls or said stupid shit. *They know how we respond in the 208.* Powers was concerned for his guard, Ryan McPherson. *A milkshake to the face is no small matter.* The state arrested cons, some carrying S.T.D.s, including H.I.V. A prisoner who spat on a guard's face might bring T.B. The cons didn't care. Milkshakes were a weapon of choice in the A.C.U. Guard Abby Tamlin had a milkshake tossed at his face last year. Lost sight in his left eye from exposure.

Powers went to Ryan McPherson. Man was having his blood drawn by the prison physician for tests.

McPherson had a Cesar haircut, tried to be nice to the prisoners. Powers eyed McPherson's left hand, noticed the man's wedding ring. Powers grabbed McPherson's hand, displayed it to McPherson.

"Don't let me catch you wearing this shit again," Powers said.

"Cons have friends on the outside ready to pay your little lady a visit."

"Sorry, Chief."

McPherson removed his ring, tucked away into his breast pocket. Inmates could not be trusted. *Too many of my new guards chat up inmates as if they were pals.* Cons used any information they received. Inmates were master manipulators eying design flaws. They read guards' lips to learn about protocol. Some convicts would beat on guards until the *spider cord* got pulled to bring the cavalry. Cons had accomplices on the outside. Willing to take a guard's family hostage to smuggle drugs into the prison.

"I'm calling a 'hell-two-four,'" Powers said. "This shit doesn't stand."

"I want in."

Powers shook his head. McPherson was too eager. Didn't have the right temperament for a hell-two-four. If a guard got too eager to beat anyone for retaliation, the inmates fought back. Better to leave it to the guys who didn't get a milkshake in their face. Powers to McPherson: "Go home and tell Rita what's going on."

McPherson sighed. No guard wanted his wife to know what took place at *The Sides. They worry enough about their husbands.* Contracting an S.T.D. was not a dinner subject.

"Rita's gonna be pissed," McPherson said. "We are trying to make a kid. Now I gotta tell her it ain't happening for a while. Even if her eggs are ready to be cooked."

"She will understand," Powers said. "Green light from the doctor comes, let me know. I will give you two days off to make it up to her."

"Thanks, Chief," McPherson said. "Means listening to Alanis Morrisette playing through the house when she gets in her mood."

Powers chuckled while exiting the infirmary. Passing by hospital bed rows of inmates who refused eye contact with him. No inmate wanted to deal with Powers when he was pissed. *No one tosses a milkshake and gets away with that shit in my house.*

"Hey, Powers."

Powers stopped. Eyed the beds, suspicious. Inmates turned their face from him. Powers searched, trying to locate the inmate begging to have his skull thumped.

"I want a refund."

Powers zeroed in on Robert Nash, Gypsy Knights member. People referred to the biker gang as the "G.K." Man was handcuffed to his bed rails. Nash's face offered stitches, bandages where Frank Gryzbowsky flattened him with a metal tray. *Frank should have minded his own business.* Inmates knew not to interfere with the GK. *The Gypsy Knights are a national epidemic.* Nash bore the tattooed G.K. member markings: A black spade for each elbow. Members earned the spades after they spilled someone else's blood for the gang. The G.K. were rumored to train pledges with medical books to kill rivals faster.

"You want a what?"

"A refund," Nash said. "King says to do it."

Powers raised a curious eyebrow, went to Nash's bed. The bounty for having the guards look the other way on Nash's attack on Brian Tuttle was five hundred dollars. Successful or not, blue never gave up a taste. "Money got you entry. What you did after that point is none of my business."

"That shit don't work with the G.K.," Nash said. "A violation happens, shit goes down."

"We did our part and you screwed up your end."

"The G.K. outnumber you here," Nash said. "If we want you, no place is safe."

The G.K. ran organized crime in the national penal system. They possessed rules, rituals. Extended out to paroled men who formed biker chapters to handle meth distribution. A man named "King" operated the Spokane Valley chapter. Fresh inmates became targets to pledge the gang. Their slogan was 'blood in, blood out.' A pledge had to kill for the G.K. to receive the black spades tattooed on their elbows. The lone exit for members to leave the gang was by their own death.

Powers said, "So, you still got Tuttle in the hat?"

Nash: "Never left."

Getting *put in the hat* meant a person's ass. The G.K. murdered targets by washing the targeted inmate's prison cell in the dead's blood. Most cons joined the G.K. when recruited. *You come into the prison system at twenty-two with a born to lose attitude.* The G.K. was not racial. The group wanted warriors. That was why most inmates joined the G.K. A recruited inmate never refused pledging when offered by the G.K. Refusal was not an option. Fifteen G.K. cons with steel shanks were eager to make a convict's pledge denial an example to other incoming convicts.

Inmates feared the G.K. more than Powers or his staff. Not only would the inmate who came within the crosshairs of the G.K. suffer, but so would the inmate's family members. Staff were G.K. targets. Two Boise guards had their cars blown up. Pocatello's prison had three staff workers stabbed to death. The Boise prison warden was threatened several times until he quit, citing stress. A guard in Walla Walla had his family murdered for denying a G.K. contract. Powers avoided those types of scenarios at *The Sides.* Took the cash, ignored preventing G.K. targets from being hit. *Every con is an animal, the strong prey on the weak.*

"What about my refund?" Nash said.

Powers said, "Let me work shit out."

"Time I ain't got much of," Nash said. "We got people all over the place in case you take too much of it."

Powers eyed Nash. *Everything I say gets back to Terry Azzure in the Cleveland Supermax. This is real shit, I need to take this conversation seriously.* Azzure ran the national G.K. operation from a supposedly secure cell. Orders were issued on paper with piss ink. The messages were invisible until the reader ran a lit match underneath the paper. Azzure got his orders out no matter how tight the prison was. *Man can have you put in the hat if you're not careful. Checkmate, Steve, Checkmate.*

"I'll work something out," Powers said.

"Fair enough," Nash said. "This is how shit gets done in the G.K."

7 Major Crimes Detective Tom Hammond waited in his department-issue sedan, ate his lunch and eyed the area with suspicion. Examined the streets surrounding the car while sitting in the afternoon light. Devoured a sixty-three cent double whammy from a 1950s-style burger stand. The area served as a haven for methamphetamine sellers. *No one comes here unless they have to*. The place was deserted except for a young black man with an infectious smile. Tom gave his change to the man, who counted the quarters and nickels at a picnic table. *What are you doing here, Tom? You should report it in and have uniforms come through to pick Angel up*.

Tom resisted the urge to go that route. *No telling who combs through my files*. Tom avoided writing many details on pending cases. Kept his partner away from his leads. *Maybe it's for Derek's own sanity*. Tom switched off his police radio, comforted by silence. *Working off the clock has its benefits*. Tom rubbed his eyes. His brain kept chattering throughout the night, limiting Tom to five hours of sleep.

Eying the area, Tom's eyes focused on the two-lane asphalt. *I'm running out of time*. Other leads on Angel were soft. Memories faded when Angel's last points of contact saw Tom's badge. *Nobody talks when Irish Pete wants someone dead*. Tom questioned if he should bring Angel into custody. *The old man scares everybody. Most cops would have known not to protect her*. Christine Gryzbowsky remained concerned about Angel. The locals had another name for a girl like Angel: *Strawberry*. Willing to let a man do anything to her for coke.

Tom sipped diet soda from a can. The taste of diet was hard to adjust to. Regular soda sweet was killing him. *I've heard stories about what cons do for sugar at The Sides*. Tom blocked those horror stories out of his mind, put the can aside. *Come on, Angel. Where are you?* Tom wolfed down another bite of his burger. Let his eyes drift along the street. Waiting.

Floating newspaper sections tumbled in the soft wind around the car. Tom's eyes caught the paper, then locked onto a shadowy figure who slipped out of the alley, down the street. Tom leaned forward, eying a gaunt male figurehead moving away from the sun. Man headed toward a collection of two-story brick buildings. Each crumbling structure wore boards and graffiti decorating their façades. *Is that where you are, Angel? Thinking they wouldn't find you here?* Tom focused on the condemned buildings, invisible to Irish Pete's soldiers. *None of them would notice this. Places too low class for even scum like them.*

Tom drove the car with his foot hovering over the brake. Wheels rolled on the asphalt at a calm pace. The burger stand came into the rearview mirror. Ahead, the figure walked faster. The man bore emaciated cheeks, dark circles sunken around his eyes. The man did not pay attention to Tom; his focus locked onto a nearby building. *He's trying to find a fix.* The man darted toward the boarded up building entrance. He latched onto a large piece of plywood, pulled it back and squeezed himself inside.

Tom parked the sedan, stepped out with the door open. Noted the broken sidewalk, covered with scattered *alley apples* from the building's façade. A glance to the building's second story window allowed Tom to spot a pale face watching him. Tom grinned, reached inside his sedan and produced a portable police-issue cherry top. Planted the cherry top on the sedan's roof, flipped the switch. The cherry top came alive. Mayhem erupted inside the abandon structure. Twenty squatters hemorrhaged toward the exits. The fiends breached plywood sheet barriers. They wore filthy clothes, running free of the building unmolested by arrest or Tom's concern.

Tom flipped off the cherry top and headed toward the unblocked building entrance. His nostrils were assaulted by the odor of methane. The fumes forced Tom to cover his face with his tie. The pungent fragrance intensified during his descent into the drug den. Emaciated people were laying unconscious on the building's floor. Tom felt his shoes *squish* as he landed in pools of foreign liquid. He checked each room for Angel. *What if she's not here?* His attention was drawn by a noise in the back.

Tom unlatched the leather strap on his sidearm. Eyes went further along the walls, examining each shadow and crevice, trying to detect what the sound was. *Careful, Tom, anyone could be back there. Maybe it's someone with a sheet that wants to fight to stay on the outside.* Tom moved down the hallway. His front toe went first, then the rest of the foot on each step. The light from the entrance waned, increasing the corner shadows. *Anyone could be hiding, ready to jump me.* A closed door sat the end of the hallway. Tom's fingers gripped his sidearm. With his free hand, Tom reached out to the door, pushed it. The door opened, revealing a desolate room.

The room held a dirty mattress covered by four people. In the middle was Angel, her skin sick and pale. The damp mattress was blackened with sweat and grime. Tom noted the tiny brown spiders crawling out of the mattress edges. The three other fiends with Angel were unconscious. The room was caked with a stench of perspiration and methamphetamine. The floor sat littered with candy wrappers, dead plastic lighters and broken shards of burnt glass. Angel stirred awake in front of Tom. He moved in close, lightly slapping her cheek. Angel's eyes fluttered. Tom noticed a long saliva string that ran from her lips to the mattress as she spoke.

"What's going on?"

"Up," he said. His nose caught a hard dose of meth fumes which dove into his lungs, causing him to cough.

Angel vomited a few inches from the man lying next to her who slept undisturbed. The man suffered from meth mouth, teeth eradicated by neglect. Tom latched onto Angel's arm, pulling her limp body to stand. Angel offered no resistance as Tom put her over his shoulder. He listened to her wheeze. *She weighs less than I would have thought.* Tom turned around to eye the hallway to exit the building.

A gaunt young man sat on the hallway floor in front of Tom. The man wore torn denim pants, no shirt. He smiled at Tom, delirious. The man rolled his shaved head with his shoulders folded, dumping his hands in his lap. *Is he going to stop me?* Tom reached down to his sidearm with his free hand, prepared. *Please don't make me shoot you. I will if I have to. But don't make me do it.*

"Hey."

"Hi," Tom said.

Move, Tom, move. Tom pushed toward the exit, Angel draped over his shoulder. Brushed by the gaunt man. *There are eyeballs on me. He's going to block me.* Tom shuffled his feet, exiting the building's entrance before the man could say anything else. Tom edged to the sedan, popped the back door open. Put Angel inside, pushed her legs in and slammed the door shut. Tom turned back, eying the building's entrance, staring into the hallway. There was no sign of the gaunt man.

Tom yanked the cherry top off the roof, tossed it inside the sedan. Jumping behind the wheel, Tom turned over the engine, drove away. Heart racing, Tom's forehead and arms were sweaty. Tom glanced in the rearview mirror at his reflection. Noticed he had dilated pupils. *Jesus, I've gotten a contact high. If a uniform pulled me over, I would piss a positive.* Tom drove a short distance to a gas station. He parked, got out and eyed Angel, who was passed out in the back seat.

The gas station stop was interesting. The pregnant cashier struggled to give Tom change off a five dollar bill. Bought a couple dollar-eighty-three bottles of water. Tom returned to the sedan, thirsty. Gunned down his bottle of water and felt the rush blow out of him. Tom's heart returned to a normal beat. Noticed Angel awake in the back seat. Tom handed off a water bottle to her and let Angel choke it down. Her skin returned a pinkish hue. *She dehydrated in that place.*

"Where are you taking me?"

Tom looked in the rearview at Angel. "Somewhere safe."

Angel didn't question it. *Maybe she trusts me.* Tom wondered if that were true. *Maybe she knows there's no escape.* He turned over the engine, rolled out of the gas station lot. Tom adjusted the rearview and watched Angel's eyes examine the details of the sedan's back seat.

"You a cop?"

"Yeah, I'm a cop."

"You taking me in, or to him?"

"No."

Angel leaned forward. "Then where?"

"Don't puke in the car," Tom said. "I don't want to drive with the smell."

She's a calm cat. Tom caught his reflection in the rearview. *You can't trust anyone. Not even Ben Dereks.* Tom had kept Dereks out of the situation to protect his partner. *He's got a wife and kid, Tom. What have you got that's so precious?* Tom turned the sedan south, headed down Highway two-seven. Leaving the city limits, drove past the Rivers End Casino. The native tribe was constructing twin tower hotels to add to its gaming complex. Five large, yellow-steel cranes worked in unison placing the beams in place. *The world keeps moving. Even if Irish Pete kills Angel, nothing ever stops.*

Twenty minutes later, Tom turned onto a gravel road. The sedan kicked up dust for two hundred yards. Ahead was a group of motel huts and an S.U.V. next to a thicket of evergreens. The five motel huts were one-room suites. Tom parked next to the S.U.V., cut the sedan's engine, got out. Saw Evan Hanaran approaching. *Man still looks like he's one of us.* In his mid-fifties, Hanaran bore a small, muscular frame. Sported a distinguished silver crew cut. Shaking hands, Hanaran grabbed Tom's elbow, sizing him up with a large grin.

"You need to lift weights again, Tommy Boy."

Tom pointed. "Cut the shit, you know I don't like that."

Hanaran winked. "Sorry, kid. Old habit."

"Who else is here?"

"Just us and the raccoons," Hanaran said. "Nothing until fishing season so I winterize the rooms to cut costs."

Tom looked back at highway twenty-seven. No cars passed. The evergreens stood quiet to the north. Tom headed to the trunk, popping it. Hanaran retrieved a pink duffle bag of clothes Tom had purchased prior to finding Angel. *You've been prepping since Christine called you last night. There's no going back now.* Tom opened the sedan's back door, helped Angel out. The girl wiped her face with her sleeves and squinted at the light of dusk.

"Where are we?"

"If you don't know, then they don't either," Tom said.

"Hell, I couldn't find us and I own the joint," Hanaran said.

The retired detective moved around Angel and Tom. Showed them to motel room five, pushing the door open. There were two beds. Each held patterned comforters. The beds sat over shag red carpet, with fake wooden paneling on the walls. An old black & white television held bent rabbit ears, sitting on a lime green armchair.

Hanaran tossed the duffle bag onto the far bed.

"Haven't paid a nickel for new stuff since I bought it three years back," he said.

Tom said, "I hope you aren't bragging."

Angel went over to the furthest bed. Pulled clothes out of the duffle bag and held them against her. *I had to guess her size when I bought them.* Tom noted that he left all of the tags on the clothes. *My mother would be horrified.* Angel turned back to the men, acting sultry. *This is her move if she wants to manipulate the situation. Convince us to let her go back to the abandoned building with her friends.* Her emaciated features did nothing to attract either man. Angel batted her green eyes. Bit her lip. Posed her backside out while doing a turn. Tom gestured to the bathroom.

"Clean yourself up."

Angel's face soured. Took her clothes, exiting to the bathroom. Tom started to follow, but Hanaran stuck his arm out to block him.

"Window has been fixed. Doesn't open more than three inches," Hanaran said. "She can't slip out."

"Thanks for doing this."

Hanaran laughed. "This is fun, Tommy. What else do I have to do?"

"You okay with this?"

"Tommy, this is beyond you to pull this shit. You know who's involved."

"You pulled shit like this."

Hanaran said, "Look where I am. You cross certain people, you gotta live with the results."

"You were a good cop. You believed in the rules. I believe in the rules."

"I was the best cop," Hanaran said. "Now, I guard twenty-two thousand barrels of rice for ten-fifty-five an hour with no benefits. By doing this, you're crossing that line too."

"Are you saying you regret doing it?"

"I wish someone with my experience had given me the option of getting out. I'm giving that to you now," Hanaran said, gesturing to Tom's right ankle. "You still got the piece down there, right?"

Tom felt the weight of his ankle for the first time. *I'm used to it being there.* "It's there."

"Someday you will have to use one from going down for doing the wrong thing."

"I can't do that."

Hanaran said, "That's the thing about you, Tommy. You'll keep going along until your life takes a nosedive. And if you have too much faith in the system, you'll snap like I did."

8 *In this world, it's all about being the last man standing.* Brian Tuttle firmly believed his personal rule of survival. Realized the trouble he had coming from outside *The Sides*. Brian's organization contact was Styles Remington. *Man means business and excuses aren't cutting it this time.* The slicked-back Italian weaved through *The Sides* Visitors Center with expert knowledge. Dressed in elegant attire to protect him from the winter. Styles' clothing made Brian feel self-conscious about his own threads. *I got the retirement home look going on.* Remington was Irish Pete's top lieutenant. *He knows how to complete dirty jobs for the old man.*

Brian didn't play tough. *I am tough. That's the difference between goons and me. I'm not a mope. I'm a force to be reckoned with.* Brian remained concerned about his safety at *The Sides*. *Things weren't as secure as I'd hoped. First, Nash pulls his shit. But Jonas gets iced.* Brian had used a throwaway cell phone to reach Freeway Phil and learn about Jonas' death. *That tub of lard fence says he ain't seen the stones.* Brian's lone option appeared to be dealing with Remington. That meant dealing with the old man by extension.

Brian wondered about the old man's involvement in giving Nash the green light. Brian wanted to dismiss the notion, but the suggestion gnawed at him. *Styles wouldn't be here if the old man were aiming to kill me.* Remington made his way across the rows of wooden cubbies affixed with wired Plexiglas. Each stall had a phone. Brian watched him sit and pick up his receiver. The two crooks stared at each other in muted silence until the phone line came alive. *We know the Feds listen. Least we can do is make it right.*

"Reunion's coming up. The old prom king is looking at the votes from back in the day," Remington said, meaning: *Irish Pete wants the stones. He's trying to decide who iced Jonas.*

"Chaperone is a bitch. Won't let us play any records," Brian said, meaning: *I don't know where the diamonds are.*

"Parties always have their crashers."

Brian paused, then said, "Crashers got to have sanctions put against them."

"Prom King wants his slice from the drink tickets after two years."

Brian said, "What do you suggest?"

"Find someone outside," Remington said. "Let the Prom King handle them after." Meaning: *Find a mope to ice after everything is finished.*

"Does he have an escort?"

Remington said, "Tick."

Brian paused. Then he said, "He's an interesting cat."

"A fair word to describe him. Man has his invitation tonight."

Remington hung up the phone. Nodded at Brian while rising from his seat, then exited the Visitors Center. *Two guys aiming for a payday who both get iced at the end of the party.* Brian shrugged. *Part of the danger of the business, but someone's going down and can't be me.* Brian left the Visitors Center and returned to his cell. Part of the issue was selling the split of the diamonds. With Jonas, the task was simple. *He was a crook who grabbed any job.* With Tick and a new fall guy, it might present a challenge. *Find someone stupid or greedy enough to want a split of the action. End of the night, it's a bullet for their trouble.*

I did the right thing holding onto the stones for this long. Otherwise Brian had no leverage. No way to keep Irish Pete from icing him after Brian's conviction. Guys screwed themselves by dealing without bargaining chips. *You can't play at the table without chips.* Every con he knew tried to bluff. Never worked. *Cops and cons always call a bluff.* Brian had prevented the score from being found by the heat. Stashed the bag in a Spokane clothing store. Did shots with The Serg at *Exit One* when the state patrol arrived. *None of the warrants were about the stones. The heist became a cold case.*

That con Lewis Harrington knows someone getting out. Brian rubbed at his chin, shook off the idea of talking to Lewis. *No, he will offer me some stovepipe: A stupid guy who holds up U-Hauls because he thinks they have lots of cash.* Things were not as easy as back in the day. *Back then, you had ten mopes ready to do anything for you. Hell, they would break out of prison to impress you.* Now, everyone was smarter. *They know how much time gets added on.*

Heading back to his cell, Brian caught a glimpse of Frank Gryzbowsky selling packets to an inmate. Brian stopped and watched his dealer, sizing him up. *He's right for this. He's out and needs work.* Desperation worked in Brian's favor. *He can handle himself. Wait until he gets a load of The Tick.* Brian motioned to Frank. The man displayed a wad of paper as he got to Brian.

"Should be all there," Frank said.

"Don't doubt it for a moment."

"I do something wrong?"

"I need a courier on the outside."

"Any heat on this?"

Brian lied. "Delivery job, low heat."

"What type of paper?"

"Half of what the fence gives you," he said.

Frank appeared intrigued. *You think you're a smooth-talker, don't you? You never met a guy like me before. I can talk you into anything.*

"What's the cargo?"

Brian put his hand on Frank's shoulder. "Are you in? I gotta know you are in."

Frank nodded. "I'm in."

He gave Frank's cheek two soft pats. "Come by tomorrow. We'll settle on the details."

Brian headed back to his cell alone with a grin across his face. Let Frank imagine the amount of paper he would make on the deal. *Styles wanted a mope, so I'm giving him one*. Brian entered his two-man cell as the lone occupant. Went to sleep that night continuing to smile. *I'm going to be the last man, as it should be.*

Spokane had three major divisions of investigation: Sex Crimes, the Gang Task Force and Major Crimes. Detective Tom Hammond had worked in "the Majors" for eight years. Any tip on a drug connection or possible bank robbery went to Tom. He was one of five detectives in the division. That meant he sat in a cubicle, overlooking a sea of paperwork. *Without forms, where would we be in life?* Tom signed his name in a scrawl. *Could impersonate a doctor's signature.* Tom shuffled papers, wondering if anyone bothered to read half of the forms he had signed.

9

Tom's job was easier than other detectives. *Dan Rahn comes to mind.* Rahn dealt specifically with the city's *John Doe* cases. *Hard enough to solve a case when you have a suspect. I cannot imagine having nothing to go on.* Rahn was loud, abrasive and other officers avoided talking to him. District Commander William Albright had attempted to rid the department of Rahn for months with little luck. *The one time the police guild fights for a cop, and they protect him.* Rahn received a promotion to division supervisor to prevent him from suing the department.

Albright had succeeded in preventing Rahn from carrying Rahn's long blade. *Who was Rahn endangering? His evidence was crime scene photographs and interviews.* Rahn also received criticism for his handling of evidence. Chain-of-custody issues from the crime scene to the evidence lab. Tom blamed budget cuts that forced the C.S.I. teams from doing proper fieldwork. That decision by the higher ups had allowed for mistakes. *I have made a few screw-ups on evidence and let a few cases die. So I understand how Rahn's cases go nowhere.* Tom still got the vibe that Rahn was a creep, though. *We're all creeps in this line of work. Few people stay married for long to cops.*

Tom's home life matched the mountain of paperwork. His left hand no longer displayed a wedding band. For the third time, he was single. *This one had promised me to be different.* Tom had taken various steps to allow her to know his work schedule. She refused to understand his duties after three years of marriage. Meant another trip to his lawyer's office, coupled with paperwork to fill out.

Tom's lawyer was sick of him. The man provided an intervention with Tom after proposing for the third time. *And I did not listen. Shows I'm the fool, not him.* Tom remembered laughing when his lawyer told Tom that he wasn't marriage material. "'You can keep paying me to get a divorce. It's like baseball. You've struck out.'" *The job application for my wife is closed. I will take applicants, but I doubt if I will make any placements.*

Tom had moved his things into a six-month lease apartment. Where he could drink a beer and watch TV in peace. His lack of martial success mirrored throughout the department. *Everyone here has been through one or two divorces.* The stupid ones put work on the back burner to save their families. Those detectives were bounced after some victim's family complained to upper administration about no progress on their case. *We're expected to be monks when we earn a shield. It's hard not to have all of your friends who are blue. Every civilian you meet acts as if you are going to bust them right there.*

Tom's eyes went from his paperwork to Rahn who moved toward his cubicle. The man wielded a mountain stomach. Rahn managed to step quietly across the carpet until he snuck up on a person. *He's a fat Mohican.* Not this time, because Tom could smell Rahn coming to him. Rahn's skin was coated in a stinging sweat. Ben Dereks had complained to Human Resources, but the complaint was shelved. *They say Rahn has a disability because he smells like rotten eggs.* Dereks wanted to file a grievance with the union to force Rahn to shower.

"You and Dereks ever find that girl?"

Tom returned to his paperwork, tried to ignore the smell and said, "Still working on that."

"She's a lost cause. We'll find her in a dumpster later," Rahn said, then displayed a file. "Garberg went into labor with her kiddo this morning. Means you share the load. This vic was found last night. See if you can do anything to help the clearance rate."

Tom took the file, opened the two-page jacket on his desk. "And suspects?"

"Dereks has got the wife in the box," Rahn said. "See what she knows."

"She ain't gonna know anything."

"Did I call the psychic hotline? Get to chatting, she might tell you who shot Kennedy."

Rahn stomped away to bother another detective. Tom picked up the file, examined the contents, then set it down. Mind wasn't on the murder victim in the jacket file. Tom's focus stayed on Angel, who remained hidden with Hanaran. Tom picked up his phone, dialed Hanaran, who answered after two rings, sounding tired.

"How is she?"

Hanaran said. "I'm watching old sitcoms. She's painting her nails, doing her hair."

Dereks walked over to Tom's cubicle. Didn't seem to care that Tom was on the phone. "Hey, Rahn says you need to be part of this."

Tom covered the receiver with his palm. To Dereks: "Give me a minute." Tom uncovered the receiver, edging it closer to his mouth. To Hanaran, Tom said, "Keep your eyes open."

Tom hung up the line, grabbed the file off his desk, heading to the interview room. Dereks followed, leaned against the threshold next to the closed door. Tom read the file: *Jonas Reed. Local bar owner shot dead in the Central District*. Garberg wrote that there were burglary tools, but that Reed had no prior convictions. *Storeowner found the body in the morning. Anonymous caller claimed a guy named Junior running from the scene. Who is Junior?* Tom eyed a smiling Dereks.

"That's why you're the primary," Dereks said. "Rahn thought I couldn't handle it."

"Lucky me."

"Every time I see that clown, I feel like I'm about to catch a disease," Dereks said. "Any word on Angel Barnes? Rahn is asking."

"No," Tom said. "I think Sully skipped on us."

"Wouldn't be the first time."

"No, it wouldn't."

Tom entered the interview room that the cops referred to as *the box*. Four walls in a tiny room to grab a confession or garner evidence from the person inside. Tom noted the large woman who sat at the table. Tears caked her cheeks. Dried herself with tissues. Mascara made black streaks on her face. Tom turned back to Dereks, who followed him and closed the door.

"Gloria Reed," Dereks said. "Her husband is the vic."

Tom sat across from Gloria. "You need water or anything?"

"No," Gloria said, her crying ceased as she sniffled. Her eyes showed angry intensity as she glared at Tom and said, "Tell me who did it."

Tom shrugged. "Tell me why he had tools on him."

"Tools?"

"Yeah, the kind you break into shit with," Tom said. "Besides, all we got is a name."

Gloria leaned in. "Who?"

Gloria balled her wet tissues, tossed them. Eyes boring in to Tom. *She put on the water works to see what I knew. But inside, she's tough.* Tom's focus broke free of her gaze first. He examined the suspect names carved into the table. *Woman wants blood. She wants details, as much as I will give her.* Tom returned to looking at her, seeing that she had finished staring at him.

"Call tags someone named Junior," Tom said. "But you don't know anyone named Junior, do you?"

"I've never heard of anyone named Junior."

Years of experience told Tom that Gloria was lying. Liars sold themselves as honest when they told a lie. *If they lied without attempting to sell me on it, I might believe them.* Psychopaths were the best liars. They acted indifferent when either telling a lie or the truth. *Like when that woman pushed her eight-month-old son out the third story window on Elm.* She acted normal whether she told a lie or the truth. *Took us three years to prove she did it on purpose. Right before she gave birth to another child.*

Tom watched Gloria rise and push the chair away. She gritted her teeth, angry. *She's going to get revenge*. She moved toward the door. Tom stretched his arm out and planted his hand against the wall to block her exit. Gloria stopped short of his arm, looking at Tom. *She could tear my arm off if she wants to. Both she and I know that. She could do it, not think twice about it.*

"Who's Junior?"

"Don't know," Gloria said. "My Jonas has his wake tomorrow at the bar."

"Sure."

Tom moved his hand from the wall. Gloria plowed past, exiting the box. *She's going after Junior. We should tail her, nab Junior, and keep him safe from her*. Tom disregarded the statement. It amused him. The city had few funds to do anything of substance, including stakeouts. *We're no longer detectives who prevent crimes. We're the cleanup crew*. Derek whistled as Gloria left.

"I wouldn't want her after me," Dereks said.

"Yeah, poor Junior, right?"

"She'll make him sorry, even if he's not the man."

Tom went back to his desk with the jacket underneath his arm. *I'm getting burned out again*. The last time, he took two weeks leave. Instead of sleeping, Tom became restless and fought insomnia. Drank about five cases of Deschutes microbrew while watching old movies. Used the empties to form a "beer-a-mid" next to his sofa. Ended up cursing out the sheriff in the movie *First Blood* for messing with John Rambo. Tom had been so loud that his apartment manager banged on his door to shut him up.

Tom noticed that his workspace had changed. Tom's eyes encompassed the area but saw nothing missing. No paperwork gone. *No one steals what they don't want.*

Then, Tom smelled foul air. The sour odor hung in the area around his chair. Tom stood, looking around. Rahn had been at Tom's desk. *He wanted something while I was in the box.* Tom unlocked his desk, withdrawing his sidearm. Holstered it deep. He moved free of his cubicle, eying Rahn at the other end of the office. *What did you want at my desk, Rahn?*

Tom followed the fat man to the back of the department. Rahn went into a stairwell without noticing he was being tailed. Tom stopped at the stairwell, counted to *thirty-two*, then entered. Listened to heavy footsteps clomp onto the concrete toward the bottom. Tom moved down the stairwell, leaving himself enough distance to escape. *Where is he going?* Rahn was two flights down and exited into the department's parking garage.

Tom went down and put his hand on the doorframe before it closed. Opened it, peered into the shadows of the parking garage. The place crawling with shadows where the halogen lamps did not bake in white light. Few cars were parked inside. Those remaining vehicles were in small groups. Tom stepped out, quiet. Drew out his Glock, kept it against his side. Tom could not locate Rahn. Searched the area until his ears caught the sound of an idling car engine. Tom moved around the edge of the stairwell. On the other side sat a black Lexus with Rahn leaning in the driver's window.

Rahn said, "You're wasting your time."

"Are you sure?"

"It's a dead end."

Tom held his Glock firm. Left his finger off the trigger. The fat detective stood free of the Lexus and moved away. Tom edged into the shadows of the corner. Held his breath as Rahn moved through Tom's location. Rahn stopped but did not turn. *He sees you and he's not saying anything. You've been made.* Tom held tight to his position, waited. Rahn moved, exiting into the stairwell. Tom exhaled, then eyed the Lexus. It sat idling with the driver's window down. Tom headed to the car and pointed his sidearm at the driver, ready to pull the trigger.

"Out," Tom said. "Now."

Tom opened the door, then grabbed onto the driver's arm and pulled him out. The driver had a cell phone in his right hand, which was tossed back into the Lexus. Light hit the driver's face revealing that it was Styles Remington, gopher for Irish Pete. Tom turned Styles around, slamming him against the Lexus. Tom worked his free hand through every pocket that Styles had.

"You sure this is necessary, officer?"

Tom latched onto an object in Styles' pocket. Drew it out, discovering that it was a switchblade. Tom's thumb pressed the handle's button. Out *hissed* a blade from the depths. Tom turned Styles around, seeing the slicked-back Italian smirking. Tom displayed the switchblade to Styles, who was indifferent.

Styles said, "Tommy Boy's got a new toy?"

"Illegal weapon," Tom said. "Gets you eighteen months in Geiger for carrying."

"You planted it. Besides, you know who makes the rules around here."

"I enforce the rules."

"How's that working for you, Tommy Boy?" Styles said. "It keep you from eating microwave slop for dinner? Tell me, Tommy Boy. Tell me you're doing well by playing by the rules."

Tom released Styles from his grip. *It's a losing battle.* Styles would walk even if busted and Tom would have to watch him leave. Irish Pete had ordered a cop's house torched once when one of his men was detained. *Everything in this city is up for grabs.* That's why no one mentioned Irish Pete's name within the department. No one trusted anyone else. Styles adjusted himself in front of Tom, displaying a cocky grin. Styles pointed at Tom's ankle.

"Got that clean piece down there?" Styles said. "You gonna make me pay by using it?"

Ashamed, Tom's eyes fell to his ankle. Hanaran had made him wear an ankle holster with a clean revolver after earning his detective shield. *Get Out of Jail Card.* That was what the other blue called it. Tom carried the clean piece on him daily. *Just in case I can't play by the rules or the rules change for me. That's what Hanaran told me I needed it for.* Guilt resided in the fact that piece remained, weighing against his ankle. *I'm so used to it, I don't feel it anymore.*

"Leave."

Styles laughed. "You need some help down the line, let me know."

Tom aimed his sidearm at Styles' face. The slicked-back Italian spat a wad that landed near Tom's feet. Styles' indifference to the pistol bothered Tom. *If I pull the trigger, he wins.* Tom dropped his sidearm, returning to the stairwell. Tom held onto Styles' switchblade. Pressed the handle's button, hearing the blade *hiss* back inside. *There's a long way to go before the department is no longer dirty.*

10 Chief CO Steve Powers resisted the urge to cry in his car. Steve witnessed his father's house painted from red to yellow. The sight would've disgusted his father. The red exterior matched the Lake Coeur d'Alene autumn. *How can I let them do this to you, dad?* Steve rubbed his forehead. Denied any retaliation fantasies. Dreams of forcing the painters to stop working, at gunpoint. Steve watched the yellow go up as his cell rang. Saw the caller was his sister, Kara.

Kara said, "Happy birthday."

"I was trying to forget."

"Nice attitude. Where are you?"

"Going to work," Steve said.

The painters coated the red walls with white primer. The house was being stripped. Whatever Steve's father had invested in the place would vanish. Some piece of trivia that a realtor tells perspective buyers. *That says nothing about the man.* Steve shook his head. *I should have found a way to keep your house.*

"Are you okay?" Kara said. "You seem distracted."

"I'm fine."

"Are you at their house again?" Kara said. "You need to stop going there."

Steve's eyes caught on the ebb of the lake. The wooden dock which stretched out twenty feet beyond the shore. Childhood memories of leaping into the water, forming cannonballs that soaked the dock, now gone.

Steve's father sat during the early morning hours with a thermos of coffee, wrapped in a blanket. Dad spent his police retirement watching the sun rise and drop over the lake. Steve made certain that his father died watching the sunset. By then, the dementia had caused havoc to his father's personality. But Steve's father always remembered the house and the lake. Steve had checked him out of the residence home one last time. When his father had asked Steve to help him die. Used a solution given by his father's physician to preserve his dignity. *I never told Kara how he died, only that he… went.*

"It's our place, Kara. I don't care what the papers say."

"This isn't helping you, Steve," Kara said.

"It's a free country, Kara. I am not hurting anyone."

Steve saw the couple who bought the place after Steve was forced to sell. A Silicon Valley set able to pay the lake's high property taxes. They had two children and a little Yorkshire mix. The dog was destroying the lawn. Steve's father had manicured the grass to sit two inches high during the summer. Hours spent installing rose bushes were shrugged off by the new tenants. Steve spotted small mounds of dirt where gophers ran unchecked.

"You remember that dog walker who put out the restraining order on dad?" Steve said.

"Yes," Kara said. "Leave a steamer on his lawn, you got sprayed with a hose."

Steve laughed. "He was a decent man."

"I remember waking up to the smell of bacon and eggs. Every time I smell that being cooked now, I think of him."

"He was there for us, wasn't he?" Powers said. "Not one of those bad guys you regret knowing, right?"

"He kept us from helping him," Kara said. "I wish he would have said he was having memory trouble. That he kept it quiet so long bothered me most."

"Dad didn't share a lot of things he should have."

He was protecting us by keeping secrets. The property taxes kept being raised and his father said nothing about it. The taxes shot up two hundred percent in five years. It started while Steve's father was in retirement. Fifty years ago when his father had built the lake house, the area property taxes were small. The boom of residential housing around Lake Coeur d'Alene changed that in the last fifteen years. Condos with lake views rose up. Neighbors sold family homes for the rich wanting vacation homes. Housing prices fluctuated, as did property taxes.

"There was nothing you could do," Kara said.

"I could have done something."

Kara said, "That's the same mentality that got you kicked off the Coeur d'Alene force."

I kept the place as long as I could. Steve set up backyard barbecues with his friends on the force. With one of his ex-wives, he attempted to make it a home. The tax bills soared after his father's death. Steve had no choice but to find money to keep the house. *I should not have had to make the choice.* The decision cost Steve his Coeur d'Alene police career. Too many successful drug busts as the Tactical Team leader. Standing over five hundred thousand dollars in unmarked street bills. Thinking about all of the good that could come if he took just enough. Not enough that anyone would miss it. *I deserved to keep my father's house. We were both blue.*

"Kara, I got to go to work."

"Okay, but come by my house. Don't go over there anymore."

"I don't know if I can promise that."

"Well, you need to follow through with your promises, Steve."

"Listen, I've got to go."

"Steve, don't shut me out. I miss you."

"Kara, it's busy at work. I'll stop by sometime this week."

Steve hung up on his sister. Each day he faced the regret of working at Sideville State Correctional. Wished instead he had his job back at the C.D.A. police department. *I used to keep this town clean. I don't feel that way anymore.* When Steve put on the guard uniform, he considered himself less blue. *I stopped being a part of something*. His nights spent hanging out at the Iron Nail bar, because it was a cop bar. *No longer welcome there, no matter what Shay Baxter says*. He quit the police softball league after he stopped recognizing the cops on his team. *Kara writes my name on her church registry. So I'm eligible for that religious league. Playing with accountants and file clerks who hit doubles for Jesus*.

The sun dropped behind Sideville State Correctional as he drove to it. Steve itched for a Hell24. The last tool of the corrections trade was the prison search. The inmates and staff called it "Hell24" because that it is what it became. No prisoner slept on a mattress. No one watched television or drank coffee. Everything stopped for a prison search. Steve had scheduled the search with outside staff on separate timetables. Purposely keeping other C.O.s in the dark prevented word from leaking to the convicts.

Normally, outside staff would come in but Powers was against it. Wanted his own staff to do the dirty work this time. Do a thorough search of every inmate, their cell and the surrounding area. Sweep out all of the contraband, weapons or purol. It was a twenty-four hour day where prison visitors, letters, phone calls, or releases were not allowed. A Hell24 got everyone's attention. The cons would know this one was coming; Fruit Loop Johnson would be on their radar. A third-strike con getting his things messed with would take matters into his own hands. Everyone's income would be affected by the action. *You toss a milkshake on a guard and everyone pays. That is how we do shit in the 208. Checkmate, Johnson, checkmate.*

He assembled three guards in the conference room. Greg Tad ran the minimum-security dormitory. Simon Christopher and Henry Trent covered medium security and the dining hall. Christopher and Trent were best friends who shared smoke breaks and gambling junkets. They had done Johnson over with the nightstick. He stood in front of them, pressing his index finger into the conference table.

"I'm calling it."

"Why?" Tad said. "McPherson doesn't do shit," speaking of the guard who got the milkshake.

Powers eyed Tad. "I'm going to pretend I didn't hear that."

"You didn't hear me?" Tad said. "I'll say it again. That boy doesn't do shit. He's lazy."

Trent nodded. "Ryan is not one of us."

"We don't let a milkshake slide by," Powers said. "Otherwise it's us next."

Each guard exchanged agreement. Christopher gestured to Powers. "What about the warden?"

"I'm going to him next," Powers said. "Make sure the animals know Johnson caused this."

He headed to the warden's office. The butterball in a sweater vest read paperwork while eating a powered jelly donut. Powers waited until the warden gestured for him to enter. "I want to do a thorough search for contrabands and weapons."

"Is this doable with your own staff?"

"Cheaper with outside group," Powers said.

"That's acceptable," the warden said. "What about Nash?"

"Nash wants a refund."

The warden said. "Rumor floating around that Tuttle is sitting on something pretty."

Powers shook his head. "I might believe it if he says that to me. But the people in here have master's degrees in lying."

"Keep your eyes open," the warden said. "He might have something worth retiring on."

"If something shakes out, I will let you know," Powers said.

Spokane's underground knew Patrick Quinn. His unofficial street name was "Tick." Criminals considered him a legend. Others got iced for crimes he escaped clean. His audacious jobs separated him from other thieves. A hood with nothing to lose, Tick got his moniker by burrowing himself into people's lives. The joke was that he would drain them if they did not cut him out entirely. His adventures were spoken of with wonderment and disdain. His reputation was scorned by virtue of getting away clean with every crime.

11

Styles Remington put in calls around the city to find him. Tick was the dumbest criminal to don a ski mask and he didn't always put one on. Three years back, he held up a Gas & Mart next to his house without a mask. He did wear his high school letterman's jacket with his last name printed on the back. There was a grand achievement to how he got away with the crime. Jonas Reed loved to share stories with Styles about Tick. Jonas laughed about how Tick escaped the noose.

'The heat catches Tick on the store cameras. So they got him. But the place is a meth front run by this Asian gang. The heat had been trying to take down those cats for months,' Jonas said to Styles. 'D.A. offers Tick a deal to serve as a witness against the owners. The kid walked even though he was the perp, the gang was the victim.

Because he robbed the only place in the city where he was the lesser of two evils.'

Tick was considered a legitimate crook after serving a small stretch after robbing this vacation cruises liner. During the overseas trip, he broke into guest cabins. He took jewels and cash while guests danced to Elvis impersonators in the showroom. Crooks avoided cruise liners because getting off one is difficult. Tick didn't realize how soon the ship went into lockdown after the thefts were reported. Again, he beat the rap. He found the sole business worried about reporting employee theft. He was declared a stowaway instead of an outright thief. He got sent up on a three-month term in county instead of facing a three-to-five year sentence. Because the company didn't want robberies reported on a statistic sheet.

He was a beauty to behold. Tick was five-six with pale albino skin, milky eyebrows against thin white hair. His Adam's apple protruded far beyond his broken nose. His cheeks littered with pockmarks. He offered beady dark eyes scoping out the next item to lift and fence. Like Jonas' DVD player, with scraped off ID numbers, sitting in *The Sin Bin*. Styles asked Jonas once about the DVD player. Jonas' reply: 'I don't want to know where it came from.'

Tick supported himself on goods he fenced to Freeway Phil in the Garland District. His skill zeroed in on a victim's stuff that wouldn't be noticed missing for two days. Tick's ability to elude the law did not include the buyers of his stolen goods. Buying a laptop or digital camera from Tick could mean a visit from the cops. *Letting him into your place while he sells you something is trouble*. He often robbed his customers if he eyed something he liked.

Tick eluded situations involving his own death. His employment with Baron Gamble's outfit came to an end quick. All because Tick had been a dumbass who got guys around him killed.

Gamble's brother Mac wanted Tick as an enforcer. Because there's 'nothing scarier than a white guy with a shotgun.' *The same goes for Devon, who may pull the trigger for no reason*. Tick was not up to the task of being an enforcer. He had too few brain cells. He had put a loaded shotgun in the trunk of Gamble's ride going to a meet. Tick hit a pothole, causing the shotgun to blast through the back seat. Sent a Gamble enforcer into the city morgue. Tick lost two fingers on his left hand to make amends for destroying Gamble's ride.

Baron Gamble was a thoughtful crook. He ran his criminal organization as a CEO. Styles guessed that after Irish Pete passed, Baron would run the city. *That's why I show him respect. You never know when you might be out of work when the old man passes*. Mac Gamble was muscle. But he had his own insight into Tick. Styles and Mac got to joking about Tick during a coke drop on South Hill.

'Man stole a roach coach. Owner was in the back serving tamales,' Mac said. 'Tick hops in, hits the gas. Sends the owner out the side window. Lands him on three old ladies waiting for their lunch order.'

Mac said Tick had crashed the vehicle into a fire hydrant a block away. 'That aluminum van tore in two pieces. Owner chased him down the street.' Styles laughed as he visualized the scene in his mind. *Some old fart dressed in chef's clothes, waving a spatula.* The Tick was original. Styles gave him enough respect.

After making his calls tonight, Styles located Tick in downtown. He was busting out taillights of parked cars. Each got whacked with a lead pipe. He had enough zeal to pretend he was at batting practice for the majors. Tick held the pipe with one hand and lost his grip with every completed swing. His last shot flew free of his hand. Sent the pipe into a Garfield doll suction-cupped back window of a Ford Taurus. He shook his head, but did not retrieve the pipe. *Maybe his fingerprints will magically wipe off the pipe.*

"What the hell are you doing, Pat?"

Tick noticed Styles for the first time. He was unaware someone would notice him. Any passerby could have attacked him from behind and gotten away with the act. When Tick pulled something, he got so involved nothing else mattered. *Tunnel vision is what I call it.* A parade of street cops could have slapped their nightsticks against their hands waiting for him. He wouldn't have known. *He's got a grape-sized brain, but a pair of plums that I admire.* He didn't avoid something because the heat might come down on him.

Styles stood freezing in his black overcoat. He attempted to dress his face with a smile, but held back. His teeth were attacked by the cold wind. The childish albino thief waved at him. He watched Tick pluck a dead filter off the street, sticking the wasted soldier in his mouth. He lit it with a cracked plastic lighter and puffed out the remaining two drags. He grinned as if his act showed intelligence. *I have a pack of Cools in my pocket.* He let it go.

"Styles Remington, in the flesh," Tick said. His sentences refused to squeak out. Instead, he snarled and gnarled each syllable on a jagged upper lip which curtained yellow Chiclets. "I make real paper here."

"Busting up cars?"

"Rates dropped with winter being shit. Snow fall makes insurance guys money," Tick said. "My guy hands paper out for this. I used to do this for free back in the day."

Styles nodded. The winter had been strange. The city received an annual dump of one hundred inches of snow before Christmas. Industries around the area were built around snowfall. Everything from snow plows to automatic car starters. Except for this year, when the city received less than ten inches. Odd for a place that resembled the Midwest, set against a mountain range next to the Pacific.

"Maybe God forgot about us."

Tick offered Styles a confused glance. "Huh?"

"Sorry, that's the West Coast Catholic in me. We only speak of God when it's a holiday or to blame Him for something," Styles said.

Tick shrugged. "You think God cares about a few cars?"

Styles laughed. "How do you target the right ones? You look to me to be hitting every car on the block."

Tick pointed a twisted finger at a sticker in a back window of a damaged car. It was of a Blue Bear, holding a honey jar, which read: Mead Man Insurance, the LOWEST rates in town. Styles eyes crept up to the other damaged cars. Several had the little sticker. He raised an eyebrow, impressed.

"He low-balls the entry rate on the customer to book the business, with a huge deductible. Then when shit happens, they call him up and sign on for a higher rate," Tick said.

"And he probably puts the stickers on the car windows himself," Styles said.

Tick grinned. "I hit some cars without the stickers. Make it so no one thinks I'm targeting anyone."

"Paper with this sounds decent, Tick," Styles said. "But with us, it's better."

Tick's eyes ignited. He wanted nothing more than to belong. It was evident that he was a true outsider. Styles had heard stories of Tick joining up with crooks doing any work offered. *He's a loser though. The ones I met in high school who hid a hot piece for you in their locker. Or who begged to be the wheelman on a grocery stick-up. Just to be a part of it.* If Tick was offered a chance to belong, he burned that bridge. *Offer him a living room to crash in and find your plasma gone with Tick by morning.*

Tick paused. Then he said, "Thought I was out. The old man didn't want amateur hour."

Styles shrugged, then lied. "Boss got a laugh out of it. He has a soft spot for you, Pat."

Tick pointed at Styles, defensive. "It could have happened to anyone."

"True, but it happened to you," Styles said. He checked himself, blocking an opportunity to smirk. Otherwise Tick would be aggressive and clam up. *No, keep him talking. You can laugh about him later.*

His actions drew the ire of Irish Pete. Stupidity was not a trait that the old man coveted. The detail was to bust into patrol cars that the heat parked unattended around high-crime areas. The County Sheriff's intention was to slow speeders and halt drug traffic. The department's program also left high value vehicles. Filled with a cadre of weapons. Sitting in the city's worst areas. The old man wanted Tick to snatch the items inside; shotguns, radios, and laptops. The goods were shipped across I-90 in less than five hours. Arrived for sale on Seattle's black market by morning.

Jonas Reed served as wheelman during the patrol car busts. To watch over Tick. Make sure he didn't do something stupid. Jonas shared a story with Styles called 'Tick versus the patrol car.' Explanations were asked for after Tick was so adamant that he would never do a patrol car again. *Even after I had orders left to fill.* The old man wanted to see if Tick was going independent like Junior Perry. So, over a few beers with Jonas, Styles received the answers. He didn't stop laughing for twenty minutes.

'Tick busts into a car. Sees this Taser in the glove compartment,' Jonas had said. 'His eyes go up like the Fourth at Riverside. To him, this ain't no Taser. It's a pistol with a box on the barrel end. Tick grabs the piece, but his hands slip. Thing hits the floor and goes off. Tags Tick with a ton of juice. I roll up to see why Tick is taking so damn long. Kid is laid out in the car when I find him. Slobbering with all of these wires on his chest like Frankenstein.'

"You guys think that stuff is simple, but you never get your hands dirty," Tick said.

"You think I've gone soft?" Styles said. He pulled out his switchblade without any emotion. Tick jumped as the blade extended. Styles did not flinch. "You were saying?"

Tick's eyes dropped. He didn't want to challenge Styles. *Tick may take two in the gut. I'll offer the old man's work to someone else if Tick dishes out sass.* Styles pressed the button to his switchblade.

The blade returned inside the handle. Tick searched the ground for another dead soldier to smoke. Jesus, *I got to watch this again?* Styles reached into his pocket. He pulled out a cigar that he had been saving. He held it out for Tick. The man's eyes grasped hold of the brown cylinder before his hands could.

"Pat, step up in the world a little."

The cigar offered was not the Cuban. That I keep for myself for later. Tick did not know the difference. He grabbed onto the cigar after Styles snapped off the end with a brass cutter. Tick stuck the cigar into his mouth and puffed as Styles lit it. The stogie's smoke made the young crook's eyes squint. The cigar burned out of the corner of the kid's mouth. Tick was sizing him up. I hate when people attempt subtlety when they haven't developed a skill for it. Tick pulled back on his yellow sweat-stained wife beater. Revealed little Taser scars on his hairless, freckled chest.

"I still got these, Styles," Tick said. "Still."

"The offer stands from us if you want it," Styles said. "Lots of paper, plus access to be back in."

Tick said, "Why did he decide to bring me back?"

Styles said, honest, "No clue. But you got an invite."

They stood there quiet. Tick coughed from the strength of the cigar. He enjoyed the taste while Styles listened to the stillness of the city night. The hum of street lamps overhead provided the sole music as they buzzed away. Styles eyed his idling Lexus a block away during his conversation with the Tick. He was starting to freeze.

Come on, kid.

Tick said, "I'm in."

Sully Brooks drove a beat-up white Chevy Astrovan, embarrassed. He wore a black turtleneck, leather gloves, slacks and boots. His face was covered with a ski mask offering nothing but lint, teeth and eyes. *I am going to do this*. He prepped himself as if he had been doing it forever. He had the urge to park the van and pee. He doubted Detective Dan Rahn would let him. Rahn sweated his foul odor in the seat next to him, ready to act if Sully ran. *Things have gone too far, man. First, we cut up Freeway, now this*.

The soccer mom deluxe headed south from the city and down highway twenty-seven. The moon illuminated the journey. Rahn ordered him not to turn on the van's brights. It forced Sully to peer harder as he made turns. *I could run off the road and spare misery tonight*. The van was not his style either. When he had asked Paco to find a burn vehicle in The Boneyard, he expected something nice. *And he tossed me the keys to this wreck*.

No one expects anything evil coming from a minivan. He held the stereotype of suburban families driving in minivans, not gangland killers. *Is that who I am? Not another player on the club scene?* He separated his self-made image as a man who pushed blow or made hot cars disappear. *Now, I'm a killer*. He questioned the tone.

"Over there," Rahn said, directing him off the highway. The detective dressed in military garb and a ski mask. *He's enjoying this shit. This is what he gets off on.* Sully pulled the minivan along a dirt road covered in pine needles. A thicket of evergreens enveloped the sides. Even with the headlights, Sully's vision was limited. *We might kill ourselves out here before we hurt someone else.*

"Kill the lights."

Sully hit the button on the dash. The headlights cooled into rust. His vision went black and he waited to collide with a tree. His foot went off the gas as the minivan rolled through the path. He imagined coasting through the air as the chilled night slapped at him. Sully pushed down on the brake. The tires locked. The van skidded on the dirt and then came to a stop. An evergreen trunk that greeted them in the middle of the road covered the windshield. *Jesus, that was close.*

Rahn sat calm and ate pork rinds out of a plastic white bag. He chewed with his mouth open. *Eating like the pig he is.* Sully edged his face closer to the open window. Kept himself from breathing in the cop's stinging sweat. Sully wiped his watering eyes whenever his nostrils caught the stench. The fat man turned as he chewed, offering a selection from the bag. Sully shook it off. *No damn way I'm eating that shit.* They sat with Santana's *Oye Como Va* coming in low from the van's damaged speakers. The music was washed with static as the frequency waned from the burnt-out panel light. *Paco's going to have to make this a "parts" car. No reseller worth his salt would take on this piece of shit.*

"You still think this is your game, right?"

Sully said, "I can handle myself."

"Sure," Rahn said. He pointed a salty finger at Sully. "Don't stare at them when you do it."

Sully lied. "I've done it before."

"Sure you have."

Rahn crumbled the bag into a ball and tossed it into the back. He belched an odor that hung in the van long after he got out. *It's like he never left.* Weight shifted as the van's shocks stretched after Rahn's girth departed. He watched Rahn disappear into the wilderness. *This isn't right, man. Even you shouldn't be in this game. You dabble in cutting chalk and do some lines. Maybe farm out a girl. But you don't do this. You ain't cut out for this.*

Sully's eyes went to the ignition. The keys dangled. Waiting to be turned over. So he could leave. *Not do any of this.* Shit that was well beyond him. Sick shit that only guys like Rahn enjoyed pulling.

You can't run anywhere. All of your cash is tied up with him. You don't nab the stones and you end up running for nothing. Sully rubbed his nose underneath the mask. I need some grain. He wanted time to fly by so he could forget tonight. Rahn had promised a snort for later. *It's in a little bag in his coat.*

Sully's cell chimed an incoming text. He was surprised after seeing one bar or nothing. The message from Junior was: *You guys find her?*

Old man is asking. Sully tossed his cell onto the dash. *You want to talk? Do it like a real person. Dial me up, we'll have a chat. None of this tap, tap, tap shit.*

He held his head. The leather glove's fingers slid against the fabric of his ski mask. *You gotta stick this out and hope for the best.*

Rahn woke Sully up calling his cell. Claimed to have found Angel. *Said some cop had hid her. Rahn had traced the detective's call from his office phone. Be ready to dance.* Sully listened to Rahn's excitement and felt terrible. Thinking about his dreams. Where Angel was touching his skin. *Why couldn't Angel just skip town and be gone forever?*

Wham! A noise shook him out of his seat. *Jesus.* He had been sitting there, numb to the world. *Gonna die like my old man did. Doing a crash and burn. Blowing out two walls of my heart.* Sully peered out the window. Caught Rahn's ski mask face smiling a set of yellow, twisted teeth back at him. *He knows how to scare the shit out of me, doesn't he?* Rahn motioned for Sully to roll down the window.

"She's here."

"Just her?"

Rahn said, "A wash-out is with her."

"Can we deal?"

"He's a crackup," Rahn said. "Now he eats pills and protects crates of oatmeal from al-Qaeda."

"So, what do we do?"

Rahn smiled. "Pop that cherry."

"Shouldn't I have a gun?" Sully said. "I should have a gun."

Rahn opened Sully's door, letting him out. *If I hadn't gotten out, he would have made me.* The two moved from the van into the dark mass of evergreens. Dirt and pine needles brushed along their boots. Sully eyed Rahn drawing out his Damascus blade from his sheath. The blade shined in the frozen moonlight that broke through the ceiling of trees. They slowed their journey to a creep as the evergreens ended into a cold wheat field.

Five motel huts sat less than a hundred yards from the trees. They were cold and dark except for one. It was ablaze with electricity. *So, this is where you've been hiding, huh? Not far enough.* Sully stepped onto the wheat field. His boots made crunching sounds on the frozen earth. *Not what you want when you surprise people.* Dank pockets of fog hid the ground below. He imagined that if the fog dissipated, it would reveal holes with an endless drop.

"Freeze, asshole."

Sully stopped in place as the forceful voice bellowed behind him. *I don't have a gun. This is why I needed a gun.* Sully spied a muscular figure with a crew cut a few feet away in the soft moonlight. The man held a shotgun and pumped it as a warning to Sully. *Never doubted you for a minute, pal.* Sully held out his hands, closing his lids. He waited to be greeted with a hot blast erupting from the shotgun. *Waiting to die. Ain't that what the game is all about? I wanted in. This is in, right?* Sully's nostrils picked up something familiar and sour in the air.

"Long time, Hanaran."

He opened his lids, noticed Hanaran was held back. A dark figure backpacked him. Across Hanaran's throat ran Rahn's curved Damascus blade. He held himself close to Hanaran and spoke into the man's ear. This is part of the game too. *This is the upper hand where the guy on top finds himself on bottom.* Sully smiled. *Probably not right, but so what? Guy was going to do me, right?* Sully reached out, taking the shotgun from Hanaran.

"Empty it," Rahn said.

"Huh?"

Rahn said, "I won't say it again."

Sully held the shotgun's slide release. He pulled back on the pump. Unspent shells belched from the chamber. They disappeared around his feet. He tossed the worthless weapon into the fog. *Rahn ain't taking chances with me. He doesn't want me to turn on him when the deed is done.* Rahn forced Hanaran toward the motel hut, pushing him forward.

The motel hut had its shades covering a large bay window. The room's yellow light illuminated the edges of the drapes. Rahn held

Hanaran tight as they moved. *Not giving him an inch of space. Hanaran is close enough that he's got Rahn's sweat lodged in his nose. Probably lost his sense of smell.* Sully followed. He listened to his heart thump in his chest. *You're doing this shit. You talked yourself into a shit storm.* He glanced at the evergreens in the distance. He entertained the idea of a mad dash escape. *And do what? Wait for Rahn to find you?*

The motel room's door was cracked open. *Hanaran didn't expect trouble on his patrol.* Rahn moved around Hanaran enough to kick the door open. The force cratered the door's handle into the fake wooden paneling. Sully listened to Angel scream. He moved toward the threshold, seeing his former strawberry standing in the bathroom. She was staring back at them, wet and covered in a towel. Rahn pushed Hanaran off his feet. The fat man sliced with his curved knife. The blade's sound hissed through the air. Sully fixated on the blade's edge but little blood. *He missed? I can't believe it. This is why I should have a gun.*

Hanaran must have had the same impression. He cracked his shoulder as he hit the ground. But the ex-cop adjusted himself and got to a knee, then stopped. Sully noted the confused look on Hanaran's face. *Something's wrong with him.* Hanaran's eyes expanded as he opened his mouth. A thin slice split across the right side of his jugular. *Rahn didn't miss. The blade's speed across his throat meant that Hanaran didn't realize it. Neither did I.* Hanaran's wound expanded, gushing rich, red blood. Hanaran grabbed his throat in a futile attempt to hold it closed.

The wound blossomed to a flood. Blood cascaded down his chest as his eyes fluttered. He collapsed with a thud, breaking his nose. Angel screamed and ran to Hanaran. She draped him as if to hold the wound closed. *You should be running, Angel. Rahn's going to slice you up next.* He noted Rahn's wicked blade offered a reflection of his smile. It was too late. *He's set his sights on you. Now you're gonna wish you would have run when you had the chance.*

Rahn used both hands on the blade and slammed it into Angel's back. The force caused her to collapse onto Hanaran's body. Sully caught her attempt to scream. A croaking sound soaked in wet filled the room. Rahn put his boot onto her buttocks. He yanked out the precious knife. Angel wheezed as blood poured from her mouth. Sully stood there, waiting for her to die. *This isn't so bad, is it?* He felt ready for her to die.

Just go, kid. Die before he decides to make it nasty. Angel started to crawl from Hanaran. His eyes followed her as she moved toward the bathroom door. He wondered what Rahn would do to her next. *Geez, kid, now he's gonna give it to you.* Angel was clawing her fingernails across the shag carpet. *She's got drive in her. Not ready to die yet.* She made it into the bathroom. Sully's eyes went to Rahn.

He caught a smile, which made him sick.

"Well?"

Sully stood confused. "Well, what?"

"Time to pop it," Rahn said. "Don't look in her eyes when you do."

"You go ahead."

Rahn pointed toward the bathroom. "This is your part to clean up."

The corpulent man plopped onto the edge of a bed. The springs whined from his mass, buckling in protest. Hanaran laid lifeless at their feet. He had bled out, showing gray skin. The carpet around him was matted maroon. Sully was unsure what to do next. *Look what you got yourself into? You thought you could act tough. Now he wants you to prove it.* He thought about running. *I run, he finds me and shoots me down like that maniac sheriff in Cle Elm.* Sully's eyes bounced to Angel who pulled herself into the bathroom. *No, I have to do this. Otherwise, he does me.*

"She ain't nothing, Sully."

Sully swallowed hard as he stepped over Hanaran's body. His boots squished on blood-soaked carpet. *She's half-dead from the wound. She will die before you catch her.* He entered the bathroom. Angel was lying against the white tile. Her back wound seeped. Two fingernails burrowed into the grout and snapped from the pressure. She continued without them. *Just die already. Pass out and go so I don't have to do anything.*

He loomed over her crawl. *Just die so I can leave.* Angel turned as he bent closer. She swung a hard right fist into his face. His back teeth loosened as they pushed against his gums. Sully fell backward with his boots slipping on the tile. He crashed against the wall next to the door. His head cratered into the drywall, jarring him into a daze. *She hit me.*

His vision blurred. Sully regained focus. He tasted blood where his teeth bit his tongue. *That bitch hit me.* Angel was pushing herself up through the bathroom window near the tub. *Shit, she's getting out.* Sully braced himself against the tile and stood. He shook off a cloud of disorientation. Angel was struggling to open the bathroom window more than a few inches. *Did Hanaran fix it so she couldn't escape on him?* He turned to Rahn sitting on the bed, sizing him up. *He doesn't think I can do it.*

Sully charged Angel. He slammed into her back. Her wound hemorrhaged, her grip holding firm to the bathroom window. His assault's force caused the frame to shake. The window slammed shut on her hands. He listened to the *snap* of bone upon impact. *Why couldn't you die? You had to hit me. You had to make me angry.* He grabbed Angel by the nape of her neck. He gripped and yanked her away from the window. Her hands gave free of the sill.

Angel turned to fight. Several shots from Angel's broken hands came at Sully. Damaged awkward clubs landed on his face. Sully pushed her into the bathtub.

Her head made a wet cracking sound against the tub's surface. Her body fell limp. Sully stood over her, upset. *You had to make me angry. You had to keep fighting.*

He sighed, thankful to be finished. Placed his hands on his hips. Prepared to face Rahn. Ready to leave the bathroom. He noticed Angel's legs squirming and his heart sank. *You're not dead yet?* Rage burned in his head. *Why can't you just die?*

He stepped into the tub. He threw a punch that split her lip, breaking her front teeth. *You want to die now? You're making me do this.* Angel eyed him as he turned from her. *Don't look at me. You're not supposed to look at me.* He spied a wet, opaque shower liner around the tub. He yanked it off the railing, snapping it off each ring. He picked Angel up by the throat and wrapped the liner over her face. He could feel her struggle. A hot air balloon of breath puffed out of the liner as she struggled to breathe.

He held her in a headlock. He held her same as his infant cousin when visiting his aunt in Miami two years ago. *Tight enough not to let them fall.* He struggled against the temptation to look elsewhere. His eyes continued to drop down and look at her face. *Don't look at me. Stop looking me.* Angel's hands thrashed against his head and back. Her broken fingers drew errant claws into his turtleneck. *Just die already. Stop looking at me and die. Please.*

Her heart beat against his chest. The rhythm weakened. Each thump followed farther apart. His eyes captivated by hers. Her hands tightened on his ski mask. He felt the tug of the mask as Angel pulled it off slowly. The fabric fought against his face. Sully caught his reflection in the bathroom mirror. His hair messed. Grime on his face. His eyes were alive with anger. *Who is this person I am looking at? It isn't me*. He almost let Angel go.

Sully questioned the alternatives for Angel had the two never met. *Would she have become a wife? Lived in a two-story house in a nice neighborhood?* Those potential life achievements Sully had erased when Angel came into his club, seeking work. He didn't care about her family in Seattle. He wanted her to stay. *Paid my girls to get her high, to erase messages on her cell from her parents. Because I wanted her*.

The two of them used to lie in bed for hours. Discussing their hopes and fears. *She understands more of me than anyone else*. That connection between them was leaving now, forever.

Sully would be the only one to know her secrets. That Angel shared her first kiss with a German exchange student in the San Francisco Airport. Or about the ten-year-old boy who sat next to on her bus who had made her promise to name her first son *George* after him. *I'm sorry, kid. Please forgive me*. He knew she loved him. Last year, he had diarrhea throughout the night. How she had been the only one he could call. She came over and cleaned me up. *She kept my secrets*. The way he felt when his twin sister asked him to touch their dead father. Telling Sully that it was the way to say goodbye at the old man's funeral. *I am removing someone who existed. Someone who loved, cried and laughed, but will do those things no longer.*

Each of Angel's fists landed with less impact. He cradled her and looked deep into those soft green eyes through the opaque film. *I'm connected with her*. The puff of plastic liner stopped expanding out as her breath ended. He felt her muscles begin to go lax. *Finally, you're going. Thank you for finally dying*. His arms felt her neck pulse churn slower until it was gone. The liner around her mouth was damp and cold. He held her up as he removed the liner from her face.

He realized he had ended the life of someone's sister or daughter. She had once told him that her mother had given birth to her at 3:39 p.m. She exited the world at 2:16 a.m. *No candles to blow out for another birthday.* No joy of knowing more in her thirties than her twenties. She was gone. He watched a little light in her green eyes dim into oblivion. Sully held her close. He brushed her hair from her forehead and kissed it. He wiped his own tears while closing her lids. *I'm sorry, kid. I'm so sorry*. He set her down gently and got out of the tub. He felt sick.

Sully looked at his hands. They felt as if they belonged to a stranger. He walked over to the toilet and vomited. He felt he was expunging an evil. *I'm part of a group that I don't want to belong to*. He flushed the toilet and stood. His eyes went back to Angel, wishing he could undo it all. *I loved her, didn't I? And this is what I did to her*. He fought back tears and turned toward Rahn. The fat man remained on the edge of the bed. He smoked a cheap cigar.

"I looked in her eyes," Sully said.

"We all do," Rahn said. "It's takes a cold-hearted person to do that and not let go."

Sully said, "How are you ever okay doing something like this?"

"Everyone else thinks they're a good person, Sully," he said. "Maybe that's my problem. I know I'm not."

Rahn tossed a small bag of chalk at Sully. He caught it. *Do I have that look? That one saying I will do anything for a snort?* He gripped the bag and left Rahn. He headed back through the thicket of evergreens back to the van. He snorted up a mountain of chalk to forget Angel. The world flashed forward into glimpses of scenes. He remembered Rahn carrying canisters of bleach from the van. He recalled how the fat man destroyed the area without setting fire to the place. *The man knows how to move. He knows what to look for to keep from being found.*

He can make anyone disappear. Sully remembered thinking as he wound down a little. He sat in the passenger's seat as the charge from the chalk ebbed. *How long before I disappear?* Rahn got behind the wheel of the van. The fat man drove out of the evergreens. Sully noted that Rahn's stench of perspiration was faint. The detective looked very clean.

Rahn smiled. "Angel and I had a shower together."

"Huh?"

"She needed to be clean."

He couldn't leave Angel alone, could he? Sully said nothing. He let his mind spin as the chalk charged in his system again. He smiled as the trip back to the city flew by. He was beginning to forget what he had done to Angel. *I want to forget tonight and what I saw in her eyes.* He waited for his apartment to come up on the road, disappointed when Rahn kept driving. *Where are we going?* Rahn stopped the van a few blocks later. At a bar, called *The Sin Bin*.

"I ain't up to party."

Rahn winked. "Trust me. This is something to see."

They entered the bar, sitting near the back rail. The dive let 8-ball become king between strangers. Twenty-five cent challenges were placed on torn green tables where everyone used bent sticks to shoot. Nine-ball was frowned upon as a money game. Sully sucked down a two-fifty Bud special. Rahn smiled across from him at a small crooked table with names carved in the wooden surface. A Blondie song with bells was playing on the jukebox. Sully noticed a gathering in the banquet room next to the back rail.

The bar crowd wore black. They were weeping. *Why did Rahn bring me here?* He peered farther. The guests descended on a body lying on a table. The body was dressed in a suit and tie. *An Irish Wake?* The set-up was similar to Sully's late father's wake. A procession of suited men each kissed the cheek of the dead man. They turned their consolations toward a large, Rubenesque woman. Rahn sat and smiled at the madness.

"This is Jonas' place."

"Thought you would enjoy it," Rahn said. "I know I do."

"Jesus," Sully said.

He moved to leave but Rahn grabbed his wrists. The fat man kept him pinned to the table. Rahn laughed, letting Sully smell the stench from his mouth. His decayed teeth were tinted green and yellow. Van Halen played on the jukebox while everyone wept in the back. Sully looked for help, but no one paid attention. Rahn leaned in.

"Two plainclothes officers are behind me at the bar, do you see them?" Rahn said.

"Yes." Sully saw two men who were not dressed for a dive. *He brought the cops here?* Sully relaxed as Rahn released his grip.

"They are watching Gloria," Rahn said. "You and I know who killed Jonas, but she is their only suspect."

"Why are you doing this?"

Rahn said, "You give orders, but your hands have been clean. You wanted to be in? Now, you are in. She will haunt your thoughts. Or whether those two plainclothes cops are tailing you or out for a meal. You see Jonas' funeral back there? Angel gets one too. Both happened because of you."

Sully left the table. *Angel could have had a kid.* He entered the bathroom. *Maybe Angel would have named him 'George.'* The walls dressed in graffiti. *Then Angel would have a story to tell her son when he was older.* He eyed the cracked mirror. *I took that from her.* He pulled out the tiny bag. *I need her to leave my head.* He did a line over the sink. *I destroyed her for nothing.* His consciousness was thrown forward warp speed.

The sun rose from the bay window in his bedroom. Sully wore black Italian speedos with his back to his bed. A club waitress named Diane had come over. During their time together, Sully eyed himself in the mirror over his bed. The world was off-tilt and he didn't know how to set it right. A Phil Collins synthesizer tune came over his surround sound system but he ignored it. When he closed his lids, his mind focused on Angel. *I'm sorry, kid.* He fought back tears as the sun shined in his room.

"Baby, come back to bed."

Sully noticed Diane waking. He had lost his virginity last night. *The world is less innocent.* He remembered his first time with a girl.

She took my hand, told me what to do. Never said a word about how smooth in the sack he claimed he was later. *Though we both knew I wasn't.* He felt nothing now. The urge to do a line was gone. The glamour of a girl between his sheets was erased. He felt apart from it all.

He cared nothing for the diamonds. *Let Rahn have them.* The club and the chop shop he owned up north mattered little. *Let someone else have that too. I need to leave.* He needed to leave tonight. *Return to Miami. Visit your twin sister who you don't talk to.* He planned on taking the four hundred grand off Rahn at the club. Catching the redeye to Miami. *Let him come after me.* He hated Spokane. *This city has no identity.*

"I didn't know you smoked," Diane said.

"Huh?" Sully said.

Diane pointed at his hand. "I don't mind if you have one of mine."

Sully realized he had a burning nail between his fingers. "I'm starting to realize a lot about myself. Some not what I ever wanted to see." The sun went up, hurting his eyes, hiding his tears.

He survived another sleepless night to watch the sun rise as he stood on the back porch. Shay Baxter's flannel robe flapped against a February breeze as he warmed with sips of coffee. He eyed his neglected yard. Used to be a beautiful lawn that other neighbors admired. Tyler's situation did not help. The flowers were dead from winter, the lawn shagged from an absent mower. Shay eyed his pond where fish swam. His morning routine included feeding and counting all fifteen. A large Crane had reduced their number to eight.

13

He woke to find his wife not in bed with him. Mariah had slept on the living room couch with a television spewing static. Internet printouts, magazine articles and books surrounded her. All related to Tyler's condition. Five years of waiting, to produce a child who suffered through this much misery. They had survived the worry that they would not conceive. Shay recalled the amount of times he held Mariah afterward when nothing didn't happened. They refrained from restaurants because small children reminded them of their infertility. Friends who had children drifted away because Shay and Mariah were bothered to be around them. *We struggled through everything only to have a sick child. Does God hate us?*

Mariah suffered through three miscarriages during that five-year period to conceive. Each time she forced herself to begin the process again. The adoption process had a ten-year waiting period.

Becoming a foster parent was a choice. But they never wanted to become attached to a child who might be taken away later. *We gave up and started to live as that childless couple people talk about. The ones that mothers pity.* Then, Tyler came.

Shay was amazed at how Tyler came as if he were a natural fit all along. He is a content little boy. Shay felt lucky to have the years he had with Tyler. *All of the things we were able to do together.* Shay had noticed several water glasses by the sink when Tyler was seven. He was angry his son would not reuse the same glass. *None of what he did registered with me as a problem.* Five days later, Tyler collapsed in the backyard with a seizure. Trips to the hospital followed with a diagnosis of Type 1 diabetes. Shay made hundreds of calls. Trying to have his son placed on the kidney transplant list. Worried that insurance wouldn't cover. *He gets a kidney that stops working six months later so now he needs a new transplant. How do I pay for that?*

The Crane circled overhead, catching Shay's attention. It dropped onto the lawn, moving to the pond. *I've got no control over my life. Everything thinks it can take advantage of me.* He dealt with gophers last year digging up Mariah's rose bushes. I fed them, collecting the bodies afterward. The Crane edged the pond. Shay's hand went to Tyler's pellet gun. He fired off a shot that missed the Crane's head by three inches.

The pellet rattled off the wooden fence behind the Crane. The bird eyed Shay's direction, flapped its wings and flew from the backyard. The bird passed overhead. Then, its wings folded. It nosedived a few feet beyond Shay's house. A small thump of metal denting and a car alarm sounded off. *I didn't even hit the damn thing and it went down.* He smiled and went inside with the pellet gun.

Mariah was in the kitchen, watching from the window. "You killed it?"

"I missed on purpose. If it died, it did it on its own."

"You missed on purpose?"

Shay: "It's Barney's problem. He flicks his butts over the fence into our yard. Let him keep the Crane."

Mariah had bags under her eyes, worried about Tyler all night. *She's a good mother.* He dismissed that. *She needs to go see him more, to be strong for him.* When Tyler was fine, Mariah worried about Shay. *She had nightmares I was dead. She doesn't understand what being in the shit is all about. The world makes sense out there, more than it does here.*

She pointed at the pellet gun. "Did you take that from his room?"

"I borrowed it."

"Put it back."

Shay shook his head. "What's gotten into you?"

"Put it back, Shay."

"Our son is not dead. We are not a couple who preserves his things like he is."

Mariah said. "I search everyday for something to bring him home."

"Go visit him. Be there for him."

Mariah slapped him across the face. "I love my son."

"You haven't been there in two weeks."

Tears welled in her eyes. "I... I can't see him like that."

"Do it," Shay said. "We have to be strong for him."

"Don't you think I know that?" Mariah said. "I love him as much as you do."

"I know," Shay said.

She sobbed. *We see all of these things happening to a little boy who doesn't deserve it.* She kept her face from him. "I'm a bad mother."

"I don't believe that," Shay said. "He wants you there with him. Visit him, promise me."

"I... I promise."

He held her for a while. He regretted parting to leave for work. Shay sat in his truck and wondered if the marriage would survive even if Tyler recovered. *Even if the transplant happens, will we last?* When he held her, Shay felt as if he were touching a stranger. *Someone who doesn't feel the way I do.* He dismissed his emotions as he parked in front of the Coeur d'Alene Police Department. *How am*

I getting two hundred thousand together to save my son? Whatever it was, he was more than willing to do it.

14 A Hell24 was survivable. The side effect was that it created more demand for sugar after the restrictions were lifted. Vic Ramsey took the sugar dealing over easy. A return trip to *The Sides* would mean that Frank Gryzbowsky would answer to Vic. The kid knew his job well. *He had a good teacher*. Vic hustled, and never shorted a tweaker when the junkie's math was incorrect. *Sometimes you get liars. Others guys have fried brains who can't think anymore*. Dealer had to have temperament. Vic proved he had the right juice to run everything.

Frank became a short-timer. Everything brushed by him fast. Millions of tasks on his mind. Each task that had to be accomplished before he left *The Sides* for good. Brian's offer had complicated matters. *I don't want to be that screw up. The guy who gets out only to fast track back into prison*. The offer held him. *Money is something I don't have right now. Brian says it's an easy pick-up.* Just do one trip and then collect and get out.

"You gonna miss us here?"

Frank offered Vic a curled brow. "Miss it as in how?"

"This place got rhythm."

"It's a prison. No rhythm here."

Vic said, "Naw, man. It got order. You screw up here, it means something. You do it on the outside, you might walk away clean. On the outside is only between you and God."

"I've never been that lucky," Frank said. "Depends on what Brian has for me out there. I'm doing it once, getting out for good and starting over."

"And if you can't?" Vic said. "I know a lot of guys who do it once, then don't get to walk away."

Vic's point was valid. *What if they put a gun in your hand, tell you to do someone? Are you willing to go that far?* He wondered if they would ice him if he walked after the pick-up job. He thought about Brian, then shook his head. *No, he's not like that. He's been square with me the entire time.*

The routine went quick for the two sugar dealers. It was strange to see everything done for the final time. Frank had a small amount of impatience attached to everything they did. *Get it over with, done and buried.* Every guard he passed gave him a common look and nod. *Don't pull any shit. Or you'll be back here real soon.*

Each inmate offered Frank a short-timer gift. Small flasks of liquor saved up for birthdays or anniversaries went down his throat throughout the day. He turned down those fellas in the medium security wing who offered shots of purol. *My gut couldn't take one shot of that stuff, let alone ten.* He avoided selling packets through most of the medium security wing for that reason.

He separated from Vic late in the day and went to Brian's cell. The old man's feet were propped up on a Barcalounger. Brian watched Wheel of Fortune on a plasma screen. *I wonder if that is what the judge considers hard time*. Frank stopped at the cell's threshold. Brian waved him forward and muted the plasma. The old man smiled as Frank approached.

"How does it feel to be getting out?"

Frank pointed at his blue khaki shirt. "I miss my clothes. Something about what you came in with being taken from you. Now I get everything back. Hits me like a dream."

"Or a nightmare," Brian said. "Good way to think is forward. The past is bullshit."

"That's why I'm here."

"You sure?"

"What else I got?" Frank said. "Except for staying at a halfway house for six months."

Brian said, "Just making sure. Tonight, you go get the stuff. You get a driver as my insurance policy. I got another man who will meet you in the house with the other details."

Brian handed a sheet to Frank. He read all of the details. *Talk to The Serg at Exit One, pick up the package. A fence named Freeway in Spokane would take the goods*. Frank looked at Brian. The job was easy enough. He handed the sheet back to Brian, who destroyed it. The contents were flushed. *Do this, collect the reward, then get out before the job gets tough.*

"Keep the details between us," Brian said. "A guy named Styles may ask, but don't trust him."

"Understandable."

"Don't screw this up, Frank," Brian said. "My friends have plans for you."

Frank was uneasy. He looked into the old man's eyes, unsure. *He's selling me on it a little too much.* He paused for a moment, but dismissed it as being too cautious. Brian's anything but a cheat. Frank remained guarded, but worried about the heat. The old man offered him a snort of Wild Turkey, which suppressed his fears entirely. *Just do the job and return to the halfway house by morning.*

Three hours later, Frank sat in a holding cell waiting to get out. The holding cell was a special area. It transferred prisoners in and out of *The Sides*. Every con who got diesel therapy to another facility was dumped in the tank first. There was a process to go through before leaving The Sides. Being released meant an inmate lost his khaki shirt and pants. The guards took an inmate's bo-bos so his feet touched cold concrete flooring during a strip search. Procedure ensured nothing was smuggled in or out of the prison. The exception was when the guards profited from the contraband. After the search, the guards tossed an inmate an orange jumpsuit.

During his residency in holding, Frank had to entertain himself.

He sat on a bench with a toilet across from him. The last vestiges of alcohol withdrew from his system. He nodded off and let his chin slack on his chest. There was a long rope of drool from his bottom lip that puddled on the concrete. Sound amplified as his gut ached and his head throbbed. Bed check rolled through *The Sides*. He listened to every inmate yell their name down the hall. Frank eyed what the boys called a "door warrior" a few doors down. The type that acts tough until the door opens, then decides to shut up. The door warrior was fresh off diesel therapy from Pocatello Correctional. He was creating a racket in his holding cell. The inmate threatened to kill a guard.

His lids opened to the steady beat of *The Sides* guards' boots marching down the hallway. Every inmate in holding shut up. Except the door warrior who continued to shout. Every inmate stood at attention when the buzzer sounded from the main entry door. Each pressed their face against the one square foot Plexiglas door window. Frank saw the door warrior across the hallway two cells down. The man pounded his fists against the cell door.

Above the main entry door sat a little red bulb. When it came *alive*, the guards entered the hallway. The silence became instant; the chatter stopped. No catcalls to guards. Every cell dweller smart enough to back off the door in unison. Except the door warrior, who refused to shut his mouth. *The Sides* had a social conditioning of the unexpected. Failure to comply meant a nightstick party by the guards, followed by going on vacation in solitary. *It doesn't matter if you come or go. No one shouts when the guards come down that hallway.*

The Sides guards moved in pack formation. They showed indifference. It was a mentality that the guards projected. They would beat an inmate for giving a look during processing. The threat kept most cons in line. Down the hallway, boots marched lock-and-step as they devoured the floor in front of them. *Scariest thing I've ever heard.* The shroud of quiet from the holding cells had the crashing parade of boots shatter it. No smart inmate wanted to draw the focus of the guards. *Not the sarcastic ones who yell shit at the judge at trial.* Not a newly minted hardcore with permanent jail muscles doing a stretch for twenty-five for kidnapping. *Cons usually aren't that stupid.*

Except the door warrior, who urinated on the Plexiglas to challenge the guards. Stories had spread about a con named George Hoob, who had been given diesel therapy from Boise. He whistled at a guard while they were processing another prisoner. Drawing their attention, he was beaten so bad that his ears bled. Frank had passed by Hoob's medium security cell a few times. The man couldn't hear out of his right ear worth a damn.

The marching of the guards stopped with a bang. The sound carried down the silent hallway. Frank detected tension in the air. He leaned to look out the Plexiglas. The guards were outside the door warrior's cell. *That means his ass.*

"Open fourteen."

The door warrior's cell clanked open. The man who wouldn't shut up became quiet and contrite. He begged mercy backing into his cell. *They don't care, man. You need to know that going in. They will beat you for the fun of it.* Two guards entered and pummeled him with nightsticks. They stomped him. Frank listened to bone *snap*. The door warrior whimpered as the guards exited.

"Close fourteen."

The door warrior's cell sealed. The march of boots continued until the guards stopped in front of Frank's cell. The production from the guards started the moment they were in front of an inmate's cell. They called out the inmate number. They warned him to move back from the door. Three guards remained in the hallway. They acted as cavalry shock troopers with Tasers and nightsticks in case the inmate refused to comply. A few cons try the patience of the guards. They receive a knee in their back while getting juice six times from a Taser.

Though he expected it, he was nervous when the guards stopped in front of his door. Five guys stared at him. Each stood ready to dance if he gave sign of trouble. The leader of the pack was Steve Powers.

He looked through inmates. His trimmed brown mustache and blue eyes hid the fact he meant business. Even the hardcore cons stepped back in his presence. He ran *The Sides* with a fury. He offered the worst beating a con could receive for crossing him. And he doesn't forget things either. George Hoob received beatings for a year after his holding experience. Powers wanted to set an example.

"Open sixteen."

Powers' voice boomed down the hallway. A guard in the security room heard him on the microphone. Another buzzer sounded. Frank's door came alive. Instinct took over for Frank. He backed up to the far end of the cell. He got onto his knees, crossed his legs, hands behind his head. All in the ten seconds the door took to slide clear. *I could work for N.A.S.C.A.R. and change a tire in two seconds flat*. He dropped his eyes as Powers and Trent entered his cell. Their shadows draped him as they blocked the cell's tiny light.

"Inmate 51307-207?"

"Yes," Frank said. Guards called every prisoner at The Sides by their inmate identification number. Only the staff gave a guy the luxury of using his real name. Stripping a con of everything meant taking their name away from them. It was the most dehumanizing thing that could be done. And in the prison system, they relished it. Trent had called out Frank's inmate identification number. Had he not answered by his I.I.N., Frank would have been beaten by the guards. If he protested further, teeth would have been lost in the exchange.

"Two minutes to dress."

Frank's eyes went to the holding cell bench. Folded clothes sat waiting. You don't have to tell me twice. He rose, stripped out of the orange suit and stood naked in front of the guards. He put on the dress shirt. Four months of dressing in front of other inmates had made Frank question: How noticeable would dressing alone be? He smiled, equating it to respectability. He noticed the dress shirt and pants were loose, half a size too big. Frank looked at Trent.

"We deloused them. They had bugs crawling all over them," Trent said.

Powers said, "Buy some new clothes. The old ones got tossed in the prison incinerator."

He's looking for a fight. Despite being processed out, Powers wanted to show who was boss. Frank returned to dressing. He pulled up his pants. Trent went down, grabbing Frank's right leg. The guard attached an ankle bracelet to Frank. Trent activated it. Frank listened to the machine whine as it charged up. Trent stood and pointed at Frank.

"Halfway house is across the street. You meet your parole officer at nine tomorrow. Failure to comply gets you a two-year mandatory recommitment here."

Powers leaned in. "Do something stupid on the outside. We'll have you back by breakfast."

Less than two minutes after dressing, Frank was marched down the holding cell hallway. Surrounded by a cadre of guards, he imagined himself as a head of state. *But they would use me as a shield instead of protecting me.* They passed by various gates as the parade went through each corridor. Each gate had a metal door, opened by a guard in the security room. The remaining guards split off from Frank as Trent moved him into the processing center. The area held each inmate's stuff where a guy's time at *The Sides* began or ended. Cons called it "The Life Room."

A staffer named Layne stood behind bulletproof glass. It keeps guys from killing him when they find paper missing from their wallet. Frank received an empty money clip. He also accepted a broken watch and a rosary. He pocketed the money clip, tossed the watch into the trash, then held up the rosary. He stared at it. *Where did I pick this up?* He noticed Trent and Layne both offered strange looks to him.

"I guess I was religious," he said.

"It wasn't working for you," Trent said.

Frank pocketed the rosary. He was escorted out of The Sides by Trent. Outside, the fresh mountain air chill bit at him. He passed through a corridor of fence with razor wire. The long fence line held the workout pile and the yard on both sides. The concrete path chewed through an empty lawn. They stopped at a final fence where Trent unlocked it, then held it closed. He looked back at Frank.

"Last chance to stay inside," Trent said.

Frank said, "Not on your life."

Trent pointed across the street. A small motel amid some decayed buildings. "Ten minutes is all you have. Take your time, the monitor goes off and we take you back," Trent said. "Don't make me come after you."

"Wouldn't dream of it," Frank said. "I'm reformed."

Trent smirked, "Sure."

The guard opened the gate. Frank exited *The Sides* as a free man. He stepped through the parking lot. The weight of his bracelet burrowed down into the skin of his ankle. He looked back at *The Sides. It seems different from this angle.* He watched Trent return to the prison. *I think I'm gonna miss it.* Frank wondered if he had gone crazy and shook off the thought. He headed into the small motel, over to check-in.

A man in a stained gray hoody sweatshirt pointed at Frank. "You're late, buddy. You got friends waiting for you out back."

Frank showed the ankle bracelet. "This gonna tie me down?"

The man smiled. He grabbed an electric wand. He swiped the bracelet twice. "This wand now produces the signal, so they'll think you are here until morning," he said. "Don't take it off though. The strap has a different tracking signal."

"Thanks."

"I served at The Sides," the man said. He displayed an old scar on his head. "I danced with Steve Powers, too."

They nodded at the mention of Powers' name. Frank went alone to the back of the motel. He opened the door, looked at the mountain range behind the building. A breeze chilled the space between his clothes. *I got to get new threads.* Two Lexus' idling in the parking lot captured his attention. A fog rolled out from each tailgate in the February cold. Headlights ignited and blinked.

As he approached, one of the sedan's side doors opened. He jumped inside, closing the door. Warmth from the heater blanketed him. The driver was a slicked-back Italian who nodded, passing over a bottle of Southern Comfort. A gift from Brian. Sobriety in holding had been too long. He broke the seal and removed the cap with his thumb. Took two-thirds of the contents down before the driver snatched it away from him. The driver looked disgusted.

"So, Tuttle gives me a blue nose," he said. The man offered his hand to Frank. "Styles Remington."

"Frank Gryzbowsky." His eyes went to Styles' hand, where he cradled the bottle. He wondered if he would get it back. Already, he could feel a good glow coming. His body loosened. *A relaxation that stays no matter what happens.* Frank eyed the remaining third of the bottle and waited to finish it off.

"Keep your wits about you," Styles said.

Frank said, "I work better when I drink. Takes the edge off what I do."

"Smells like you've had enough."

"You want to find someone else? Maybe wait a few weeks till someone that Brian doesn't trust as much comes out?" Frank said. "I can sit in my room for the next six months then walk."

Styles shrugged and appeared to review his options. "What did Brian tell you about the job?"

"He wants me to pick something up," Frank said.

"You still up for it?"

Frank motioned to the other sedan. "Who's the driver?"

"Insurance," Styles said. "You get the package to the fence, you separate. The payout on this is once in a lifetime."

Styles offered a piece. It was hidden in a rag. Frank looked at the clean Beretta held out for him to take. "I don't do guns."

"You do for this," Styles said. He shoved the Beretta into Frank's hands. "Rounds are with your driver."

Frank held the Beretta, unsure. "I need this for a pickup job?"

"Helps get your point across," Styles said.

"I need to get my point across when I'm picking something up?"

Styles said, "You would be surprised."

The slicked-back guy handed Frank a few playing cards. Each card was of the King of Hearts. "Show this to anyone who gives you a hard time. If they need to know who you speak for, this will send them the right message."

Frank paused. The King of Hearts meant Irish Pete. *Get out of the sedan right now, Frank.* He imagined himself pushing out of the Lexus only to be shot by Styles. Brian would never let him walk away after he said yes. *And Irish Pete means business.* "Are you expecting stuff to go wrong?"

"I don't expect anything. That way, I'm never surprised," Styles said. He handed Frank the Southern Comfort bottle. "Don't drink it all until the night is over."

"Sure."

Frank exited the Lexus and Styles pulled out of the parking lot. *Frank, what have you gotten yourself into?* Styles headed out back toward Spokane. Frank's eyes went to the other Lexus. The driver sat in the car as it idled, hidden by tinted glass. *This is going to be one hell of a night.* Frank downed the rest of the bottle in three seconds flat.

15 Irish Pete's estate was located west of the city in the plains of the Palouse. Finding it was difficult as the sun dropped. Junior Perry had been there once prior when the old man offered the job. His cell dropped to one bar and GPS was useless. His ride ran gravel roads cutting down into valleys of brown wheat. He fought temptation to turn back. The old man would want to know how the girl had been handled. Irish Pete's request to find the stones had ceased. *It means I do a face to face to get the lowdown.*

An hour later, he stopped at the estate's entrance. He was impressed by its layout. Irish Pete had bought an old church, restructuring the façade into an elegant ranch house. The building stood amid thirty-foot barrels of wheat in a valley unmolested by neighbors. A private gate served at the end of a long asphalt drive. It ended with a circle at the house's entrance. A large concrete fountain spewed water to the heavens.

Junior's cell chimed a text from Baron Gamble: *Man, where are you?* Junior sent back: *The old man's place.* Baron shot back: *k.*

A cadre of security cameras decorated the outer wall. Each lens viewed angles beyond the shrubs. The lawn held a parade of embedded lights beaming to the sky. *The man spends his paper to flatter himself.* Junior touched the security panel to open the automatic gate. He noted the house's façade with a workman's scaffolding. Along the exterior were several large work lights affixed to the temporary metal frame. Junior used his arms to shield his eyes from the illuminated front.

He touched the TALK button on the gate's intercom. "Kill the lights, man. It's blinding."

Seconds later, the white light cancelled. The bulbs powered down orange, then dead cold. The house's shadow rose. Junior saw the church's transformation. New additions included a red brick façade with looming white columns. The steeple was dismantled with a dome in its place. The old man talked to Junior over his cell about the reasons why. Irish Pete was remodeling the structure after the house of a dead president.

Irish Pete gave Junior a quick five-minute overview of his plans for the estate. *The man is full of himself.* He let the old man talk. Irish Pete loved to regale in stories of the past, including the minutiae of any deal. *Keep him talking. He will tell you what he knows.* Junior sat in a chair opposite of the old man's large oak desk. He held back his boredom as the old man talked about days, which no longer mattered. On his desk sat various handguns, ranging from a Luger to a Desert Eagle.

The place held a menagerie of stuffed kills. Junior's vegetarian girlfriend *would've gone ape shit if she were invited over*. The old man brought down each animal during the thrill of a hunt. The beasts were mounted on walls or poised from the floor. The illumination of firelight kept the room from total darkness. *Kid's nightmares come from places like this.* The corners offered weapon cabinets. Irish Pete recited tales of hunting grey wolves by helicopter in the Alaska Tundra. Junior pretended interest.

"Where was I going with this again?" Irish Pete said. The old man rubbed his temples in an attempt to remember. He offered a blank stare. "I guess that's what happens when you get old and forget your point."

Junior said, "I'm sure it will come back to you." He shot Baron Gamble a text: *He's rambling.* Baron sent back: *He is old. They do that.*

"I was telling a damn good story," Irish Pete said. "Let's get down to it. So, Jonas didn't carry the stones."

Junior lied. "Tuttle is playing you. Jonas was empty."

"Styles visited Tuttle. He swears Jonas had them."

"Two years he holds the stones without telling Nash or Jimmy. You think he's going to tell you now?"

"We were partners."

"So were they," Junior said.

Irish Pete shrugged. "You make an interesting point. If you're lying to me, I'll find out."

Fat chance you will, old man. He eased up a little and refused to appear nervous. Rumors floated the city about what Irish Pete was capable of. *Hell, I've seen it.* But the score was worth crossing the old man. *You can't walk from that much in stones for twenty large in cash.* He decided to play himself off as a man who needed the cash, not the stones.

Junior sent a text to Baron: *Old man is off the scent.* Baron shot back: *He is playing you.*

"So, you got my end?"

Irish Pete appeared shocked. "You ain't found shit. You dropped Jonas. He was a friend of mine."

"He was fencing off your score on the side," Junior said. "I can't believe you're so focused on the stones. Been two years and you ain't let the matter pass."

Irish Pete slammed his fists onto the desk. The thump caused the guns to bounce on the desktop. "It's not the diamonds. It's the principle. I planned this heist for three years. I organized men, listened to their bullshit on how good they were. The place turns wild west, cops get tagged and Tuttle hides the stash while he stands trial."

"And he's a liar," Junior said. "He got them to his fence without Jonas."

Irish Pete shook his head. "His fence is being watched. No one is bringing him anything. If they do, I know about it first."

A stillness between the two occurred for a minute. Neither spoke. Both stared at the other, waiting for a response. Junior understood that he should feel intimidated, but didn't.

He wants me to confess. Thinks I'm stupid enough to give up that easy. The diamond score had turned into a mess. Freeway hung out in the Garland and sent texts asking about the status on the stones. Man was nervous about being watched. Junior had to improvise until then. He had given Baron Gamble the diamonds to hold until the old man stopped looking for them. *But it doesn't seem like he's giving up soon, does it?*

"You wanted to talk to me, boss?"

Behind Junior, one of Irish Pete's goons entered. He was dressed in a black leather jacket and had short blonde hair. *I met him last time I was here.* His name was Beau. Junior's eyes followed Beau as the man walked closer. Hand fell down on his sawed-off. Ready to blast the old man into oblivion if Beau made a move. *Do it already, Beau. Try me as I ice your boss.* He watched as Irish Pete gestured the goon to the couch near the fire. Beau sat and Irish Pete moved from the desk to stand next to him.

"Beau, you've been part of my crew for what, five years?" The old man said. He put his hand on Beau's shoulder. Junior saw Beau's eyes turn to him. "If I find out someone double-crosses me, what happens?"

"You take him out, boss," Beau said.

Irish Pete stared at Junior. So did Beau. *They know everything.*
Junior slid his finger into the trigger. *This is a set-up.* He would have
to fight his way out. *He knows everything.* He tensed waiting to find
out what the next move would be. Beau smiled at Junior, ready to
take him down if the boss gave the order. *They believe Tuttle's story
over mine. I'm going down for this one.*

"I don't put up with it, do I?" Irish Pete said, staring at Junior.

"No," Beau said. "You nip it right away."

Irish Pete turned to Beau. "That's right."

The old man drew out a garrote. The wire wrapped around Beau's
neck as the two ends met at the nape. Irish Pete gnashed his teeth
as the goon reacted to the twisting wire in his seat. Beau's hands
flailed. Eyes bulged. Feet stomped loud bangs into the floor as he
tried to fight the old man off. Irish Pete held his ground behind Beau
until the goon's face was red, then dark purple. The wire cut deeper
into Beau's throat drawing blood. Beau's muscles relaxed as his
hands fell limp. The old man twisted a little more as the last breath
fell from the goon. He released the garrote but left the wire hanging
around Beau's neck. Irish Pete smiled at Junior, straightening his
hair.

"He double-crossed you?"

"Beau grew a conscience. That doesn't work in my world,"

Irish Pete said. "He intervened with some pregnant lady who he convinced not to take a loan with me. Cost me a three bedroom in Brownes Addition."

"Your mortgage loan shit is that big?"

Irish Pete: "I don't do mortgages, Junior. I do commercial notes. Mortgages have protections and requirements. I make commercial loans, charging ten thousand percent interest the second they sign."

"The government lets you do that?"

"I'm a licensed loan officer by the state," Irish Pete said. "It took some paper, but I got it going. Best time happened once the recession hit and loan standards tightened. I had a lot of desperate fish coming to me to save their family home."

"But you take it, right?"

"All I need is a pulse and the legal ability to sign," the old man said. "I charge sixty-seven percent interest on loans each week. The person must meet me in person and hand me the cash."

"And you don't make yourself available to meet," Junior said.

Irish Pete nodded. "I set them up. Did them as commercial loans. A twenty-two thousand dollar loan, adding a promissory note of two hundred thousand. Sign each sucker to a quitclaim deed. It gives me their place without the six month waiting period and consumer protections."

"And people sign that shit?" Junior said. "Straight out?"

"You would be amazed how trusting people are. Beau is a good example," Irish Pete said.

"But he was loyal," Junior said. "How does your thing survive if you do a loyal guy?"

"This thing takes nothing to get going," Irish Pete said. "Three or four guys are enough. The main ingredient is fear. You gotta have people fear you, otherwise it all falls apart."

"Is that why you got dirt on your forehead?" Junior said. The comment drew the attention of the old man who returned to his desk. The smudge laid on his faded widow's peak with white eyebrows that crept onto wrinkled skin. He offered a smirk to Junior and rubbed at his forehead until the dirt was gone.

"It's a religious thing."

Junior said, "You think it offers you some protection?"

"The life I've led means there's no amount of penance or forsaking indulgence that will ever make up for what I've done," he said. "But we all have our rituals, don't we?"

He is worn down. It happens when anyone does it too long. Irish Pete displayed a full head of hair, blondish red, not yet white. Junior's eyes ran through the cavernous wrinkles that make the old man stand out. He walked with a little limp and his hands had a shake once in a while. He was a good shylock. He tossed guys out of moving cars for not paying up. Used a baseball bat to get his point across. Irish Pete led a young life. He frequented city restaurants with strawberries on his arm. *I'll have that life the second this deal is over.*

Irish Pete's face reflected an overhead light where he showed his age. His gaunt face created shadows of despair over the dents that hid his eyes. Junior's first impression was the man was older. But his bruising hands said otherwise. His eyes show what his territory costs him to manage. Hair stood in strange forms with his left ear popped out. The nave of the old man's arms had decorations of scattered tattoos and faded scars. Junior saw evil in the old man's eyes. Those tiny brown beads had fixed angles. Both running twelve moves ahead to keep Irish Pete alive.

"Do you think you're too valuable to not be iced?" Irish Pete said. "I get this feeling you got this low opinion of me."

Junior said. "I'm an independent contractor. If you don't want to find your stash, send one of your guys after me. I know how to find shit. It's all up to what you want to do."

Irish Pete shrugged. "Your generation is hard to read. None of you sell anything. You are content to be order takers, nothing more."

"Not every bride is meant to wear white."

The old man laughed. "Maybe generations have their own way of doing things. Back East, I ran from Fed dragnets. This city is a one-eighty. Patrol car cruised down there every two hours. Here, it's ten days or so by the county, if you're lucky. Back East, it's every two minutes. That's the beauty of this place. It's so spread out that you can get away with anything."

"Well, my generation wants to be paid," Junior said. "You could do that for the work I've done."

Irish Pete said, "My generation wants results first."

"I gave you results. Jonas didn't have it on him."

"All I have is a dead body and more excuses. Come back when you find the stones, I'll bring you the cash."

Junior eyed Irish Pete. "You don't have the cash, do you? Even if I brought you the stones, I wouldn't get paid, would I?"

"Give me time to put it together," he said. "I don't keep it lying around."

"What kind of crime boss are you? There should be stacks of clean paper filling up your place," Junior said.

Irish Pete said, "It allows for someone to abscond with it."

"I'm wondering if there is anything to abscond with."

Irish Pete pointed at Junior. "Get me the stones. I'll give you a good share. I want results, Junior. I tell the guys building this house the same thing. They get paid when they finish the job."

"I don't get the whole house thing either," Junior said. "You're flushing a lot of paper."

"Thomas Jefferson was no ordinary president, Junior," the old man said. "Monticello was no ordinary estate. It's one-thirty-eighth scale and trust me, when it's finished, you'll be impressed."

"Never heard of Monticedo."

"Monticello. His estate is called Monticello," Irish Pete said. "You kids have no passion for history. You're part of a bankrupt culture."

"Yeah, and you raised us," Junior said. "Come to think of it, I've never met a guy with no people. No serious paper around to peel off and hand me. You can't tell me it's all wrapped up in this house."

"It is what it is."

Junior's eyes wandered the large room. He noticed beyond the décor that the walls held rotted wood, bounded by dust and webs. *The lights are off. My eyes only catch what the firelight lets me.* He worried whether Irish Pete would give up hunting the stones. *He needs it to survive. That's what he's been hiding. That makes him more dangerous to me.*

Patrick Quinn drove the Lexus as a car that belonged to him. *Good living is what it is*. He wished he had stolen a Lexus before. He targeted Fords or Chevys with breakable steering columns. Cars stolen minus those backseat GPS trackers that help the cops locate later. *Good American cars*. Pat considered stealing the Lexus. Driving to the coast to see the Ocean for the first time. Night fell over the world. Pat drove west on the interstate sitting next to a drunk pretending to be a badass.

16

Frank sat silent in the passenger seat. He offered a false image of a tough hombre. *He acts as if I don't see through it*. Pat had heard stories of Sideville State Correctional. *I don't believe any of them*. Cons spilled tales of sugar dealing. Random guys getting shanked. Guards beating you for a stray glance. Pat eyed Frank's way of falling into the Lexus. It was awkward. Man put his piece off to the side. *As if he never handled one. That's why I see through his bullshit tough act*.

Pat sized up Frank. He wore cheap clothes and stank of alcohol while donning a ten o'clock shadow. Pat had encountered the type before. Smooth talkers hired without the skills to finish the job. Life in prison sounded simple. *You fight for territory and keep your pride. That is what I would do*. The streets were no different. *Herman Gantz never understood*. Pat remembered how Styles burned the mule during an illegal card game on the South Hill.

Gantz had it coming. He was stupid enough to talk shit without the willingness to fight. The mope had suggested Styles took longer than a woman to get ready. The slicked-back Italian grabbed Gantz by the throat. Held Gantz's face to a stove surface until the room stunk of melted skin. Gantz's left eye was dead. After the mope swore payback, he disappeared. *Styles did him and buried him in the Highland Quarry.* Pat wondered how many bodies had been laid at the Quarry.

That is why Pat did not give an inch of respect to Frank. *He doesn't deserve it. Plus, I can take him.* Pat had tossed an envelope of quadruple fins into Frank's lap. The drunk had offered a stare that showed he could not handle himself. *Man looks at a bunch of twenties and wonders why. Man thought his look was powerful enough to have me drive off the road, kill us both. Man ain't shit.* Pat threw the drunk one back. *My face says you best watch yourself, otherwise you ain't seeing much of anything.*

Something about Frank bothered Pat. *Hard to put a finger on, but he ain't a professional. He's a career minor-leaguer getting his first shot at Yankee Stadium. I'm a veteran at this shit.* Before he had gone missing, Gantz had called Pat a 'minor leaguer.' Never thought Pat was good enough. Even when both were kicking down bedroom doors at an old folk's home during recreation time. Pat had been trying to get used to being called Tick. *When they ask for Tick, everyone knows who they're talking about*. Gantz had a different view.

Gantz thought a nickname was an insult. The man hated the idea of people knowing who he was. *Said he didn't need a nickname for someone to remember if he cut 'em. He figured they would remember him. For slicing up a mope who owed a dime. Bet it on the Colts when they lose by 13 with a 15-point spread*. That was before Gantz displayed a damaged eye or stovetop grill scar on his cheek. *Gantz was an asshole. No one remembers him. If I went down, everyone would spread adventures of the Tick.*

His sole instruction from Styles was to watch Frank closely. *If anything ain't right, I call him*. In his pocket, sat a burner cell programmed with Styles' number. *If Frank goes ape shit on me, I dial it and Styles brings muscle*. Pat eyed the drunk. *I might stop him by myself. That would really impress Irish Pete and get me back in*. The two rode down the interstate ready to perform Old Testament shit to complete the job. Styles wanted Pat to buddy up with Frank to find where they were going. *Then, Styles takes down the drunk and I am in with the old man.*

"These yours?"

Pat glanced over. He saw the drunk holding up a pair of shades. Pat had jacked the sunglasses off a Gypsy Knight biker last week.

"Yeah?"

"You mind?"

"No," Pat said. He did not know why he lied to the drunk. *He is some nobody with information. Someone who thinks he is down.* He watched as Frank put the Gargoyles on his face. *Those are now his, my man.* Frank checked himself in the rearview mirror. *You lost them to a drunk.* When Pat wore them, he was invisible. Frank appeared to feel the same way. He caught the drunk nodding. As if to say *yeah, that's me there, ready to do my thing.*

Pat became less of himself. He was back to being little Patrick Quinn. The kid bullied by everyone in Hillyard. With a momma who never thought he amounted to much. The type who was second to any guy she brought home. Who took beatings because his dead-beat daddy ditched momma for a slut in Seattle. *There is no going back to that. No matter how many times she tells others that she misses you. You got a life now. You got to leave that old one behind.* Part of his new life included driving through a cold night, to an unknown destination. *Let him have the shades. By morning, I will be back in and he will be a memory.*

"Pull off and head to Exit One."

He pulled off the interstate. Fog-covered wheat land and small trees ahead. The Lexus chewed up a dirt highway. Toward the unofficial landmark separating two northwestern states. The Exit One gentlemen's club served as a ratty joint notorious for seedy clientele. Everyone had screwed up too much to live in Coeur d'Alene or Spokane. Inside held illicit options: purchase of an illegally modified gun; a mail-order bride fresh from two months in a Chinese shipping crate; or a bag of chalk run down from the northern border. It was the home to Tony Hell, the human cock-fighting show in the basement.

Pat had been tossed out seven months back. Too touchy-feely with the girls they said. *All I wanted was Sapphire's number. She gave it to everyone else. Why not me?* His jaw still ached where Exit One's bouncer Donovan had punched him. He recalled lying on his back for hours watching the Exit One sign. Where the electronic woman in French Stockings parted her legs underneath the club's name. Almost revealing the naughtiest part.

He cut the Lexus' engine in the parking lot. He turned to Frank. "Let me handle this one."

The drunk shrugged. "Be my guest."

Pat grinned. He exited the Lexus, slammed the door shut, then marched over to the club entrance. *Man thought he was doing his thing. Didn't know he was with a professional.* Pat rolled up his sleeves and stepped into the club. *Being little Patrick Quinn ain't no life. This is the life. And there ain't no going back.*

Pat's ten steps into the club was greeted by Donovan's fist. He knocked Pat back through the club doors. Pat spilled into the parking lot. The world spun. Pat tasted blood. He looked up to see the drunk standing over him, smiling. *What is that man smiling about? Doesn't he know I'm the Tick? I'm a legend around here.* Pat attempted to get up and watched Frank step over him into the club. *He thinks he can do better. Let's see him try.* Pat saw the drunk enter the club and waited for him to be thrown out. He waited a while sitting on that gravel parking lot. *Maybe he needs a nickname too.*

Brian Tuttle had aged years in a few days. The dye in his hair was going. The stuff got gray but he left it be. *Too many things to worry about right now*. After surviving Robert Nash's attack, Brian was edgy.

From what he heard, Frank had caused the biker to spend another week at the infirmary. *I should arrange to go visit him and make sure he doesn't get out. That is how I send messages*. Safety at *The Sides* was a concern for new guys. Not for guys with connections.

Jimmy Carcetti was his next challenge. Crazy junkie wheelman on the diamond job had entered the pit. Brian sat in his cell and planned what to do. Decided to screw over Irish Pete to get at Carcetti. *No loyalty in this business, inside or out*. Word got to Brian that Carcetti had Brian's daughter. He had to give up the stones. Otherwise, Cassie Tuttle would be floating in Lake Coeur d'Alene by morning. He was unsure of the answer. Family was supposed to be off-limits by rivals. *I have done it myself some times. I shot a guy's old lady while she was taking a shower. It is what you have to do to get your point across.*

A few years back, Brian would have panicked in this situation. Now he was a veteran of the "wait." He could sit through anything. He could think of whatever and let the "wait" roll on. *Used to think waiting was worse than getting stuck with a knife or shot with a gun. I know better now. Sometimes you have to wait it out.*

His wife, Lynn, provided the longest "wait" that Brian had ever been through. *Sit next to her and keep up appearances. Let her body finally give out.* Then, the agony he had was gone. His mind drifted toward the length of the "wait" that he would be forced to endure. *Will Jimmy get the message that I don't know anything?*

The junkie had been the world's worst wheelman. He remembered the craziness of Jimmy's driving on the diamond job. *Kid got the bright idea to drive on the opposite side of the sidewalk.* Brian recalled Jimmy's laugh. Women with downtown mall bags leaping out of the way as Jimmy tried to run them down.

Brian held a photo of his girl, Cassie. She was twenty when he went in. A strained smile on her face. *She's ashamed of her old man.* He wished she was better about what he was. Lynn had tried to get her to understand. *The kid never asked how the credit card bills got paid because she didn't want to know.* If Lynn were still alive, she would have made Cassie visit him often.

Brian expected one of the guards to notify him of a visitor. He imagined Lynn arriving, telling him that Cassie had run off with a boyfriend again. *Like I can do anything about that. I tried to convince Lynn we're each out here on our own.* She never realized. *She always thought I could step in and do something.* He shook off negativity regarding Lynn. *She's been gone two years and it isn't right.* He remembered hospital room stays with her. He let all of the nurses and doctors see him. Showed how much he cared about his wife. *Appearances are important.*

He had survived the "wait" every time Lynn went into surgery. Each time she came out more exhausted than before. His back aches from long hours in uncomfortable chairs. Wondering when Irish Pete or Styles would show to pay their respects. Lynn's heart monitor beeping. Every ten seconds. Hearing the respirator inflate, then collapse, with every forced breath the machine made her take. *She couldn't die like a normal cancer patient. She lived on. She made me sit beside her and keep up appearances.*

His trial had been postponed numerous times due to Lynn's health. *She kept talking about finding a lump while in the shower. Even when I mentioned I might be going away.* The conversation had become tense. The trial was secondary to her. *She didn't understand I wasn't facing a straight eight before a chance at parole. It was twenty-five to life.* He recalled the night after she had discovered her cancer. Brian had screamed at her to shut her trap. She responded by dropping her head at the dinner table. Landed her face in a plate of microwave spaghetti.

The hours Brain spent watching a static-filled black & white in her hospital room. Ignoring trial prep ate at him. He had worried too many times about Styles arriving with flowers and wondered where he was. *They didn't care about me.* He felt anger toward Lynn for humiliating him. *Making me feed her bits of mush and getting her to drink sips of water. She kept getting worse but wasn't dying.* In the end, he hated her for continuing to live. *She was toying with me and getting my hopes up that she would beat this thing.* He watched her improve for two days, almost lucid, then crash. Repeat it for another week, and another.

Cassie never understood. She would tell me how mean I was to her mother. She was an expert without any experience. She acts like I'm a pariah. But she never turned down money from him. *She acted as if I was in the wrong when the Sheriff's Office came to our house. She never backed me the way Lynn did.* She had never visited him at *The Sides. She's too good to have an old man inside. But now she needs my help. Maybe I'll take my sweet time getting her safe.* He stopped his anger. He knew it wasn't about Cassie. *It's about Jimmy thinking he can do this. He's disrespecting me. If he gets away with it, cuts her up because you don't pay. Gives someone else the idea to challenge you.* Guys would begin to form a line. *Nash thinking he got the green light to do me. It's not right. How long before five guys are waiting to kill you at once?* He knew it would happen if Jimmy got away with doing Cassie.

Brian rose from his Barcalounger and killed the plasma. He stretched then nodded at his plan. *No better way to screw with wise guys than to bring in the heat.* Brian exited the medium security wing minus the catcalls and hoots that followed other prisoners. *The cons know better than to disrespect a connected guy. After tonight, Jimmy will know better too.* Brian approached a guard named Christopher at the end of the row. The guard appeared shocked to see him come forth.

"Need the warden," Brian said. "It's important."

"How important?"

"From me, everything is."

Ten minutes later, he had an audience with the warden. The man appeared unimpressed by Cassie's kidnapping. Until Brian mentioned he knew the location of the stones. Then, the warden was interested. *Those stones get people's attention.* He knew better than to believe the warden was honest. Man had also used some excuse of budget cutbacks to switch out the sugar with artificial sweetener. *Because, he's sadistic enough to want to see what would happen.*

"So where are they?"

"You rescue my kid first."

The warden shook his head. "You're lying. I can see it in your eyes."

"What's the difference?" he said. "Lying or not, you make the papers for saving some girl from being iced. If I'm not lying, and I'm not, you get the stones."

The warden remained interested. *Those gears are turning. He's thinking of that new car that he can buy off of this.* The common method for extracting inmate information was to beat it out of them. But Brian knew he held his connections over the warden. *I can do a lot with my reach. Maybe blow up his car when he turns over the engine. Or let him come home to his wife with a Colombian necktie.* He refrained from smirking. He planned on doing it after Jimmy was screwed over by his deal.

The office door opened behind Brian. He turned to see Steve Powers entering. He was a sadistic guard who had beaten an inmate for whistling. Brian knew better. Powers was mean. I approached George Hoob, tried to get him to whistle for me. Guy couldn't do it for shit. That's when I knew Powers was a nut job. Brian guessed Powers had beaten the guy without charge. Probably made up the whistling claim as an excuse. *You gotta keep your cool in this game. You never know who is watching.* Powers presented a tactical map of Coeur d'Alene's streets.

"We ran a trap-trace," Powers said. "Found them in an abandoned complex."

The warden appeared cautious in tone. "Yes, but how do we extract her alive?" *They want to keep me happy. They want those stones for themselves.*

"Shay Baxter runs my old tactical unit," Powers said. "He can make it quiet."

The warden faced Brian. "You are lucky you came to us."

"I feel it is in good hands."

"After we extract her," Powers said, pointing at Brian. "I want the location of the diamonds." *I bet you do. I never doubted for a moment.*

18

Frank Gryzbowsky entered Exit One and felt the need to bathe. The music pumped between low lights and offered a point of no return. *You think you can walk away but you know you can't. Even left the piece in the car. Otherwise, you might have to use it.* He felt the bottoms of his borrowed shoes squelch off the stickiness of the floor. *If someone does a germ test here, they walk away in disgust.* Men with new suedes had them ruined entering Exit One. He imagined a back dumpster full of destroyed new sneakers from the filth licking the floor.

He stood behind a velvet rope coated in grime. A hot little number approached. Ready to do her hostess thing. Kissed a stamp on the back of his hand. Her gloss was ultraviolet. Patrons received entry after having the hostess read the rules preventing solicitation and weapons. Frank doubted customers or workers adhered to the rules. *They have their own set of rules.*

"I am here to see The Serg," he said in her ear.

His eyes grabbed the club's interior. Inmates spread rumors of the Russian mobster who ran the joint. The illegal fighting den downstairs fueled the stories from inmates at *The Sides*. He had survived Federal raids and mafia debts from his homeland. The hot little number directed Frank with a fake thumbnail toward the back of the club. He palmed her two twenties that found home in her thong. *She earns better tips doing that.*

The scent of lust took hold in his nose. Sex singed his eyes. He noted a pair of blonde identical twins. They were kissing at the behest of a man making it rain large paper at their feet. It was a club fronting for a brothel. *Brian spoke about the underground fights where you had to be invited to attend.* Money rolled in from different club components. The club's edges showed coke hustlers and the burlesque venturing behind side curtains. Exit One paraded girls with fake tops and false smiles for a clientele eager to pay.

Two men grabbed his arms tight. He was lifted from his feet and carried toward the Champagne room. The main floor sped by. His body was slammed against the room's door and through it. His eyes caught a dancer and patron having sex on the room's couch. He was tossed onto the carpet, which blew the wind from his lungs. *I need to wash my face.* The dancer screamed. He felt the men searching him for weapons. He watched as the dancer and patron were moved out of the room. Frank was lifted to his feet and forced to stand.

The Serg entered. One of the men spoke Russian. *They are telling him I am not carrying.* He hoped that was what they said. The Serg wore a cheap black sport jacket with dark shirt and pants. In his hand, he smoked hand-rolled cigarettes that produced loud puffs of odor. He smiled with his salt-and-pepper goatee and sized Frank up. *Now try to talk your way out of this one. You should have gotten out when you had the chance.*

"Brian Tuttle sent me."

The Serg appeared surprised. He looked at his two men, exchanging Russian words. The language was fast. Frank focused on The Serg. *He knows English. He doesn't want me to know what is going on.* The two men released Frank, letting him ease up. The Serg leaned forward. He patted Frank on the cheek.

"American cowboy," The Serg said. "That is what you are."

The Serg wrapped his arm around Frank and led him back to the main floor. The two men shadowed them. A retro hit blared over the speakers. Frank's eyes caught an eighty-three percent plastic number walking to the stage. She placed her purse to the side, heading up the steps wearing impossible heels. She shook her can and did a five-dollar dive in front of an excited customer. The Serg moved Frank toward another room with a descending staircase.

Brian had told Frank about Exit One's original owner, Angelo de la Castro. *Said place was for beat-out strawberries entertaining bikers and dealers doing a stretch-run from Missoula to Seattle.* Frank remembered Brian recalling how back then, Exit One was a place of criminal status. *Buy a used Glock or a cheap V.I.N. for those cars with ignitions started by screwdrivers.* Angelo let the club run down. Brian said he collected the paper and looked the other way until The Serg arrived.

Angelo's tenure ended when an offer was made for him to walk away from the business, alive. Brian said it was a good deal. No cash exchanged hands but Angelo got to breathe. *John Caspin got tossed off a bridge after he wouldn't leave his front.* Frank felt uneasy as they headed down the staircase. He smelled stale sweat floating on the ceiling. *What are you doing here, Frank? You should have walked away.* He noted a circle sand pit in the middle of the room.

The pit's décor was comprised of rotten wooden panels held by electrician's tape. A blood-soaked bulb hanging from a chain served as the source of light. *This is the place where the fighting happens.* Inmates at *The Sides* spoke of Tony Hell with reverence held for saints and mothers. *He is a god to them.* Frank saw the large metal door with a small rectangular opening. *Someone is staring back and watching me in the dark.*

"You have message for me?" The Serg said.

Frank stood across from The Serg and the two men. The Russian offered his full attention. The music poured large bass beats upstairs. He could feel something staring at him from behind the metal door. *Whatever it is wants to come out and devour me.* He acted firm, but not tough in front of The Serg. *Man might take it as an insult.*

"Brian says you have something for me to pick up," Frank said. *Be that guy you see in the movies.* Frank drew from his pocket a playing card. He displayed it for The Serg. *Show him who you speak for. Let him get a good look at it*. The Serg held a calm reaction to the card only a few inches from his face.

"Now, I know that if Frank Gryzbowsky was getting out, he would call me."

Frank looked at the staircase. Howie Sims headed down. He rubbed his nose acting as a fiend. His curly black hair meshed with a trimmed beard. He could be a stockbroker or lawyer for the dress shirt and sport jacket he wore. He noticed Sims' casual manner. *He's been expecting me*. Frank looked at The Serg. The Russian backed out of the pit. Sims entered displaying shark teeth. Frank felt The Serg's goons ready to grab him so Sims could get a few shots in.

"You owe me a new piece," Sims said.

Frank slammed his foot into a goon's knee. He felt it collapse. His ankle bracelet scraped his calf. He resisted the temptation to tear it off. Frank threw the base of his palm into the second goon's throat. It sent the man gasping for air. Frank focused on Sims, who dropped his smile. You never did fight fair. He kicked Sims in the chest. The shot sent him into one of the wooden panels. Sims' head smashed through it. Beyond Sims, Frank listened to something bellow a blood lust at the violence behind the metal door.

He pounced on Sims amid the thump of bass. I lost four months of my life for him. Frank slammed fists into Sims' face causing his mouth to bleed. His eyes went groggy. *Maybe the white light is coming for him*. Frank refused to stop hitting him and struck Sims several times in the chest. *I couldn't stop even if I wanted to.*

A hand clasped his shoulder and threw him off Sims. Frank went back across the sand pit. He crashed apart a wooden panel. His vision dazed as his senses dropped. Frank tasted blood. One of the goons helped Sims stand up. The other goon held his knee, screaming from the initial exchange. Frank stood and felt the ankle bracelet weigh his leg down. Sims moved to the side of the pit, wiping blood from his face. Frank locked eyes with the remaining goon. *I'm a pit bull. Like those Gypsy Knight biker dogs. The kind who tear each other apart in the valley.*

The remaining goon lunged at Frank and missed. The goon charged until he crashed against the metal door. A cavernous roar from behind the metal door overtook the room. Two muscular arms came through the small rectangle opening. They grabbed the goon's face. *It's a human animal in there.* The goon screamed as his face was torn apart.

Sims brandished a switchblade. The knife hissed as it extended. He offered Frank a look of *Come on, let's do this thing.* He charged at Frank with blade pointed out. Frank slid by, grabbing hold of Sims' stabbing arm. He sent him into the goon with the broken kneecap. The blade plunged deep into the goon's chest as Sims toppled the man. The goon and Sims exchanged shocked looks. Sims held the handle with the blade lodged in the goon's chest. As if an apology were waiting to take place.

Frank took advantage. He latched onto Sims' wrist and pushed hard down on the handle. The blade snapped at the stem. It left the remainder in the goon. The move was common at *The Sides*. *You stab a snitch in the shower and break off the handle. Let him grab at nothing trying to pull it free until he bleeds out.* The goon was dealt the same hand. Sims shook while holding the handle. His eyes focused on it. *He's never been this close to losing before.* Together, they stood silent. The goon heaved, clawed with his big fingers at the metal end stuck inside his gut. The goon shook. He fell onto his side in a puddle of his own tissue. His eyes yellowed, ballooning as they puffed out.

Frank took a broken wooden panel and smashed it over Sims' head. His former friend dropped and passed out on the sand pit next to the dead goon. Frank looked at The Serg. "Brian says I got something to pick up. Where is it?"

"Boneyard," The Serg said.

The Russian sat calm in a folding chair and puffed his hand-rolled cigarettes. He enjoyed the show. *To him, this is sport.* Frank eyed the metal door. The goon was a mess of blood, a face torn in shreds. Whatever is behind that door was inhuman. *At least, it's not human anymore.* From what he had done, he wondered whether people would say the same about him. *God, I need a drink.* He looked at Sims, seeing his blue jacket. *Howie's my size too.*

Frank struggled to get off the sport jacket. He put it on and felt better. Something heavy in one of the pockets drew his attention. His hand fished out a pair of brass knuckles. He tossed the knuckles up in the air and caught it. Frank headed up the staircase, ready to see what awaited him at The Boneyard. *Brian said this was an easy pickup job. I guess I should have asked his definition of easy.*

19 He felt a stranger among his former crew. Steve
Powers missed being real police. Getting shit
done. *The Sides* had its moments. But there was
no comparison to being in *the shit*. Powers had
the sense of "owning the situation" during his time running CDA
Tactical. *Better than being a wet nurse for cons.* If an inmate
messed with Powers at *The Sides*, consequences happened. So did
paperwork. But Coeur d'Alene Tactical gave him a real taste for
the action. *Stakeout a house for ten hours. Get the routine of the
inhabitants down. Know the situation. Come charging through with
four guys in body armor behind you. Nothing stopped us back in the
day.*

Running *The Sides* got dull. CDA Tactical never had. *Watching
some tough asshole go soft two seconds after an eight-cell Mag-
light gets flashed in their eyes.* So did red beams from five carbines
aimed at their skull. Steve loved every minute of it. His mind would
be alive at night. Excitement from the job made him pop up each
morning, hoping a situation was called in. *That's the juice talking.
Something they never had in a street drug.* Times he knocked out the
front teeth of some wife beating asshole with his baton. Subduing
a punk who held a baby at gunpoint. Some jobs had side benefits.
CDA Tactical was no exception.

He was back in *the shit*. Steve got a hard-on talking to his old team on the phone. The set-up was a dank building one hundred yards from where Cassie Tuttle was held. *I miss this*. He climbed the staircase to the second floor, skipping steps to get there faster. The odor of bad coffee brewing. His ears caught mindless chatter on the walkie talkies that the boys made during the stakeout. *I want back in. Work at The Sides has been okay. But nothing compares to this. This is real life. I want it back.*

His commanding officer's signature on his resignation form made sure those days were gone. Commander Coll had never been in *the shit*. The *paperweight* had never donned a helmet or raided a building full of meth heads. *The asshole was a press hound trying to get his face on the tube. I made the hard choices.* Coll set the CDA police department back about twenty years. The man caved by allowing civilian panels and watching every move a cop made. *Who cares if we get a taste off some dealer's cash? It should be a reward for risking our lives.*

The commanding officer had entered the department with a blood lust for cops. He wanted every good cop off the force. Steve heard stories from his old Minneapolis post. None of the blue there could stand Coll when he ran that department. After being hired by the mayor, Coll gathered names of CDA's finest whom he didn't like. *He made an enemies list like Nixon.* Coll let anyone with a beef against a blue brother into his office. Then the investigation would start.

Department claimed it was broke. But it had the money to pay a forensic accountant to go through a cop's financials. Anything I took was from bad people. Not civilians. Who says I shouldn't drive a nice car because the city denies me a merit raise? It doesn't seem fair. Coll never saw it that way. He found out what Steve was pulling on the raids. *Man thought all of the money should be turned in. That no one should get a taste. Sometimes, cops need a taste to get by.*

Steve entered the stakeout of on Cassie Tuttle as a civilian. *It's weird not to be part of it.* He noticed the difference when he called up Shay Baxter to give details. *It reminds me of the retired cops who visited when I was running Tactical. I'm one of those guys with history but no real future.* He wanted to enter as an elder statesman. But he knew that was not the case. Most of his team had moved on, bringing in new blood to CDA Tactical. *I don't recognize any of these guys.* He searched for Baxter and found him overlooking maps. His old partner noticed him and met him halfway.

"You look good, mister," Baxter said.

Baxter wore a brown beard. Made him appear old when he trimmed because it revealed the gray. He was more muscular than Steve. They greeted with a grip at the forearm. Steve noted the bags under Baxter's eyes. *Shay's worrying to death over that damn kid of his. I wonder how much longer he can put his father through this.*

"What have you got going?"

"Solo act," Baxter said. They examined a monitor. It displayed two heat signatures. One was in a sitting position, the other paced in front of them.

"Any muscle?"

"He's working on a deadline," Baxter said.

"Can we extract her alive?"

"Possible," Baxter said. "Why don't we discuss the details outside."

They went to the building's roof. Hid behind a dead transformer to prevent Cassie Tuttle's kidnapper from spotting them. Baxter pointed at Steve, letting him know their conversation was serious. "My guys got questions about this being off the grid."

"Couldn't say it over the phone," Steve said. "Not in front of your guys."

"Cute," Baxter said. "I'll be put in front of a disciplinary board because of you."

Steve shook his head. "No, you won't."

"You don't understand what it's like to have a family to worry about. Tyler has been worse and I can't afford to be suspended."

There it is. Tyler is more important than I am. He makes Shay weak by caring about him. Steve never understood the paternal instinct of others. He left one of his ex-wives because she wanted a kid. *Said she changed her mind after she got married.* Steve was betrayed and she called his bluff that he would leave. He called up his lawyer and got the papers ready. Walked out before she could trap him. *No couples counseling or reconciliation no matter how much she begged me.* Steve saw Baxter's weakness was his son's health.

Steve lied. "I'm thinking of Tyler with this thing."

"How so?"

"Guy who tipped me off on this, that's his daughter being held."

"And this helps my kid how?"

"Bring her out alive, we get about two million in diamonds he stashed."

Baxter: "You believe that?"

Steve shrugged. "The guy is connected. My boys and I don't mess with him. He'll line us with a fence and we'll cover Tyler's bills for the next hundred years."

"Don't do that," Baxter said. "Don't use my son to justify what you're saying."

Steve leaned toward Baxter. He sold his lie that he cared about Tyler: "Your kid matters to me, Shay. How long before your insurance stops paying? Don't make him suffer because you get cold feet."

"I don't want to end up like you," Baxter said. "Taking a taste and getting bounced. That doesn't help Tyler either."

"I run a state prison," Steve said. "And it's got rules."

"What are the rules?"

"Do as I say or it means your ass."

Shay: "So, nothing has changed since you running the show."

"Nope."

20 One of the more notorious places talked about at *The Sides* was The Boneyard. It held the bankrupt name of Baker Auto and every con hot-wiring a car ended up there. A car thief named Peanut with a bad sugar habit had been there too many times. *Said he busted out into tow trucks. Took their industry book of every key made. Stole any car he wanted.* A short drive to The Boneyard had the car dismantled into unrecognizable parts stacked high overlooking Division Street. The road separated the city from the outskirts. It was where organs of hot cars with dead VINs are laid to rest.

The yard held carcasses of every make and model from 1952. The hollowed-out rust shells piled high enough to block the city skyline when commuters slashed up the hillside southbound on their commute. A car buff restoring his 1967 Chevy Impala never ventured into the yard. His exploration would be fruitless. It was a graveyard for cars mangled by screwdriver starts. Water-filled headlights that loomed from faces of dead car fronts monitored pedestrians venturing the sidewalk near the Boneyard.

The kid stopped the Lexus a block from Baker Auto. The kid whistled at the sight. Frank agreed with his assessment. *What have you gotten yourself into, Frank? Could you walk away and pretend this never happened?* He considered then dismissed the idea. *You screw with guys Brian knows and they send people after you. If you run, you have to keep running.*

Frank to the kid: "What's your name?"

He had noted the kid's silence after he returned from his Exit One visit. The kid saw the blood splatter on Frank's shirt and let his imagination play. *But it's really not far from the truth.*

"My name is Pat," he said.

Pat's attitude offered little respect to Frank. *He needs my respect to get through tonight.* The more silence from a guy, the more serious people took them. *Because no one can read into what they say when they say nothing at all.* He wished he had been less of a talker at The Sides. *Maybe I wouldn't be in this mess.*

"I'm thinking I was talked into some heavy shit," Frank said.

Pat said, "Who are you?"

"Frank," he said, offering his hand. Pat did not take it.

"No, I mean, who are you?" Pat said. "You act like I'm your DUFF. You're some hottie with a DUFF trying to make yourself look hotter. You ain't shit. You're an accessory for someone like me who also picks up the bar tab."

"You should be smarter about this, kid."

"You're some drunk who bullshitted his way into this," Pat said. "I'm only good at this and working at Mickey Dees doing lot check for cigarette butts and spent burger wrappers."

Pat is an arrogant ass. Frank turned toward The Boneyard. He wondered what awaited him in there. Pat grabbed Frank's piece off the dashboard, exited the Lexus. Frank watched him cross the front of the Lexus then dart in between traffic toward the chop shop. Two cars slammed their brakes to keep from knocking Pat out of his sneakers. The kid disappeared through the entrance.

"Jesus, kid," Frank said.

Frank exited the Lexus. He crossed as the evening rush began and made it to the mouth of The Boneyard. The sidewalks sat empty. Frank's eyes went down the descending path of the wrecking yard. No sign of Pat. *Where the hell did he go?* Frank headed inside. His eyes went from a fractured car to a mini-van shell. He felt the looming headlights and broken windshields monitoring his movement. The carcasses of metal cadavers displayed cold, twisted portions.

A few feet into the dirt drive, Frank questioned his intent. He saw no sign of Pat. He moved around halves of a white Chevy Astrovan. He placed his hands on the crushed anatomy of a dead engine and ducked down as he saw a worker move in the distance. The worker headed toward the end of the drive where a white building sat at the center. *This place feels alive for all the wrong reasons.*

Frank crept around the engine manifold and headed closer to the heart of The Boneyard. He remained close to the edge of stacked cars to keep hidden. His eyes caught twin hangar doors cracked open at the entrance of the white building. To the left of the building, he spotted two workers tearing apart a car with a hot blowtorch. The metal screamed when kissed by the torch. The car's contents vomited out fractional pieces onto the concrete flooring. Liquids oozed through large cracks littered around the yard's base. You should get out of here now, Frank. He felt a gun push up against his neck.

"Are you lost, friend?"

A hand placed on his shoulder pushed him forward. He was moved to the men dismantling the car ruins. The men spotted him and set aside their work. The torch was cut. The metal abandoned. The men hooted with the anticipation of fun. *I'm the most interesting thing to happen tonight.* Frank was pushed toward the crack between the two hangar doors. As he was forced inside, Frank's eyes caught Pat hiding behind a smashed up Ford to his right. *How in the hell did he not get caught?*

21

He was not crazy. Jimmy told himself that all of the time. *No matter what they say, Jimmy, we ain't crazy.* He heard his older brother Tim telling him what a good kid he was. *You're swell, Jimmy, a real sport. You gotta stop listening to other people.* Tim was gone now without even a picture for Jimmy's wallet left. So hearing him say those things was all Jimmy had left. *We ain't crazy.* The buzz that went through his head was hard to keep out. Dreams of Hawaiian women were interrupted by the buzz crashing through his skull. *It hurts bad. I want it to stop.* He pounded at his head still hearing the sound. *When I get a taste, the buzz stops. It goes away for a while.*

Out came his little baby. A snub-nosed Saturday Night Special of cold black metal. It weighed under his scrawny grip but it was good to him. *Ain't that right, baby? Just you and me fighting against the world.* The piece was his true friend. *Back when Mrs. O'Henry's dog wouldn't stop barking after pop worked a nightshift.* He had been a boy when it happened. Pop had used Jimmy's little baby. Squeezed the trigger. Barrel aimed at O'Henry's pooch. So he had some quiet and work in the morning. *Did its job in one shot. After that, the little baby got passed down to me.*

His power came from the piece. His finger caressed the trigger to let the smooth, cool tooth become a dagger. With the girl, his little baby played. The skin of the little baby snub-nose went across Cassie

Tuttle's skin. The barrel rested between her brown eyes. *Betcha she smells gun oil. I'll pull the trigger before her daddy calls back with the stones.* Jimmy questioned his will power to hold back from a party. *When I get the stones, I can have my medicine.*

The barrel pressed against Cassie's forehead. *Feel it? Don't it feel nice and good?* He eyed the lanky brunette. He liked brunettes because they had style. *This one is twenty-two going on thirty.* She had legs skyrocketing past her age. *She is asking for it, ain't she?* Jimmy noted her left eye's shiner was growing dark. *She got mouthy with me. That's what happens when you get mouthy with old Jimmy.* Her mouth sealed by duct tape kept her from annoying him now. Her hair hung in sweaty strands, coated by the human stink of fear. *There ain't nothing to fear, my queen.* Her eyes sat on the floor. She was worried about Jimmy's little baby snub-nose being on the stage.

"Your poppa did bad stuff, ripped friends off," Jimmy said. "That's why I'm getting the stones. I need my medicine to stop the sounds so I can sleep."

Jimmy's momma was a shrink. She put him on all sorts of stuff when he was young. If there was one person who should never be giving advice to others, it was Jimmy's momma. *She made me take that syrup.* The stuff that made the colors of the world leave. He blamed his momma on the buzzing sound in his ears. The syrup she gave him made the buzzing sound happen. *And it won't go away. No matter how hard I try, it stays buzzing. I hate it.* Momma's new man tried to get Jimmy to believe in second chances. *Tried to say that we do the best we can, screw up and try again.*

Momma's new man was making his move on Jimmy. *He wanted to sap my strength. Put me in a hospital bed so Momma's new man felt ten years younger.* Momma's new man tried to write him a check to leave. *Said it was for my medicine and a new life.* He was leaning over, signing the check when Jimmy hit him. Over and over again until Momma's new man was in a pool of blood, dead. But still somehow talking from beyond. Wouldn't shut up. Even after Jimmy unloaded his little baby six times into the man's back.

That was when the lies started. Momma not understanding him. Not trying to save her son. Jimmy's momma lied on him in court, said he got a disease from his old man. It wasn't his fault Jimmy couldn't sleep. *That's why I had to put my little baby to her chest and pull the trigger. So I can sleep.*

Jimmy was sent to a hospital after the diamond job where his momma was the head shrink. She was wheeling around in her chair showing what her boy did to her. *Said I was a menace and had to be stopped. She said she loved me.* She hopped him up on drugs and put volts through his skull. *She called me a bad seed. Said I would never be out.* But Jimmy showed her. Never swallowed the syrup. Knew it wouldn't keep the buzzing sound at bay.

Jimmy put his hands around his momma, choked until her face went blue. Stole his little baby snub-nose out of her desk, escaped. The buzzing sound haunted him on the street. The residue of the syrup his momma gave him must have lodged in his brain. Then, Jimmy discovered medicine to open the flower that beat back the buzzing sounds. But he needed more to keep it away. He went to old friends in need of cash. They told Brian Tuttle to use him as a wheelman. *I don't crack under pressure.*

Brian Tuttle was like Jimmy's momma. Saying Jimmy was a loon. *I was a good wheelman. He shouldn't have burned me.* Jimmy had done the diamond job right. *I drove away when Nash and Brian got in.* He raced through intersections, hit pedestrians, and managed to crash into a hotel lobby. With Nash unconscious and Jimmy restrained by the airbag, Brian took the stones. For two years, I never got the green light. Then the old man gave the okay. *I've waited to get my medicine. And I intend to get it.*

"We're going to have fun, you and me." Jimmy said.

He flashed a broken smile. The sweet urine hit his nostrils. His eyes focused on her crotch. The girl wet herself in the chair. Her denim bore dark blue patches and streaks. He giggled and stared into her nice eyes. *I haven't had medicine long enough not to be tempted. It's not my fault she wants it. Usually the medicine would make me want to stop.*

"I don't mind a little extra with the party," he said.

Jimmy listened to her muffled cry underneath the tape. He had handcuffed her to the chair. She struggled against her restraints, rocking back and forth. *Now, it's getting good.* He thought of dancing in front of her, clapping as she fought. *She's playing hard to get. I like that.* Jimmy remembered his first with that little Marie girl with Down syndrome. He took her hand, did her business, and his shrink momma covered it up. *Said I needed help, I needed medicine.*

His attention left Cassie. The windowsill held a dirty needle and burnt spoon. A few grains of heaven awaited him near the window. *I need to have some. I can hear the buzzing sound and I can't think straight.* Amid the building's rats that made sounds, the buzzing in his head amplified. Jimmy held his head, stamping his feet on the ground. He clenched his teeth and prayed that it leave. *I need my medicine. I need to take it now.*

I'll take the medicine when I get the stones. I promise. Jimmy rubbed his lip against his teeth. The medicine went through him. The buzzing sound would leave as the flower bloomed in his mind. *I forget everything until the flower closes.* The need to open the flower wide. He had stolen medicine from a pharmacy. Escaped with a few grams before the police arrived. *Not a drop since I grabbed her. I'm supposed to wait until the job is over.* He attempted to resist, but the need burned inside him and called him over to the grain.

"Your poppa's been a bad boy. Thought he snatched my slice of the score," Jimmy said. "Now we see how much he loves you."

He tried to stay clean. *But I need my medicine.* They forced him to enter rehab after deals with the D.A. to avoid prison. His shrink momma thought she was able to cure him. Did it to her little baby by shooting him up with ten-thousand volts. Right to his temples. The buzzing sound returned. He begged for it to stop. *I don't want to be clean anymore. I want to sleep. I want the flower to bloom.*

A taste wouldn't hurt. As long as it stopped the buzzing sound, it would be worth it. Jimmy stamped the ground again. He wanted to sleep, bad. The aroma of white fear touched his senses. *I need my medicine.* He had done well by staying clean before taking Cassie and being a professional. It was now a waiting game. *When the stones are mine, I will get more medicine.*

"I'm getting a little for a bit," Jimmy said. He offered Cassie a nice, fat wink of coming attractions. "Be back soon."

He thought of the time he would wink at her again. *Right after her poppa calls in. When the coast is clear, that is when you do it. Right after you do your thing to her. When she looked different, it's because she knows you own her.* Jimmy knelt down and wiped away Cassie's oily hair with his little baby snub-nose barrel. He kissed her with his chapped lips on the forehead. *I'll be gentle with her later so she understands everything.*

The sky fell on Jimmy Carcetti. The crash of ceiling followed by armored men shooting smoke canisters through the window. It destroyed the little bag of heaven and created a powder finality. Black masked men pointed large guns with red beams and screamed, aiming right at his chest. Jimmy got tossed to the ground, hog-tied and put on his back. A black masked storm trooper smacked Jimmy with the butt of his rifle. Jimmy saw his front teeth fly free of his mouth. His vision went black as blood, vomit and mess covered his face. Jimmy passed out and knew the flower would have to wait to bloom.

The building's nerve was cavernous. The ceilings covered by humming halogen strips. Several autos hung ten feet off the ground by chains and hydraulic

22

lifts. Catwalks and shafts zigzagged through the upper interior as chrome bumpers reflected off the light. A Firebird slept on a metal lift in the middle of the room. Attending underneath its hood was a tall, tin man of suspect origin. Frank Gryzbowsky waited with his hands bound, assuming the man was who he needed to speak with.

The man donned a pair of sculptor's frames on his skull. Swatches of grease caked on his cheeks and arms. His thin patch of hair continued beyond his neck in a tiny ponytail. Frank eyed the man's long-faded blue coveralls. The fabric held a year worth of oil and fuel in its fibers. The Firebird's lift was tethered into metal chains that dangled from the ceiling. The man stopped his craft at the sight of Frank and beckoned his workers for an explanation.

The worker named Eric said: "Hey, Paco, we found this one searching the yard."

"Yeah, maybe Sully gives us a bonus." The other worker named Zed said.

Paco stretched as he straightened out of the Firebird's engine. He wiped with a spent rag. "This one is ready to go."

The two men left Frank with his hands bound. They ran to the

Firebird, tested the chains against the lift. Paco went to a control podium a few feet from the lift. He pressed a button that let the Firebird rise. The car went twelve feet above the floor. Paco left the podium and went to Frank. He leaned in, examining Frank's eyes.

"I don't like thieves," he said.

Frank said: "I'm here to see somebody."

"Sure, pal," Paco said. "That's what they all say."

"Where's Sully?"

Paco sent a knee into Frank's stomach. The blow made him collapse onto the oil-stained cement floor. Frank coughed and blinked. He attempted to refocus on Paco. The blond giant kicked him twice more. Frank spat hot mess. He waited for another attack but did not receive it.

"I don't know you, pal. So why do you want to know me."

Frank's attention went to the far end of the building. A man stood on the catwalk leading to an office. He was dressed in a double-breasted suit. Frank guessed he wore loutish cologne that made eyes water. The man's flippant hair floated in a perfect shell and hid his large forehead. *This is a trap. The Serg set me up. Why didn't I walk away when I had the chance?*

"What do we do with him?" Paco to Sully.

Sully sighed, appeared tired. "I don't care."

"I'm here for the pickup," Frank said. He adjusted himself to turn, then sit up.

"What's he talking about, Sully?" Paco said.

Sully shrugged. "No clue."

Frank to Paco: "My left pocket."

Paco and Sully exchanged looks. Paco reached forward and threw a punch into Frank's cheek. The force threw him to the ground. He groaned, then felt Paco's hands fish around his pants pocket. It took a minute, but Paco closed home on the playing cards. Paco looked uneasy as he displayed the cards for Sully's attention. *Irish Pete sent me. That's all you need to know.*

Paco tossed the cards onto the floor. To Sully: "You wanna tell me something?"

Sully shook his head. "I know what he's talking about."

"The Serg told me to talk to you. Brian Tuttle has something for me to pickup."

Sully tensed on the catwalk. He attempted to play it smooth but Frank caught his freeze. The man knew something he didn't want to share. Not with Frank or his partner Paco. He left the catwalk and went to Paco. "He's playing us."

"He's got those cards," Paco said. "No one's stupid enough to run around with those cards if they ain't from the old man."

Sully said, "We don't answer to him."

Frank to Sully: "You're damning yourself."

Sully left Paco and went to Frank. He gave him a kick in the chest. Sully knelt a foot from Frank. "We're all damned. It's the price we pay for the things we do."

"What do we do with him?" Paco said.

"Have Eric get that rust bucket," Sully said. "And make him stay gone."

Frank watched Eric dart into a corner. Seconds later, the roar of a car's engine ignited. The gas was laid on quick. He caught the odor of exhaust belch from its backend. Eric drove back a 1950s Plymouth with California plates with its back end rolling toward Frank. The vehicle crept. Black smoke plumed out of rusted holes in the broken tailpipe. The trunk popped up and down as it waited to devour him. The Plymouth's balding back tire halted on the slicked cement floor when the brake was applied. But the rubber slid until it rested less than two inches from Frank's head. Sully kicked Frank in the shoulder.

"We got a Turkish roll for you, buddy," Sully said. "Eric drives this heap north past Chewelah, then you stay gone."

Paco: "What about the old man?"

Sully to Paco: "Don't worry about the old man. This ain't no regular muscle. He's a burned-out drunk playing bad guy."

"You sure?"

"Trust me," Sully said. He checked his watch as he headed back to

Paco. "Take care of this."

Paco appeared surprised. "You ain't staying?"

"Gotta go," Sully said. "Club business."

"Sully, what's going down?"

"Don't worry about it," Sully said. "Just take care of the drunk and we're good."

"Can I use the torch?"

Sully nodded. "Knock yourself out."

Sully went off to the other end of the building. He leaped over the driver's door of a yellow Porsche. The engine turned and purred with excitement. Zed and Tyrus went to the hangar door and opened it for Sully to leave. The man drove past Frank, offered up a military salute that transformed into one finger. Sully drove out of the building, leaving a trail of spent sound behind.

Frank felt hands grab him. He was pulled to his feet. Bound at the wrists with chains, he wondered if his mitts would fall off. He attempted to untighten himself as Zed and Tyrus backed away. Then he figured out why. Paco held court displaying a large torch handle with the flame off. Off to the side, Zed grabbed a crowbar and Tyrus offered a large wrench. Ready to go if there is anything left of me after Paco starts. Frank spat at Paco's feet. It was a large wad of snot and blood.

"Why do they call you Paco?"

Paco shrugged. "Maybe because I'm French."

The torch spewed out contempt as a stream of blue heat stretched three feet from the handle. Paco waved the handle, knifing the oxygen. The torch light reflection made Paco's teeth appear to dance. The temperature in the room rose. Yeah, you should have walked away. But it's too late now, isn't it? Zed and Tyrus stayed clear for their own safety as Paco descended on Frank.

Frank's eyes caught Pat creeping by in the far corner undetected. His attention returned to Paco as the man edged closer with the blowtorch. The blue heat was less than nine feet from him. Sliding closer with Paco aiming at his crotch. A gun blast ripped through the air. The shot sucked out the flame's sound as the bullet lodged into Paco's back. The man fell forward on his knees and impaled himself on the torch. Paco engulfed himself in the fury of flame.

Both Zed and Tyrus waited precious seconds gaping at Paco's death. Pat was able to hide behind a vehicle as Zed turned, tossing his crowbar. The tool went end over end until it planted itself near Pat into the building's drywall. Tyrus charged at Pat and received a dose of five blasts from Pat's gun. Three shots were errant. One missed Frank's cheek by an inch as it cut by. Two rounds planted into Tyrus' stomach. The shots knocked him off his feet backward. His head hit the cement floor and made a splat sound of a crushed melon. Zed tackled Pat against the wall. Pat dropped the gun, which discharged a round that blew out the Plymouth's back window.

Eric erupted from the Plymouth. He threw fists at Frank who ducked and dodged. Frank charged Eric and knocked him into the car's trunk. The force caused the trunk to close and latch shut. Frank turned to Pat. He was wrestling with Zed in the corner. Frank moved around Paco's smoldering pile and slammed into Zed's back. Zed threw him off and into the control podium. Frank knocked his chained wrists against a large red button. The Firebird above them went horizontal. The car dropped right into the Plymouth's trunk as Eric was breaching the lid. Eric turned his head up to catch the lift dropping the Firebird. The metal frame plummeted twelve feet down, erasing him.

Frank knelt down and grabbed Pat's Beretta off the cement floor. He squeezed off one round that embedded itself in the wall near Zed. The man released Pat who ran toward Frank. Zed turned toward them, revealing a bad set of teeth adorning a sinister smile. Pat went to Frank and pulled off the chains. They looked over at Zed who'd discovered a pump action shotgun. Both jumped clear as Zed fired a round. They went behind the body of a blue sedan as Zed descended. Zed dumped another shot into the sedan's body. The pellets tore through near Pat's head. He lifted his head over the body to glance at Zed. A follow-up shotgun blast forced Pat to hide again. Pat checked the Beretta.

"We're out."

Frank said, "Not yet."

He slid to the far side of the sedan. He noted that Zed pumped the shotgun, then squeezed off another round at Pat. *He's shooting anything that moves.* Frank eyed a wielding tank on a cart sitting at the end of the sedan. Frank kicked the cart, which rolled toward Zed. The man fired a blast at the tank causing it to explode. Zed transformed into a flaming arrow. He was thrown headfirst into the side of the Plymouth and tore through the body.

Paco's wielding tank exploded from the heat throwing it into several supply gas canisters. Frank and Pat escaped as a large explosion consumed the inside of the structure. Half of the building collapsed while the rest filled with flames. Heat and ash came down on them as secondary blasts singed their heels. They tore down The Boneyard's path and spat out the entrance. The internal organs of the city's largest chop shop collapsed behind them. They dropped onto the sidewalk outside the entrance, watching the place consumed with fire and explosions.

"What do we do now?" Pat said.

Frank said, "We catch a Porsche."

"I've kept up my end. So, out with it. Where are the stones?"

Brian Tuttle sized up Steve Powers. The main goon at *The Sides* was serious. *Man is a shark. Something I gotta respect about that. He's tied up all my loose ends. Now, it's my turn to dance.* He resisted the urge to mock Powers. Brian sat in a holding cell where Powers had placed him after the meeting with the warden. *We both know what can happen in here. No cameras, no way of telling what Powers can do if he wants. Ask George Hoob about Powers' reach.*

He returned Powers' cell phone he had used to speak with his daughter. She was in the hospital, safe. *If she got hurt, it would look bad and no one would respect me after.* Now, he felt no one would challenge him. *They see what I am capable of doing to get my point across.* Brian eyed Powers, capable of doing anything, too. *He gets his point across because he's a shark. He wants those stones so bad he can taste them.* Brian was certain Powers was not letting the authorities in on what was going down. *This is an inside job between him, the warden and a couple of other guys for muscle. He's already spent his cut and is just waiting me to drop the location.* He did not doubt that was the play. Powers leaned closer and glared at him. *He will do whatever he has to get the stones. What it takes.*

"Gryzbowsky," Brian said. "He's got your stones."

23

Powers sat back, confused. *Ain't it rich?*

Brian kept a straight face. *You gotta find Gryzbowsky first, otherwise you lost the stones for good.* Brian figured that Frank had picked up the diamonds and brought them to Irish Pete. *After that, I'm in the clear. No more green lights offered by the old man.* By the end of the night, Frank and Tick would get a bullet each for their trouble. *That's the game right? They wanted in, so that's the way it plays.* Brian looked at Powers. *He wants to play the game too.*

"Frank Gryzbowsky?" Powers said.

Brian: "I needed a bagman who was getting out. He fit the description."

"He got out three hours ago. You gave him the location before we made our deal?" Powers showed frustration with Brian. *That's the game, ain't it?*

Brian offered a nod. *Never trust a con, Powers. We don't deal anything but shady.* He was used to working with real police. The goon squad leader was too dumb to pass the academy test. *You got that look about you, Powers. Don't you see it in the mirror each morning? You swallowed a shit burger and asked for more ketchup.* Brian sat cool as could be. *Jimmy Carcetti will find that out when he wakes up at County. He's getting a beat down message from the boys that you don't mess with Brian Tuttle. No way, no how.*

"He broke his parole to do it," Brian said. "You got grounds to catch him and the stones."

It was a faint solution. But he offered it to Powers. *Acting like I care*. There was no need for Powers to suspect Brian was screwing him over now. *After the old man gets the diamonds, no one will say shit to me*. Powers would have to explain why a tactical mission was performed without the command of CDA's finest. *From where I sit, I got a negotiating tool down the road.*

"You're lying," Powers said. He watched Brian with suspicion. Brian suppressed his smirk. He fought temptation to act offended because it wouldn't wash with Powers. The man was too hard to let compassion persuade him to give up the score.

Brian displayed his cuffs. "What can I do here? You know where to find me if I'm lying."

"I should beat your ass for stringing me along."

Brian: "I made it easy for you. Just find Gryzbowsky and you will get your stones."

"Why did you let him in on this?"

"He's a good bagman."

Steve shook his head. "He runs his mouth."

"We see in people what we want to see."

"What do we do now?" Powers said. "Wait for him to come back?"

Brian shook his head. *You gotta lead these dumb goons down the path*. Otherwise they never bit. "Frank's got a bracelet. You can find him."

"Why can't I sit on you and just get a taste on your end?"

"I'm out of the deal. Gave up the location and my interest," Brian said. *That's the truth. Powers don't need the reasons why.*

Powers sat silent. Brian could tell he was thinking hard. *He does his thinking as if he's doing his business on the toilet. Or he gives up because it's too much to go after the score.* Brian examined Powers' face. *No, he's thinking he can do this. Excuse I gave him about going after an escapee sounds legit enough. Let him and his buddies go after Frank. That's what he's thinking. I'm sure of it.*

Powers nodded at Brian. "I'll take it from here."

"What are you going to do?"

"That's between me and Frank."

Brian fought back a smile that would have brought a nightstick across his temple. He offered a solemn face to Powers as they rose together. *Give these goons enough rope, they hang themselves for you.* Powers escorted him out of the holding cell. He rubbed at his wrists, wishing the handcuffs would be removed. *Don't seem right letting other cons see me cuffed. But Powers has to keep up appearances, too.* Brian beat back a chuckle while entering the medium security corridor. *It's hard to beat a man on top of his game.* He strutted when he was sure Powers was not looking.

He caught glances from other cons sitting in the dark reaches of their cells. The doors were closed for everyone but him. *They don't get the special attention I do, where their door stays open all night. You gotta have a lot of game to be at that level.* Tonight, he had gotten a few guys off his back. Powers would be next on Brian's list. *And I kept up appearances with Cassie, too. Maybe now she won't be so ashamed of her old man and visit me for a change.*

Brian guessed Lynn would be proud of him too. His strut became more evident as he walked past some of the lifers. The odor of purol was brewing somewhere down the corridor. He thought of the bottle of wine he had stored in his cell. *Saving your kid does something to you. Making sure no one can screw with you does as well. I'm invincible at The Sides. No one can touch me.*

Powers moved in front as they drew closer to Brian's cell. Part of prison protocol. *He has to keep up appearances too, don't he?* He entered the dark cell, smiling.

The sound of Powers closing the cell door behind Brian was a surprise. The lock slammed shut. Brian turned and glared at the guard. *Hey, that don't work for me. I get my cell door open. Otherwise, I'm caged in.* He walked to the cell and put his wrists through the slot to have Powers uncuff him. Instead, Powers smiled and turned, heading down the medium security row. *He thinks I'm some regular con now?*

The light inside Brian's cell clicked on as someone pulled on the bulb's chain. Brian turned, seeing Robert Nash standing inside the cell. Nash's bandaged face drooled foam as he reached out and grabbed Brian by the throat. Brian squirmed and pressed his face against the cell door. He pushed his chins into the cell bars in a futile attempt to squeeze through. He tried to scream and caught the sting of Nash's shiv bury deep into his side. Hot ooze of blood poured down his legs. Brian listened to the soft march of Powers' boots as the guard exited medium security. *He's a shark.* Nash held Brian's mouth with his hands to prevent him from screaming. He drifted into darkness, dead.

The Blacklight was the epicenter of the city nightlife. Every bar in the downtown core had last call at eight on a Wednesday. Except The Blacklight which stayed packed until a minute before two in the morning. The music thumped a beat of a New World Order remix. The bass carried whenever the club doors opened to offer passage inside. The brick-and-mortar façade carried over from its former banking tenant prior to the last financial collapse. The marble interior spread sound through a menagerie of dancers; single or swinging. The alcohol long pours covered for short conversations.

No cover required upon entry. The audience was selected by the preference of the changing elite staff holding court at the entrance. The management imitated carnival barkers before a sea of eager patrons. Most had heard mere rumors of the debauchery inside. The exclusiveness spread so deep that a drunk, womanizing actor and his entourage were turned elsewhere. The boast of a major acting award thirty years prior did not grant the access it once did.

Stories of lust fueled by contraband and cash pushed people toward the Blacklight. Frank and Pat noticed the yellow Porsche sitting out front. The yellow car separated other vehicles by VIP status velvet ropes on metal stanchions. Pat hit the brakes and parked across the street. Frank eyed the surroundings. A little manager stood with two muscular bouncers on each side.

24

"This is trouble," Pat said.

Frank to Pat: "Stay here. I want to avoid blowing the place up this time."

Pat held up the Beretta. "You want this?"

"It's empty," Frank said. "Give it to me."

"When you bring a gun, you end up using it," Pat said. He handed over the Beretta to Frank who tucked it into the waistband behind him.

Frank said, "Who told you that?"

"A guy I know."

"Smart man," Frank said. "Leave the engine running."

"No offense, but you look like shit."

Frank eyed his reflection in the rearview. His face held grime. He smoothed his hair to no success. His clothes were torn along the right sleeve of the sports jacket and both pants knees. *I'll be fine in there. Especially after I see Sully. I ain't running from him. Either he gives me the stuff or…* He didn't want to finish that sentence. He didn't want to believe he was capable of being a bad person. *I'm tough enough to survive all of this shit.*

"What are you going to do if there is trouble?" Pat said. *He has a good point.*

Frank drew out Sims' brass knuckles from his sport jacket. The surface shined from the streetlights. "I'm using the soft approach."

He exited the Lexus. The Blacklight's overkill of bass rattled the car's frame. The streets wet from a light rain hissed as passing car tires collided with damp asphalt. As he crossed and stood before the club, Frank caught the expensive perfumes. His eyes went to gold necklaces and pinkie rings. Frank pushed through the crowd to the front. He stood less than a foot from the little manager. The small man was dressed in a three-piece and was obnoxious.

"No more in, goddamn it," he said.

The little manager shouted obscenities at the crowd unafraid at losing customers. People gathered as he increased his rudeness. The Blacklight was notorious for people to be dissuaded by horrid customer service. They want inside to see what is in there. The crowd refused to dissipate. They witnessed a ritual of exiting patrons freeing space inside so they could enter. Frank tucked his hand into his pocket. He slipped his fingers into the brass knuckles and clenched a fist.

His eyes ran across the broad continents of muscle mass. Two bouncers guarded the door. Both wore ripped gym shirts reading *Shockley's Body Shop*. The pair monitored the crowd behind pairs of shades. Christine had introduced me to them once when we were still together. Frank recognized the five-ten Samoan with a bald skull as Blye. The other bouncer was Kyle. Man was juiced. Enough that other men admired his mass but women stayed away in fear of it. No way would Frank be allowed in. *Not even to see Christine, who wants nothing to do with me*. The manager sized Frank up and offered a look of disgust.

"Homeless mission is on the next block, pal."

Frank drew out his brass knuckles and popped Blye in the nose. The shot collapsed the overgrown child. Blood spewed. Blye passed out while Kyle reached around the manager to get at Frank. Kyle received a shot to his knee, which caved inward. Frank used his knuckles to clock Kyle in the face. Everyone in the crowd reacted as they heard Kyle's jawbone break. Kyle dropped out of commission. Frank turned to the manager who reached for the sky to offer no trouble. He felt the crowd move back from him as he headed inside.

The Blacklight's bass cloaked him as he slid the knuckles into his sport jacket. The atmosphere thrived on young body scents of sweat and sex. Little blue and red beams shot from the ceiling to cut the vapid crowd. The club speakers pushed giant waves of sound. Frank noted the illuminated tables making guests into ashen-faced ghosts. On the second floor, Absinthe was consumed regardless of local laws. Young Asian escorts serving as ornaments and silent concubines eager for the fast life accompanied the VIPs.

He looked to the bar and saw his estranged wife Christine. She made married men consider infidelity to be with her. But the years had taken their toll. She was pale and tired. *There are enough miles between us*. He recalled the touch of her tumbles of curls that cascaded her shoulders and back. The thing he enjoyed was her sparing use of makeup to compliment her natural features. *I'm still in love with her*. Frank dropped a few deuces and fins on the bar and winked at Christine.

"How in the hell did you get in here?"

He called her close. "Need the driver of that Porsche."

Christine: "What you need is to get out of here. Before they find out you snuck in."

"I came through the front."

Christine shook her head. She looked at him. "Let me guess, two shots of Bourbon?"

"Not a bad choice."

Christine leaned in: "And the guy who drives that Porsche is behind you, asshole."

She snatched the paper Frank laid out and lined up the twin shots. *She's pissed I'm not here to see her. That's what it is*. Frank eyed his reflection in the mirror behind the bar. Sitting to his right behind him was Sully. The man was sharing a table with a tough hombre in a fedora and trench coat. Underneath the table, the hombre pushed a briefcase toward Sully. *Might be what I'm picking up*. Frank grabbed a shot and let the rim touch his lips. Christine grabbed his wrist. She stared into his eyes, serious.

"It's a long time, Frank. You could have at least said hello."

Frank shrugged. "Would it made any difference?"

"To me, it would have."

Christine released him and moved away. He watched her exit into the far reaches of the bar. *She cares about me too much. She'll come back because she'll feel guilty.* He shook his head. *Why am I such a shit? She loves me and I treat her like dirt.* He knocked back the shot. The Bourbon eased down his throat and coated his stomach. A good glow was coming on. *I'm going to get this job done and get out.* He felt a large finger burrow into his back.

"Come outside now. So this place doesn't get messy and shit."

Frank caught the mirror reflection behind him of the club's main bouncer, Stew. Who had a body mass that towered two feet above him. Christine had mentioned Stew before. Man had played defensive end for Boise State. Pissed a positive during his junior year and got bounced off his full ride. Rumor had been that he and Kyle had served time for robbing a parking lot. Frank turned and received a stare down from a pair of eyes apart by a huge nose. His neck chain could hold up that Firebird back at The Boneyard. Stew's arms veined and ripped. Next to Stew was Blye. The Samoan held a washcloth full of ice against his nose.

"You asked nicely," Frank said.

His right hand dove into his pocket and he slid his fingers into the brass knuckles. Stew intercepted him. He latched onto Frank's wrist and pulled it out. The big man yanked off the knuckles and slammed them down on the bar counter. He leaned in. Frank smelled his hot, rancid breath. "Last chance to go," Stew said.

Frank reached behind him and grabbed hold of the empty Beretta. He whipped it forward and aimed at Stew's arm, squeezing the trigger. Stew winced back as if he expected the shot as the hammer snapped. *Imagination works miracles*. He smacked Stew with the butt of the gun, collapsing the bodily perfection to the ground. Frank pointed the Beretta at Blye's face. The man stumbled backward facing the empty gun. Frank kicked Blye in the crotch and sent him down next to Stew.

Sully erupted at the sight of Frank. He pushed back from the table, leaving the tough hombre behind. Frank moved but was restricted by Stew's hand clenching his leg. Frank crashed onto the dance floor. His Beretta flew out of his hands and skidded across the dance floor. Sully drew out a small piece and squeezed off a few rounds that embedded around Frank's head. The crowd's drug-addled dystopia crashed into a sobriety of self-survival.

A confusion of people rammed the exit. The stampede overtook Frank. Both he and the bouncers were caught in a flood of hysterical screams and shoves. Sully squeezed off another round that found home in a woman's leg and dropped her. He aimed square on Frank again, but was silenced by a beer bottle crashing over his head. Frank turned to the bar, seeing Christine had thrown the bottle. Sully leapfrogged over the dog pile of people and ran toward the exit.

Frank struggled against Stew's grip on his leg. He used his free foot to kick Stew twice in the face. The bouncer released Frank as his nose cracked open. Frank rose and scooped up the empty Beretta. His eyes went to the bar counter. He saw that last shot of Bourbon waiting there. He shook his head in disgust at leaving the shot behind. Frank exited the club amid the chaos that spilled into the streets. Everyone gave Frank a wide berth as he moved to the sidewalk.

Sully hauled ass down the empty street on foot. Ten blocks beyond the club. Frank eyed the Lexus. Saw Pat slam on the gas. The car shot forward with him after Sully. He watched the man's head bob over the ridge of the street. The man was running for his life as the Lexus closed in. *He's running him over like a dog.* Frank closed his lids, listening to his heartbeat. *Stop him before there's no turning back.* Frank opened his lids and chased the Lexus. The tires roared as the Lexus chewed up asphalt with its headlights closing in on Sully. A few blocks from him, the car's engine growled at the stylish man. Pat drove the Lexus onto the sidewalk.

"Oh, shit," Frank said.

Upon impact, everything blurred. Sully was thrown over the hood and smashed into the windshield. Flesh, bone and mass met against the car's metal frame to create a deafening sound. The airbags ignited a shotgun blast that filled the interior. The horn erupted into a non-stop blare. Sully was catapulted over the Lexus' roof. He landed headfirst on the pavement with a splat. The luxury car's engine blew and its tires locked, skidding to a stop. Frank ran up to the Lexus, smelling the gas aroma that plumed inside the vehicle. Pat stumbled out of the Lexus holding his shoulder.

"I think I broke something," he said, then collapsed.

Sully was a broken mess a few feet behind the car. The man was coughing blood. He grabbed at Sully's fashionable shirt and drew him up so the man could breathe. Sully rasped as Frank shook him back to consciousness. Sully's eyes rattled, fluttering into his head. He slobbered blood with a large gash in his head. His legs and arms fractured and bent in wrong directions. Sully offered Frank a delirious grin of broken teeth.

"I'm... sorry... kid," Sully said in a whisper. "So, sorry Angel..."

He's already seeing angels? Frank placed his fingers against Sully's neck. The pulse was distant. He lowered Sully gently back onto the ground. He let the man's eyes gaze up into the stars as he went. The light went out in his eyes. *He sees Angels coming for him.* Frank fished around Sully's jacket. He discovered a ring with three keys and a black car alarm. Sully's cracked cell rang. Someone named Junior was calling. Another search brought him a money clip with real paper attached. The other find was a license listing Sully's home address. Sully's life collapsed while no one noticed.

Twelve blocks away, the crowd of club patrons stared back at them. Frank turned to Pat. The kid was wheezing and clutching his shoulder in pain as he attempted to stand. "You need a doctor, kid."

"No, I'll be okay," Pat said.

He fell back to his knees and screamed in agony. The Lexus' blown engine hissed as the radiator cracked. The front bloomed a hot steam cloud on the cold February night. Frank attended to Pat. He knelt down and patted the kid's cheek. "We need a ride and to see a doctor."

A roar erupted from the club. Frank's eyes were attracted by the noise. He saw the crowd part in front of the Blacklight. Sully's yellow Porsche gunned its engine and powered through the crowd. The VIP ropes surrounding it were knocked away. The headlights shined down on Frank as it pushed toward him. The Porsche reached him in ten seconds flat. The tires squealed as the brakes were applied and the car pulled alongside Frank and Pat. Christine was driving.

"You sure know how to make an entrance, Frank," she said. "Get in before I change my mind."

A wail of police sirens filled the city night. The three went away from them. *She loves me.* Frank's eyes turned toward the sky. He saw the stars lit everywhere. He wondered what Sully saw when he looked up. *Was he saying he saw Angels? Or was he apologizing to an Angel?* The question stumped Frank for a while as Christine drove the car from the scene.

25 CDA Tactical Leader Shay Baxter was uneasy about tonight. The entire plan hatched by his ex-partner Steve Powers sounded suspect at best. *Get out of this while you've got the chance, man. A reprimand won't happen over the Cassie Tuttle stakeout. If it did, you would go to the press and be in the right. But this, Shay, this is different.* He fought temptation to turn the CDA Tactical van around. *Because Tyler deserves better, doesn't he?*

The northern end of Coeur d'Alene used to offer a twenty-four-seven diner. One of those breakfasts for two dollar joints where they poured coffee and handed out white toast to the local blue. Three kids set fire to the dumpster in the back over their winter break. The prank turned into a four-alarm job that made the diner a hollowed-out charcoal shell in an empty parking lot. *Now those kids sit up in Green Bush Juvenile for the next two years.*

Shay pulled the van into the diner parking lot. He wondered if those kids would realize how lucky they had it. *They get to run and jump, do things that other kids can't.* Shay's thoughts turned to his son, Tyler, as they always did. The little boy Shay loved with all of his heart sat in a hospital room. His youth was peeled away on dialysis. *We're all ignorant of things when we want to* be. He fought another urge to drive the van back to the station.

He had lifted the CDA Tactical van on previous occasions. But none had been as serious as this. *The brass ain't going to understand this one. We've done midnight runs before but this one is a treasure hunt.* Midnight runs remained a highlight when Shay and Powers ran together. They would go after Idaho's worst and extract them. *We would find their place, wait until bed time, then bust in with five guys in body armor.* Shay enjoyed extracting bond jumpers. *I got that kick from yanking a low-life out of his girlfriend's pad and getting him back before someone saved his bond.* Bounty hunters were former convicts helping current convicts slide by the rules.

Shay eased the van into the lot and eyed the area. A sedan flashed a burst of headlights. It came from Powers' ride. *He's ready to go on this one, ain't he?*

Shay's eyes fell to Tyler's photograph taped to the van's dashboard. He was a good kid who had a rotten deal. He wondered how long the insurance company would keep paying the hospital bills. Already the company was getting testy with medical procedures that the doctors had used on Tyler. *What good am I if my kid can't count on me to do something?* Shay pulled the van alongside Powers' ride and cut the engine.

I'm staying on this one because my kid needs me. Shay rubbed at Tyler's photograph with his finger and thumb, smiling. He exited the van and saw three Sides guards standing with Powers. *If he trusts them, that's good enough for me.* He went up and shook hands, meeting each. The guards introduced themselves as Trent, Christopher and Tad. All were hard-cut men. They had been chiseled from years of guarding guys who'd slice a person's throat without thinking twice. The kind of guys that make a midnight run work.

Shay to Powers: "We all set?"

Powers nodded. *Like old times.* Powers led the men to the back of the Tactical van. *He's feeling it again. Like back when he ran the unit.* Shay got excited. With Powers leading the pack, there was a sureness of himself. He made every man in the unit believe in each other. *I try, but I know I come up short.* Powers made his men believe. *Nothing could mess with us back then. If they did, it was their ass.* He watched Powers do the honors of opening the van's back doors. Inside were a cadre of body armor, helmets and M4 carbine rifles. Everything that could take down a small army would be used to take down one man.

"This parole jumper has an ankle bracelet on," Powers said. "We find him and take him down hard. My guy fingered him for the stuff. In less than ten hours, we each get more than all of our pensions combined."

He's got the touch. Makes everyone ready to do what he says. Powers had a keen knack that he used daily when he was Tactical leader. Shay had witnessed it several times. *People do what Powers wants his entire life.* Powers would be leading the Tactical team still if the Ridgemont bust had not happened. *He never mentions the bust. You don't, either, because you know it might end your friendship.* Every time he saw Powers now, there was a debt unpaid. *I should have been there for him.*

The Ridgemont Housing District was a collection of low-income housing that served as a stash house for drug king pin Clemont Jones. Right before the bust went down, Tyler got sick. Shay had rushed to the hospital and left Powers without his wingman. The bust moved as scheduled and it spelled the end of Powers as Tactical leader. The bust went smooth, but a fresh-faced beat cop caught Powers taking a taste of Jones' paper. The CDA command forced Powers out to "clean up" the department. *I would have watched out for him had I been there.* Those in blue understood that everything, including them, had an expiration date. *Right now, the milk in me has soured.*

The truth was that every cop took a cut when it was a drug dealer's money. The CDA Tactical slammed through doors, eliminated threats and ended up guarding millions in dirty street bills. The paper filled with grease and grime fresh off of being wadded up in a guy's pocket for two weeks. And before evidence control could arrive, the CDA Tactical took tastes of the cash. Every cop had the same concerns; worry about making grade and living on an unlivable wage. Drug busts meant cops were guarding street bills, the dirty cash that every junkie used to pay for their fix. *Why should it go to some city excess fund when we risk our lives to obtain it?* Personally, skimming drug money had helped with Tyler's medical care. *Shouldn't it go to those risking their lives serving the community rather than back to a dealer stringing out a twelve year old on H?* None of the civilians cared about cops from the way they slashed pensions and healthcare benefits.

The struggle to save his son was unbearable. It drained his bank account, strained his marriage, and made him feel helpless. Tyler's nine-year-old body strained against the dialysis machine. *You had to be there, right? To show him that you weren't afraid either? Otherwise he would be scared, wouldn't he?* Tyler's Type 1 Diabetes meant daily treatment from the dialysis machine. And round the clock care when his body went into shock during the night. *If I hadn't been taking tastes, Tyler would have died.*

Shay had guilt over not being there on the Ridgemont bust for his friend. *I would have watched the door. I would have made damn sure some punk beat cop would not have spotted us.* Things had changed between Powers and Shay. *I keep wondering when he's going to bring it up to me. If the next time we talk, it will be the last time because Ridgemont will be mentioned.* Powers handed Shay his body armor and slapped him on the shoulder. Shay smiled at his friend, seeing the team prepped and ready.

"Just like old times, huh?" Powers said.

"I was thinking that," Shay said. "What if it turns into Hightower 394?"

"God," Powers said, "Anything but that."

They shared laughter and shook their heads in disbelief. The other guards shrugged at the two men bonding over a private joke. During Powers' days running CDA Tactical, one of their CIs gave the team a phony address. Hightower Avenue, house number three-nine-four. The information given was for a haven of drug dealers with a million in loose cash. The team breached the front door at three in the morning. They discovered it was a nursing program's house for several young, barely legal college-coeds.

The sight of a dozen women running around terrified in towels and nightgowns was etched in Shay's mind. So was the director of the nursing program. She was not angry. She was *pissed*. The cherubic squat woman transformed into a wild animal. *I thought about Tasering her to get out of the house.* Powers was not as lucky. He got cornered in the living room and received an earful. *We can only be so lucky this time.*

"Hey, something good did come out of it," Powers said. "I married one of those girls."

"Yeah, but you ended up divorcing her too."

26

"It reminds me of Fallujah."

Junior Reed sat in a Cadillac Escalade with Baron at the wheel. *We're watching apocalyptic shit going down across the street at The Boneyard.* The walls of broken cars collapsed. Streams of water hammered the flames by Spokane Fire. The place was a smoldering pyre of death. *Whoever did this was a bad ass. You don't do something like this without an evil streak in you.*

"Where's that?" Junior Reed said.

"Fallujah is an Iraqi province transformed into chaos," Baron said. "It is where I got my hometowner in the leg. And it is what has allowed me to return to run the family business."

Baron's family business was a drug cartel. His reach was smaller than Irish Pete or the Gypsy Knights, but Baron had his pull. Various sections of the city dealt with him and answered to the old man. *He's small time, him and his brother. But I still wouldn't want to cross them.* Baron ran the show while Mac was the muscle. *Mac is a beer guy. Baron talks about books I don't read.*

"You don't sound like any black guy I ever met," Junior said.

"Speaking well is color-blind," Baron said. "It is not the providence of white people, either."

"Huh?"

"You would not understand," Baron said.

They had history between them. Baron split off to go a four-year stretch at some college doing an ROTC scholarship. He got Uncle Sam's request to liberate the Middle East and played Rambo for a while. Junior stayed behind and did some hardcore shit of his own. Both had been weak kids from Hillyard. *How in the hell did we grow up so different?* Junior had no answers. *He's got your back, though. Holding the diamonds without screwing you, that means something. Now, you have to keep Irish Pete happy and ignorant until the stones can be moved.*

"Who do you think did this?" Junior said.

"Streets say Tick was part of it."

Junior: "Tick? He's a lousy thief. He ain't no killer."

"Have you heard from your friend?" Baron said.

"What?" Junior said, then realized what Baron meant. "No, he ain't picking up his cell."

Sully had been missing in action since this morning. He ran The Boneyard and Junior wondered if the guy was in trouble. *Maybe he turns me in to Irish Pete for his own protection.* He tried Sully's cell a few more times. He was told to please enjoy the music while his party was being reached. Then he listened to some crap top forty hit before getting a bland voice from Sully asking people to leave a message. Junior hung up the line.

"This ain't like him."

Baron: "Maybe Devon and Mac need to go to his place. See if he's hiding out."

"You think?"

"It is worth the chance," Baron said. "Whoever did this to The Boneyard is hardcore."

Junior eyed a city meat wagon cart off black bags big enough for a human body. "You're telling me."

"Irish Pete brought in a heavy to deal with his issue," Baron said.

Junior: "I'm going back to play nice with the old man. See what I can find out."

"That would be wise."

Three more Spokane Fire trucks arrived at The Boneyard. Each began battling the blaze. The fire crackled, hissing as cold streams of water attacked it. Black tumbling clouds of filth covered the skyline for miles. Irish Pete let loose a bad guy. *Some hardcore who will take a lot to put down.* Junior tried Sully's cell again. Bad music and voice mail options at the end of the call. *He could be burning me to Irish Pete while I am sitting here.*

"What happens if the heavy comes after you, Baron?"

Baron did not react to Junior's question. The smooth man appeared to think, then nod. *He has the diamonds because I know he'll defend them with his life. He can be trusted. Few qualities you can find in a crook these days.* Junior knew Baron held his own when the stress level was high. He recalled that back alley bust two months ago.

An undercover cop tried to pin Baron for selling. After beating the cop down, Baron doused him in lighter fluid. *He would have lit the man on fire and walked away, if not for you stopping him.* Baron had a mean streak in him. The diamonds were safe. *But what protection do I have?* Junior wondered if he should bring more firepower when he visited with Irish Pete. *Maybe he's setting you up like that goon Beau. Lulling you into submission before he shoots you with a needle and suffocates you slow.*

Baron: "Too many people brag about being the man. Thing is, if you're the man, you never say it. People just know it."

27 Cons at *The Sides* raved about Dr. Shamus
Moreland. Known as a dive doc, he would pull
fifteen bullets out of an escaped fugitive fresh off a
police shoot-out. Vic Ramsey had gone to Moreland
once. *Said man fixes knife wounds without questions. All you do
is pay in paper.* Moreland's own troubles with the law had made
him notorious to crooks. His failure to stay off the juice made him
accepted by the criminal element. *That's why guys go to him. He's
been as low as we have.*

No one at *The Sides* suggested Moreland bounced on any small
time crook when the heat or Feds knocked on his door. He repaired
men in his two-story gothic with cons offering enough paper for
him to be on twenty-four-seven call. Brian Tuttle had recommended
Moreland to a few cons planning their maiden heist when they got
out on parole. *Said the doc had mended Brian after a tough gunfight
where he took a ricocheted bullet out his side. No questions asked.*

Moreland's specialty was not human surgery. He was a veterinarian
by trade. The doctor had been expelled from practice after his
signature was found on several large drug shipments. The addict
did a three-year stretch at old McNeil Island coming clean. The
man knew how to fix dogs. The Gypsy Knights biker leader King
Garrison kept Moreland on the payroll. The GK owned thirty of the
meanest pit bulls alive. From what Frank understood, Garrison kept

the doctor a constant prisoner. If he denied a wounded patient, con or animal, or attempted to skip town, the GK would kill him.

Frank spotted an old station wagon sitting out front of Moreland's house as they pulled up. Christine edged the Porsche around it and went up the driveway. The doctor greeted them in his bathrobe. *He's used to late night customers.* Moreland controlled the automatic garage door, which lifted. Christine pulled next to Moreland and let Frank help Pat out. Moreland took over and guided Pat up the back steps into the house. Christine parked the yellow Porsche in the garage.

He stopped her attempt to get out of the Porsche. She looked at him with those eyes as he placed his hand on her cheek. *She doesn't know what to expect from you.* He kissed her. She did not resist. He noted she was blushing afterward. *That's how you treat a woman. Get her to think you don't want her. Then, show her how much you need her.* Sometimes, Frank surprised himself at how good he was at this.

"I thought you were beyond it," Christine said.

Frank said, "I convince myself of things that aren't true."

"Tell me about it."

"Put it out of your mind and move on," Frank said. "I have to do my job."

"You're a contradiction. You know that?"

"I'm human," Frank said. "I figure that plays a part in it."

"You've got choices, Frank," Christine said. "It always comes down to the choices you make."

"You're right," Frank said. "I do have a choice."

He lifted his leg and displayed the ankle bracelet tethering him back to *The Sides*. *It doesn't matter now, does it? They catch you, they tie you to Sully and you got back.* Frank yanked at the strap. It took effort. He managed to pull the bracelet off. Frank exited the Porsche and tossed the bracelet in the garbage. He turned to Christine who remained inside the car. She gripped the wheel, thinking. *She doesn't know what she wants. That makes two of us.*

"I can't go with you, Frank."

"You sure?"

"No."

Frank went around the Porsche and opened her door. He offered his hand. "Let's check on Pat, then get out of here for good."

"Are you sure?"

Frank: "Yeah."

They closed the garage door. The yellow Porsche dropped into darkness. A little red flashing light from the bracelet emitted from the garbage. Neither noticed it as they headed to the back door of Moreland's house. The two entered into the operating room. Polyethylene plastic sheeting bound to the walls by duct tape shielded the surfaces from the gore of surgery. He's used to doing a lot of these things daily. Two different sized tables sat in the room. Pat was on the large one with an IV in his arm.

Moreland was tending to Pat. He had opened the crook's shirt to reveal an albino chest. He used his hands to detect the damage. Moreland placed a stethoscope to Pat's pecks and tapped several times. Pat winced each time Moreland touched him. *The good doctor appears to know what he is doing. At least one thing is correct tonight.* Moreland eased Pat onto his back. He felt a few more times, then turned to Frank.

"A lung has fluid. His shoulder is broken," Moreland said.

The doctor investigated his cabinet. He produced a syringe and vial. Pat appeared ready to protest. *Sorry, but this is the best we got right now.* Moreland fed the vial's juice into the IV bag. Pat attempted to yank the IV tooth from his arm but Moreland held him in place. Pat's head bobbed as he tried to hold it up. Moreland held him firm until a sea of narcotics deflected the kid's defenses. Pat's hands went limp, his eyes glassed as his pupils became vacant.

"What about the lung?"

"I can insert a tube through his chest wall and drain it until the lung re-expands," Moreland said. "Anything more than that and you would have to get him to an emergency room."

"You fix a lot of cons?"

"Everyone but that maniac employed by The Serg," Moreland said. "He bit me on the shoulder the last time I went there to stitch up his wound. Thought I was his brother, Mikhail. That one can find help elsewhere."

"What did you give him?"

Moreland: "Animal tranquilizer. It's all I have in stock considering my usual clientele. It works for a guy his size though."

"You got a john?" Frank said. His bowels ached from dosing himself in Southern Comfort. Moreland directed him down the hall. His tired legs crossed from plastic sheeting to a wooden floor heading toward the living room. His eyes caught a hallway door and guessed it was the bathroom. He opened it into a dark room. *What in the hell?* Several cages holding pit bulls came alive upon his presence. They barked in an excited low hum. The dogs gnawed at the cyclone cage fencing and frothed hatred. Frank backed out of the room as Moreland headed down the hall.

"That's not the bathroom," he said.

Frank: "No shit."

Moreland slammed the door shut. The excited low hum was muffled but not retired. Moreland guided Frank through the hall. "The bathroom is on the far left."

Frank hit the head and did his business. He let relief of empty bowels wash over him. He flushed with his shoe, leaving the lid up.

At the basin, his hands were coated with soap to remove all of the grime. The reflection offered in the basin mirror showcased a man with blood-shot eyes, uncombed hair and a face which had witnessed better days. *It's nothing worse than every morning after you used to tie one on the night before.*

I've got to get out of this mess. I don't want Irish Pete and his men coming after Christine either. His eyes went to the back of the toilet. A small picture frame of Moreland with a young woman sat on the back lid. Both sat happy on a porch swing. The photograph was older and faded by age. He picked it up and examined it. Frank rubbed the glass cover with his thumb. *Christine deserves a life like this. A happy one, not the one she's got.*

He exited the bathroom and went through the living room. A blue sofa greeted him. Frank teased the notion of crashing and putting his feet up on the glass coffee table. *Won't get me too far. Irish Pete knows where this place is too.* Frank left the sofa and table, passing through the hall. The muffled sound of excited low hums continued as he went by the door. *They sense me walking by. They want to come out and get me.* Frank entered the operating room.

"Your usual clientele is calling," Frank said.

The doctor's attention went from Pat to the hall. "Excuse me for a moment." Moreland passed Frank and down the hall, into the room.

"He's multi-talented," Christine said. "Seems nice."

"He's a con," Frank said. "We all seem nice until we don't have to."

"You're such an optimist, Frank."

Frank shrugged. He moved around the operating room. His eyes wandered the interior. The cabinets were filled with small vials, bandages and bottles of chemicals. There were three large plastic bags marked with a yellow sticker warning of toxic waste inside. The doctor had been busy. Frank focused on the wall next to Pat's table. Behind the plastic sheeting, he saw a large red button. Frank reached out to touch it.

"You don't want to go there," Moreland said. The doctor was returning from the hall. "Sorry, one of my patients is waking up from his last match. I had to repair his stomach and intestines to keep him alive."

Cons at *The Sides* talked about the city's notorious underground dog fighting circuit. It was a sport hidden by back alleys and basements. Gypsy Knights in the valley would hand-check their pit bulls while the dogs ran alongside their chopper unleashed. Men would sit on their porch for hours and wait for someone with a dog to challenge his. Some fights lasted until death in a backyard. Moreland served as an animal hospital between the valley and South Hill. Frank noticed Christine stood off by herself, attempting not to engage in the dirty conversation.

"Why don't the dogs bark?" Frank said.

Moreland: "Keeps the neighbors from complaining. I have nine back there without voice boxes."

Frank pointed to the red button behind the plastic sheet. "What does this do?"

"Releases the cage doors and lets them out," Moreland said. "I've never used it, but in case there was a fire or something, I would not want them trapped inside."

"But loose on the street?" Frank said. "They could attack you if they got out."

Moreland: "They've been trained on when to attack. The Gypsy Knights train the retired fighters to work in packs to serve as guards. They won't attack your friend or me, unless we become a threat. Dogs are instinctual. They know who and what to fight."

"And if they got out, you are sure animal control could put them down?"

"No," Moreland said. "I implanted pieces of Kevlar underneath their coats around the jugular and stomach."

"Why?"

"The Knights want them fighting longer. It makes them harder to kill and allows for more bets," Moreland said. "They are trained to find advantages. If a rival gang comes on the GK property, they fight the dogs as well as the Knights."

Frank said, "They sized me up when I walked in there."

Moreland nodded. "You hit one, the others react. If you stayed in there, they would have destroyed the pens to get at you."

"Touching," Frank said.

Pat moaned. It drew Moreland's attention away from Frank. The doctor checked Pat's IV. The kid turned to Frank. He smiled a happy grin of loopy pleasure. *Get well, kid. I'll do what I have to do. Whatever it was I was supposed to pick up, I'm going to do it and get us out of this mess.*

Moreland: "How hot is the car in my garage?"

"Scorching," Frank said. "When Styles comes by for Pat, he will take care of it."

"Styles Remington? He's an interesting choice of friends."

"He will take care of the bill," Frank said.

Moreland said, "I figure as much." The doctor fished a set of keys from his cabinet. He tossed them to Frank. "Take my wagon. It burns more oil than gas, but it will get you where you want to go."

"Seems to be the story of the night."

"This vic looks familiar."

28

Major Crimes Detective Tom Hammond leaned over the body. His partner Ben Dereks pointed a latex-covered finger at the face of the dead man. The body was a twisted mass. Tom bent closer and adjusted his glasses to get a real good look. *Where have I seen this cat before?* He went through a thousand mug shots in his head. *Yeah, this one does seem familiar. But who is it?*

"Is this Sully?" Dereks said.

Tom eyed Dereks. "Someone found him before we did."

"He ran those home invasions out in Shadle Park last summer. Allegedly," Dereks said.

Tom grinned. "Yeah, allegedly."

Both rose sharing a nod. Tom pointed to the Blacklight Club down the street. "Shoot-out goes down there…" Tom's finger moved to Sully's body, "and he gets dumped here."

"Nasty way to go," Dereks said. "He was an asshole though."

"Pretty much," Tom said. He thought of Angel but said nothing. *She was safe from Sully. I should go relieve Hanaran tomorrow morning.* He had not called Hanaran since the night before. *Too busy doing all of the other stuff to follow up.* Tom looked at Dereks. "Who do you like for this?"

"What about Lieutenant Goering?" Dereks said. "Maybe we get

him in the box, ask him where he was tonight."

"In his defense, this asshole kept saying 'lawyer' every time Goering asked him a question. I might plead temporary insanity if I had to listen to that."

Dereks: "I remember Goering say 'what's your name' and Sully would say 'lawyer.' Didn't matter what the question, he kept saying 'lawyer, lawyer, lawyer.' And it worked for him too."

"Not in this case," Tom said. He reached down and checked Sully's wrist. The man's gold Rolex worked behind broken glass. "They took his wallet, but not this?"

They stood and eyed the streets. Both attempted to figure out the action without saying a word. Then, Dereks said, "Guy makes like a deer, does a Peter Pan off the hood and all they take is his wallet?"

Tom's eyes caught an alleyway staring the scene. A fat man stood in the middle. He was dressed in a trench coat and wore a tan fedora. He was holding a briefcase, smoking large cigar puffs. "Any help would be welcome, Dan."

Dan Rahn shook his head. "I'm off duty and have kicked back a few. I saw the lights, thought I should ask."

"Don't know much right now," Dereks said.

"Keep me informed," Rahn said. They watched the fat man turn back into the alley and vanish into the dark. *He doesn't want to be caught in a lie by staying around too long for questions he can't answer*. Tom looked at Dereks who was shaking his head.

"You think he's involved?"

Dereks: "No. I was thinking of something my Grandma Grace always said. 'No matter where you go in life, you will always meet people with no redeeming qualities."

"Hey, the devil has to work for somebody," Tom said. "We appear a logical fit."

"Delightful," Dereks said. "You want to go interview witnesses? Five bucks says everyone's back was turned to the shooter."

"You're the primary, you go ahead," Tom said. Uniforms at the Blacklight held the crowd back from leaving. "You think it's hard to find a yellow Porsche in this city?"

"If The Boneyard hadn't gone up, I would say yes," Dereks said.

"What the hell happened to this place? I used to think it was safe. Now we are like everywhere else."

Dereks: "The city just grew up."

Tom went to his sedan and sat in the front seat with the door open. He jotted down notes for his file on the late Sully Brooks. Dereks had begun interviewing patrons from the club. None of them would see anything. That's what happens in the city nightlife. No one stands for anything or anyone after the night is over. Tom thought about Hanaran sitting there with Angel. Maybe I should call and let them in on the good news about Sully Brooks' death. He reached into the glove box for his private cell.

An object fell out of the box and onto the sedan's floor. Tom leaned over and grabbed it. He brought it into the light. It was the switchblade he had taken from Styles Remington last night. His thumb went over the handle's button. He pressed it and listened to the hiss of the blade extend. He had no clue why he had not destroyed it yet. He didn't have time to take care of it now. Tom pressed the button again, the blade hid inside the handle. He returned it to the glove box and retrieved his private cell.

Eight missed calls from his soon to be ex-wife. All with promises of reconciling that resulted in sex, promises of change, and fights until morning. I need sleep and I'm sick of dealing with her. I can't do it anymore. Tom erased the missed calls and instead dialed Hanaran's cell. As the cell rang, a uniform cop walked to Tom's sedan. He held his ear to the cell but paid attention to the uniform. "What's up?"

The uniform pointed back to the club. "One of the bodyguards wants to talk."

"Where's Dereks?"

The uniform pointed to Dereks, who was interviewing club dancers. "Over there."

Tom shook his head. "I'll take care of it." He hung up his cell before connecting with Hanaran. We can get together later and discuss what comes after Sully Brooks for Angel. "Yeah, I guess the city has grown up."

The uniform cop looked at him. "Huh?"

"Never mind."

29 The CDA Tactical van was parked on South Hill across the street from a large gothic house. Steve Powers eyed the area with binoculars and saw little movement. *Frank's inside sleeping. Wait until we come in and wake his ass up.* The coordinates from Frank Gryzbowsky's ankle bracelet had the fugitive at or near the house. Steve licked his lips in anticipation of the score. *Too bad I can't have a beer with Brian. Maybe I'll spill one over his unmarked grave.*

The neighborhood was still. Steve's heart pounded against his chest. *I'm back in the shit again. Ready to bust into a place settled down for the night and catch some perp while he's with his honey.* The chance to nab a large score did not hurt either. *I'm taking a vacation to celebrate.* Steve turned to his men inside the van. Each held their M4 carbine rifles. They had donned their shielded riot helmets and body armor. *We're ready to do this.* Shay Baxter used the van's computer system. He brought up the homeowner's information on screen.

Baxter said, "It's registered to Shamus Moreland and he's got a sheet. He served two and a quarter for drug possession at McNeil."

Steve to his men: "Control says the fugitive is inside."

He eyed the house. *Frank, I got you so it's checkmate and you lose.* The place stood two stories and sported white walls with dark trim. The shutters colored dark in the nine windows reminded him of tombstones. A chimney shot out of the pitched roof. Above the porch was a landing accessible from a bedroom window. *If Frank runs, that is where he is going to go.* Steve's eyes caught the area below the landing. It was covered in rose bushes, making any exodus detectable.

To the men, he said: "Prep for anything, boys."

"How do you want this?" Trent said from the back. "What about Moreland?"

Powers smiled. "This one is off the grid. We take anyone inside down hard. Gryzbowsky has what we're after. If we work wet, we work wet."

The men exited the van in unison. They gathered around the van opposite Moreland's house. The neighborhood remained quiet. Every house was asleep in the early morning hours. *No one is going to expect this raid coming down.* Trent latched onto a two-handled battering ram. Christopher adjusted his body armor. Baxter drew out a picture of his son, Tyler and a sterling silver St. Benedict medal pendant around his neck. He kissed them both. The photo went onto the van's steering wheel. The necklace was tucked underneath Baxter's armor.

Baxter: "Steve, I need a minute."

They moved to the far end of the van away from the men. Doubt needed to be eliminated before it spread. *Damn kid is making him weak. He's not the partner I used to know.* "You can't back out on us now, Shay. Not now," Steve said.

"What are we doing here?" Baxter said. "This ain't us, man. This is criminal shit we're about to do."

Steve put his hand on Baxter's shoulder. *He is never going to be convinced if it's about the money. He needs something more to go through with this.* Steve said, "Then don't do it for the money."

"What else is there? This guy didn't do anything wrong?"

Steve lied. "He's a level three guy, Shay."

"He is a copperhead?" Shay said.

"I didn't say anything because it didn't matter before," Steve said. He knew how to get his partner motivated. Shay hated sexual predators because he had kids himself. *Sometimes you have to lie to win the game.* "Why do you think he got out so early? He is one of those jackals people keep trying to reform. Don't do it for the score. Do it for Tyler. Do it for all of those little kids who don't have childhoods because he had urges."

Baxter eyed him attempting to ascertain if he was being fed a lie. Steve held his gaze until his partner decided to look away. *I sold him. I got him amped up to take down a bad man.* Steve knew Baxter would learn the truth after. *But once we take this guy down and get the diamonds, he can't say a word. He will be in the game then. And once you are in the game there is no way out. Checkmate, partner.*

Checkmate.

Shay cocked his M4 carbine. "When he's contained, you give me five with him."

Steve smiled. "You want five? I'll give you ten. Hell, if you want, I'll give you twenty or thirty. We're off the grid and a copperhead never has friends. The boys and I will smoke Kools Filter Kings. Play some Jackson Browne on Trent's IPod so you get time with him."

They rejoined the huddle. Steve to his men: "Shay takes Christopher and Trent to breach the back. Tad comes with me. We go straight up the gut."

The team suited to match the dark night. They wore gloves and had radios affixed behind each with a stem in their ear. Their vests held various pouches decorated with concussion grenades, pepper spray canisters and a loaded Glock for close combat. Each helmet was designed with a small blue light to increase night vision but remain dark enough to keep out of sight ten yards away. The blue lights whined as they came to life. Steve checked each suit himself and slapped them on the back when finished.

He led a swift charge around the Tactical van toward the house. Five men ventured through the peaceful neighborhood. They hid in shadows split apart by random working vapor lamps scattered along the street. Trent bumped a metal trashcan but caught it before it could spill. *Come on, kid. This ain't amateur hour.* They moved at Moreland's two-story abode undetected with their carbines drawn. The night air was warm for winter.

Steve moved with Tad across the front lawn. Their boots made a light wisp as they brushed through soft water collected on the grass. Baxter led Trent and Christopher down the drive until they disappeared. Steve and Tad edged the porch steps toe first and then foot to reduce the weight on the planks. They pressed against the front door to avoid detection from the windows. *I'm in the shit again.* Steve clicked his walkie-talkie button once. It signaled Baxter to breach the house from the back.

Steve moved to the side as Tad swung his battering ram at the door. The barrier blew off its hinges. Steve went first with his carbine out with Tad following. Baxter's team blew off the back door. The burst of chaos destroyed the house's calm. The blue stems on each helmet cut the black interior. *Show yourself Frank before I get pissed.* Tad tripped and crashed through a glass coffee table in the living room. The shattering sound banged off the walls and caused Baxter to rush through the hall to add support from the back.

"Freeze. Show me your goddamn hands."

Steve moved past Baxter to the back. Trent and Christopher continued to yell at someone. Okay, Frank, we got you. He joined them in a room covered in plastic sheeting. The person the two men aimed their carbines at was lying unconscious on a table. Steve noted the IV stuck in the young man's arm. His team took no chances. Steve put his finger against the young man's neck for a pulse.

"He's out," Steve said. "Go upstairs and bring anyone down here. Someone's got to be keeping this guy alive."

Christopher and Trent exited into the hall. Steve searched the room and found a switch. He flicked it on. He removed his helmet and listened to the beat of boots as they stomped around upstairs in search of Frank. The room he stood in was strange. *Why is there so much plastic in here?* He noticed the large plastic bags with toxic stickers on them. *It's a medical room for escaped convicts.* The translucent plastic covering was duct taped over large portions of the walls. It left the room devoid of esthetics.

His eyes caught the cabinets and two tables on either side of him. The young man was lying on one table. The other was smaller, three feet in length. *Does he fix up kids in this hellhole?* Steve nodded as Tad entered. His face was fine but his helmet's shield bore slash marks and grooves from the glass. He put his arm around the guard. *In a few days, we'll be sitting on a beach laughing about this shit.*

"You okay?"

Tad said, "Yeah."

Steve pointed to the garbage bags of medical waste. "Our fugitive got tagged by a shot and this guy had to fix him up."

Steve guessed Moreland was the thin guy in a bathrobe who was led down the hall toward him at gunpoint. *He better have answers. God help him if he doesn't.* Behind Moreland were Baxter, Trent, and Christopher. As the first three entered, the room became crowded. Christopher stood in the threshold to allow space in the room. Moreland appeared worn and carried bruised bags of exhaustion around his sockets. Steve pointed a gloved finger at Moreland's chest.

"Tell me where he is," Steve said. "Tell me before I decide to get mean."

Moreland blinked. "Who the hell are you?"

Steve grabbed the thin man by his bathrobe collar. He weighed nothing. Steve lifted him off his feet until the man's toes touched the plastic floor covering. *I love this shit.* He could play bad cop with this asshole all night. "Frank Gryzbowsky. You sewed him up tonight. Where is he?"

Moreland shook his head. "Dunno who you're talking about."

He's lying to you. He thinks you don't have the balls to do anything. No one screws with me. Not here and not at The Sides. Steve snarled and released Moreland. The old man dropped onto the plastic sheets. He crumbled as the Tactical team towered over him. *I've already put one body in the ground today. Another one won't make much difference.* Steve turned to Baxter and smirked. *The old man wants to be tough, huh? Let's see how tough he is when he messes with the 208.*

Steve pointed a gloved finger at Baxter. He carried his finger down at Moreland. Baxter didn't question. *He knows this part of the game. We've done it too long for him to question it.* Baxter stepped in and fired a round from his carbine into Moreland's leg. The specialty barrel muffled the shot so it sounded as if someone had slammed a door shut. *Let's see if you remember Frank Gryzbowsky coming to see you now.* Steve lowered onto his haunches and leaned into Moreland. He took a handful of the old man's hair. He heard a strange hum from inside the house but ignored it.

"Tell me where he is or you never walk again."

Checkmate, Moreland, checkmate. Moreland's eyes displayed fear but he resisted saying anything. He spat into Steve's face. *I saw it coming, that's why I closed my eyes in time.* He wiped the waste away with his sleeve. Steve rose, hearing a hum which grew louder. *It's got to be wiring. It doesn't sound human.* He dismissed it and turned to Baxter. *Let's see how Moreland likes his other leg. Maybe he will talk then.*

Christopher swatted his gloves together to alert Steve. Every team member went from Moreland to Christopher. *He hears something in the hall.* The electric hum was all Steve heard. *Christopher must be hearing something else. Something I can't.* He motioned Christopher to investigate. The guard slid down the hall with his carbine drawn. Steve got a sick feeling as the electric hum ceased. The bad wiring in this place must keep Moreland up all hours of the night. He looked down at the thin man.

Steve to Moreland: "Next one goes through your skull."

Steve could see the doctor was not going to talk. *I can make him talk. Put one round into his stomach. He'll talk until he passes out.* Steve was ready to motion for Baxter to lay another shot into Moreland. Christopher broke his concentration by swatting his gloves together. It caught everyone's attention. Christopher stood halfway down the hall. He pointed at a closed door. *You hiding in there, Frank?* Steve nodded at Christopher. The guard put his hand on the knob, twisting it with his weapon drawn. *Checkmate, Frank, checkmate.* Steve saw Moreland move out of the corner of his eyes. He turned to the thin man as Moreland smacked at the translucent plastic sheeting covering the wall. *What did he do?*

Moreland dropped to the floor. *What was he doing?* Steve's eyes darted across the wall. He wanted to know. He glared at the plastic sheeting attempting to see beyond it. Steve put his gloves against the plastic and smoothed it for a clearer view. Then he saw the red button. *It is Moreland's alarm system?* He fixated on the button's use. *Are we going to have to deal with cops now? Some ten dollar and eighty cent an hour rent a cop is going to come up against my boys?* He laughed at the thought it would protect Moreland from him.

Sounds of metal clanks drew his attention from the button to Christopher. The team member stood with the door ajar. He was frozen in place. *He's terrified of something.* Steve glanced at Moreland. *What does the button do?* More metal shifted from the hall. The sounds were louder with the open door. Christopher did not move or raid beyond the door. He stood in place, scared.

"Trent, I need you, man," Christopher said. "This guy's got a goddamn dog. And it's mean."

Trent left the operating room into the hall. The electric hum returned and was louder. *It's focused.* Trent's body blocked most of Steve's view from the hall. Steve could see a dark animal staring back at Christopher. The hum grew louder. *Jesus, what is making the humming sound?* Christopher remained overtaken by the animal beyond the door. The only light offered was from Christopher's helmet. It shined a soft blue beam about ten feet forward. *I can't make out the dog. Must be hiding in the room.*

"Jesus," Trent said.

The second guard stopped short of the doorway. Trent drew his M4 carbine slow and expended a muffled round at its target inside the room. A flash filled the hall. Steve heard a flesh object hit the ground. Good, if that's all Moreland's got, it's no big deal. He offered Moreland a smirk. *Get ready to get a round for putting your doggy on us. My team is better than that, asshole.* Steve saw Trent inspecting Christopher.

Trent to Steve: "You should come see the size of that thing, Powers. It's a tank."

"No time. We need to find Gryzbowsky," Steve said. He gave Moreland a kick in the side. To Moreland: "You better talk. I'm not playing around here."

Trent was attending to Christopher, who was in shock. *This is what happens when you put people untested in the shit. They get all worked up to go Rambo then they turn soft when the shooting starts.* Steve and Baxter had faced several bad dogs unleashed by owners during their time at CDA Tactical. *Guy thinks he's got a Cujo that's tough. You drop that dog with a round to prove he ain't so tough.* Steve's ears were attracted to the sound of more metal clanking from the room. Trent appeared oblivious and was putting his hand on Christopher for comfort.

"Trent, what is going on down there?" Steve said.

Trent faced Steve and said, "We got the situation handled, sir."

An object leaped from the other side of the door and landed onto Trent's back. *Jesus, what the hell was that?* The creature latched onto the nape of Trent's neck. *Moreland's got another dog?* The electric hum was louder. The guard screamed as he struggled to stay in the hall. Trent squeezed off a small burst from his M4 carbine in the confusion. The rounds went from floor to ceiling. Half tattooed Christopher in his leg, torso and chest. Christopher was thrown onto his back. The floor pooled blood around him.

The dog's weight pulled Trent back into the room as he cried for help. *What the hell is happening?* It was the first time he had been in the shit and confused about what to do. Steve, Baxter and Tad began to breach the hall for a rescue. They were held back when several rounds fired out of the side room and lanced over their heads. Trent continued to scream. *Hang in there, Trent. We're coming. The cavalry is coming.* The three remaining team members went down on their haunches and slid into the hall. Baxter turned to Steve.

"Gryzbowsky?"

Steve nodded. Baxter confirmed his suspicion. *Frank's got some dogs waiting for us, huh?* It increased his willingness to put a round through Frank's skull. *We've been through this before. After the dogs get put down, we'll find him cowering in some corner. He'll beg us not to kill him.* Steve looked at Christopher's body. Frank would get a couple dozen rounds for his trouble. *You don't do that to a blue.*

"Frank, we're not playing around here. Come out right now," Steve said.

Back in the operating room, Moreland said, "I wouldn't go in there if I were you."

Baxter to Moreland: "Shut up, old man."

Trent's screams ceased. Steve heard the weird electric hum grow louder. *It's coming for us. Whatever is in there is coming for us.* The light from the operating room emptied away as the tactical team members blocked the entry to the hall. Baxter and Tad provided blue light visual from their helmets as they crept into the black hall. Steve noticed his helmet off back on the small table in the operating room. *No time to go back for it now. Push forward and slap myself for forgetting it over Miller Time.*

The three men approached Christopher. Steve made out where Trent's carbine had chewed up the guard. Christopher had three wounds. One bullet hit his torso, another in the gut and a final round that shattered the right side of his neck. Baxter slid to Christopher. The guard attempted to speak. He breathed out words that made no sound other than gasps. Christopher belched blood balloons. His face was chalk. *This ends now.*

Steve edged toward the doorway. He was inches from being able to see inside the room. He slapped his gloved hands together. The team members were to pull Christopher to safety. Baxter slipped around Steve and put his back to the room. Tad latched onto Christopher's body armor. Both ready to fill the hall with the sound of fabric rubbing against wood. Baxter turned and his gaze went inside the room.

"Oh, shit," Baxter said.

A creature leapt from the shadows at Baxter. It centered on his face. Another charged out and tore at Tad who opened up with his carbine. The rounds exploded the creature's skull. Gore expended everywhere. Steve bent his carbine around the threshold into the room and opened up a burst. The flash lit the room. Tad followed Steve's lead. He fired off a succession of shells. Steve drained his clip faster than he imagined possible. The smell of hot death erupted. *Whatever you got in there with you, Frank, we can handle.*

A concussion grenade from Trent's belt exploded inside the room. The blast threw Steve against the wall. His head cratered the drywall surface two inches. He was jarred, his vision blurred. Steve refocused on Baxter. His partner was on his back, struggling against the creature on top of him. Its mouth was latched onto his carbine. Steve shook off the grogginess of the concussion grenade. He headed to Baxter. Steve used the butt of his carbine and smacked the creature's head. It had no effect. *What kind of dogs are these?* Steve drew his Glock from his vest, firing twice into the animal's head. Gore splashed Baxter as the animal collapsed onto him.

"What the hell was that?" Tad said. He removed his helmet. The guard snapped off a pepper spray bomb from a ring on his vest and pulled the pin. He held it, ready to release it in the room.

Steve to Baxter: "You okay?"

Baxter coughed and spat out waste from the dog's skull. He pushed the animal's body away. "That was scary, man."

Baxter remained on his back. He wiped his face with his gloves. Steve examined the dead dog. *Moreland has some pit bulls, huh? They ain't so tough.* The stillness in the house put him at ease. *It's over now. That is all that matters. We beat back his best and it's over.* Steve stood comfortable and sure. He offered his hand to Baxter to get him on his feet. He smiled at his partner. "Get up, Shay. You're embarrassing The Brand."

Another dog launched out of the dark room. It flew into Tad and clasped onto his throat, biting down deep. Tad released the pepper spray bomb. It ignited. The hall was covered in a searing heat. Steve stumbled and rubbed his eyes in pain. Baxter screamed as the sudden burn of acid filled the air. He placed his gloves over his eyes for protection. Steve's boots skidded on the wood floor. He tripped over Tad's body as he fought blurred vision. Baxter screamed louder. Steve tried to clear his eyes to see what was happening.

Two dogs riddled with bullet wounds charged the hall. Steve emptied his Glock into them to no avail. He spun around and dodged the beasts. The dogs centered on Baxter who remained lying on his back with his gloves covering his face. The dogs clamped their mouths down on Baxter's legs. They then pulled Baxter *back* into the room. *They are containing him.* Fabric rubbing against wood flooring wisped as Baxter was skirted across the room on his back. His hands whipped out in every direction. Baxter screamed as he latched onto the doorframe. The dogs pulled harder leaving his fingers the only thing visible in the hall.

Steve stepped to aid Baxter but was cut off by another dog, which burst into the hall. The animal's momentum coupled with the slime of gore in the hall caused it to slide across the floor. The dog slammed against the wall. Steve took a step then saw the dog recover. It growled fangs at him in a hot, nasty intensity. The dog stepped at him. Steve's eyes went to Baxter's fingers on the frame. They went from tense to limp. Baxter's screams ceased. *Come on, Shay. Don't die on me.*

He stepped back out of the hall and into the operating room. The animal followed. Large smashed rounds were embedded in the dog's coat. *And it doesn't die. Why don't the damn things die?* He went into the room's light with the dog matching his step. *It's hunting me and saving the moment. It knows it's got me. Now it wants me to realize that.* Steve's eyes fell on Moreland. The doctor had strapped a belt around his wounded leg. A needle stuck out his flesh to ease the pain.

"I warned you," Moreland said.

The doctor blew Steve a delirious kiss. The dogs in the hall continued to maul his team members. They devoured their flesh after death. The horrid beast entered the room and stalked him. One of the dog's eyes was shot out but it remained fixated on Steve as a target. It frothed blood-drenched saliva with teeth stained pink. Steve glanced behind him to see the back door was clear. The door smashed off its hinges where Baxter's team had breached less than ten minutes prior. *I can make it if I try. I can out run this thing.*

He spilled from the back of the house. The dog charged behind him. Steve scrambled across the grass and leaped over the neighbor's wooden fence. The dog snapped its jaw shut less than an inch from his face as he toppled over into the next yard. He crashed and felt his right shoulder jam from the collision. The electric hum of the beast continued as it tore at the wooden fence. The dog chewed at the planks unwilling to give up.

Steve held his arm and pushed away with his feet. He sat in the middle of the yard. The electric hum carried on the other side. He closed his eyes and prayed this was all a dream. Steve wept soft tears. Both his old friend and his dad's house were gone. For good. *Checkmate, Steve, checkmate.*

"There are two people inside you, Frank. The sweet guy and the one after you've had a few."

30

Frank Gryzbowsky parked in front of Sully's apartment. Christine was trying her best to start a fight so she could leave. *You can't do that, Frank.* He worried about what would happen if she left. *They will kill her. Cut her up in little pieces if you don't find the stuff for them.* Sully's apartment was his only lead and he didn't know what he was supposed to pick up. *You can't let her leave. No matter what she says, she has to stay with you.*

The cold night wind smacked heavy against the station wagon's windshield and whistled as it bore through the cracks. The traffic light rocked on a wire as it blinked yellow caution in silence. Few cars passed by the place. *She thinks I'm bad for her. She wants to leave and never speak to me again.* If he thought it would help her, Frank was willing to put her on a plane tonight. *But we both know what Irish Pete will do if he finds out. He will kill her to make an example.*

"Sometimes, the only thing getting me up in the morning is a drink," Frank said. "Other times, I can't get to sleep without it." There had been long nights at The Sides where his drinking did him no good. *Staying up late and smelling the dead farts by men around me.*

Christine: "Don't you want to be free of it?"

"I've tried," Frank said. "It doesn't work that way."

"What are you doing here, Frank?"

Frank said: "Whatever Brian wanted me to pick up, Irish Pete wants. We either get it to him or we die."

"Don't drag me into this."

"They'll come after you to get to me."

"I'm not a part of this thing."

Frank shrugged. "At The Sides, we pay for the mistakes of others. Muscle asks 'where's the paper he stole?' or 'why is his count short?' and it don't matter if you didn't do anything. They will break your arm to make an example to the others."

"This isn't prison, Frank."

"I know," Frank said. "Prison has order. This is a jungle."

"Do you love me?"

Frank said, "Never stopped."

He was surprised that she kissed him. *It's been a while since she felt this way*. Every day in prison, he wanted for the divorce papers to be mailed. *But she kept waiting for me. Even though I figured she wanted nothing to do with me*. They pulled apart from each other's lips, but he held her as they stared at Sully's apartment. *We got to do this thing and get out of here. I'm not going back to The Sides*.

"Let's find what Sully was supposed to give me. We do that, drop it off, and leave tonight."

"Together?" Christine said. "Where do we go?"

"It doesn't matter to me," Frank said.

They opened Sully's apartment to the sound of an alarm system ready to go off. *Shit, I didn't think of that.* Frank turned to leave. Christine went to the alarm panel, typed in five digits, and shut it off. *How did she know how to do that?* His wife smiled and shrugged.

"You were gone a long time, Frank."

Frank: "I'm starting to believe that."

He eyed the living room. The place was decked out in neon colors. Everything was a pastel color of pink, blue, green or fuchsia. Frank moved around to the couch. A packed duffle bag with plane tickets on the top. He showed the tickets to Christine. Frank opened the duffle bag, spilling out pairs of white linen pants and t-shirts.

"He was skipping town," Frank said.

"What the hell were you picking up?"

Frank shook his head. "I don't know. Brian said it would be easy."

"If anything comes easy, there's usually a problem with it," she said.

They went to the bedroom. On his knees, he searched underneath the bed. It could be anything that Brian wanted picked up. *And it doesn't have to be here, either.* Christine picked an object up next to Frank. She held it as he stood. It was the rosary beads that he had him when he left *The Sides.*

"This came out of your pocket," Christine said. "Are you getting religious on me, Frank?"

He touched the beads with his fingers. *I can't remember how I got this in the first place. Maybe they made a mistake with them back at The Sides. He wondered if some con being released would look forward to seeing them and be upset they were gone.* Frank shrugged at Christine.

"Maybe I got them in AA," Frank said.

"They gave you a rosary?"

"Sobriety is a religion. You surrender to a higher power, admit you have no control and hold hands praying. The only thing they don't do is shave your head and make you sell flowers at the airport."

Christine handed it to him. "You might need it."

"What's that supposed to mean?"

"We all need a little faith now and then," she said. "Even you do."

Frank pocketed the rosary. He took the empty Beretta from his waistband and set it on the dresser. His tumbling mess of hair could not be smoothed in the mirror's reflection. *How did I get here?* He could explain all of the ways how, but logic told him it was impossible. He stretched his back and wondered if he could continue. *I need to find whatever it was to pick up for Brian. Otherwise I'm going to be dead by morning.*

"We should go," Christine said.

"And go where?"

She shook her head. "Frank, you spend way too much time convincing people not to love you."

"That's what my last wife said too."

"Why didn't it work out the first time?"

Frank rubbed his face. "Debbie just bugged me."

I tried to make that one work too. I didn't want the divorce. But the marriage had problems. Debbie nagged him. She wanted him to quit drinking. *Go work for daddy she would say.* He couldn't stand the man at holidays, let alone work for him. *Then it was the sobriety coins where she made me go to meetings. Coming home, I would give her the coin and she would be civil for a few hours.* The idea worked until Debbie noticed it was a collection of thirty coins, all-marking first day sober.

"I don't settle down, Chris," he said. "I told you that when we met."

"What are you, a wandering Pole? I thought that was reserved for Moses' people," she said.

"I'm American," Frank said. "I am who I want to be."

"But you have no people, Frank. In all the time I've known you, I still don't know where you come from."

"I'm from all over."

Christine put her hand on his cheek. "I love you. It's insane to say that after tonight, but I do."

What do you tell her? None of it sounded easy without the charm. *She sees through my bullshit. If I say it wrong, she leaves and dies.* He rubbed the back of his neck with his hands and waited for something to come to mind. *What do I tell her?* A sound from the living room drew his attention. *We've got company.* The front door opened to Sully's apartment.

Frank put his finger to his mouth to Christine. He grabbed the Beretta off the dresser and moved to the bedroom door. He closed and locked it. There were footsteps as the intruders went through the living room. They spoke to each other in muffled tones. He guessed there were two or three of them. An intruder stumbled over the living room furniture and kicked it in frustration. Christine moved close as he eyed the closed bathroom door. *No, I would have to shoot myself out of that place.* Frank noticed the bedroom closet. *The steps are getting closer. They are coming back here.*

He grabbed Christine and headed to the sliding closet door. Inside, he closed the sliding door except a crack of space to see back in the bedroom. He put his face against the crack. The footsteps halted. Frank focused on the doorknob. It was tested with a slight turn. *Now, it begins.* The door exploded from a shotgun blast in the hall. Spent fragments blew into the bedroom. The frame collapsed onto the carpet.

Blooms of smoke filled the air. Frank and Christine covered their mouths in order not to cough. Two black men entered the bedroom. Both wore nice suits with gold chains. The first was small and held a smoking pump action shotgun. The second one was three hundred pounds with a large combat blade. Frank squeezed the handle of the Beretta. *It's empty, but they don't know that*. He brought the Beretta next to his face against the sliding closet door.

"Damn, now that's what I call answering the bell, son," the small one said.

"Devon, do the bathroom. Ain't got time for games," the large one said.

Devon aimed the shotgun at the bathroom door. He blew a large hole in the middle. *He's enjoying this. It's a damn video game*. Frank looked at Christine. She tried not to scream though fear sat in her eyes. Devon kicked the bathroom door free. He hooted and hollered. He fired another blast and blew apart the shower. A stream of water gushed out of the bathroom and soaked the bedroom carpet.

"Damn, son. What you think, they hiding in the toilet?" the large one said.

"Sorry, Man. Got carried away," Devon said inside the bathroom. "I take it they ain't home."

"They here," Mac said.

Mac stabbed his combat blade into the mattress. He pulled it free

from the frame. *He's looking for us. He isn't going to give up easy.*
Mac kicked the mattress to liberate his blade. Frank watched Mac's
eyes fix on the closet door. As Mac approached, Frank edged away
from the closet's crack and hid in the shadows. He squeezed the
door's inside handle and placed the Beretta's barrel at the door. He
glanced at Christine who was terrified. Mac's large fingers punctured
the crack between the door, then latched onto it. Frank pushed all his
weight against the closet door to shut it. The force slammed Mac's
fingers in the jam. Crack. Mac's hand broke as he dropped the knife,
howling in pain. Frank threw open the sliding door and tucked the
Beretta's barrel up against Mac's fat chin.

"You found us."

Mac's eyes widened. He didn't expect anyone inside. He was doing
his rounds so they could both go home. Frank saw Mac was holding
his left hand. It was broken. Frank pushed Mac back as he exited the
closet. He turned Mac around and placed the Beretta against the nape
of Mac's neck. Christine moved behind Frank and picked up the
knife, throwing it back into the closet.

"Mac, I'm telling you, they ain't here," Devon said as he exited the
bathroom. "Tell goddamn Baron if you…"

He stopped talking as he saw Mac standing with Frank and
Christine. Without thinking, Devon turned his shotgun onto Mac,
ready to fire. Devon looked jittery and upset. Mac held up his arms,

waving off Devon. *Mac looks more pissed that Devon has a gun on him than the one I've got on him.*

"Don't you shoot me, Devon," Mac said. "Man's got a gun on me and he ain't shooting. You pull that trigger and I'll kill you."

Devon looked at Mac, then to Frank. "He'll kill us anyway."

"No," Mac said. "Man wants to talk." Mac to Frank: "You want to talk, right?"

"Sure," Frank said.

"Mac, you don't know this man," Devon said. "Look at him, he ain't got no clue what to do."

"Can't look at him, I got a gun to me," Mac said. "Chill, you hear me? Chill."

Devon shook his head, frustrated. He wants to have more fun blasting off a few more doors. The small gangsta tossed the shotgun onto the bed. He stayed put while Christine retrieved it and put it on the far side of the room. Frank released Mac. The big man stumbled to the bed holding his broken hand. Frank motioned with the empty Beretta for Devon to join Mac. When Devon sat down, Mac used his uninjured hand to slap Devon upside the back of his head.

"What's that for?"

Mac said, "If you have to ask, then you already know."

"You always doing that, acting like my pops," Devon said. "Ain't right, Mac. Ain't right."

"Shut up," Frank said. "You two are giving me a headache."

Devon looked at Frank. "Oh, I'm so sorry mister white Republican gun rights man."

For the first time tonight, Frank wished he had a bullet. *Trouble is, with Devon, I would use it.* Frank to Mac: "Who's the Baron?"

"Man sent us," Mac said. "You come after him, he goes for you first."

Frank to Christine: "We need to pay Baron a visit, don't we?"

"He ain't gonna talk to you," Devon said.

Before Frank could retort, Mac slapped Devon upside his head again. *Baron will talk. A man worried enough about me to send two goons will talk my head off.*

"Why are you so concerned with the diamonds, Junior?"

31

The way that Irish Pete spoke made Junior Reed suspicious. *He knows something. He wants me to say it first.* The old man sat at the helm of his oak desk and drank a glass of Jamison with a cadre of handguns. Junior's eyes went beyond the old man. He watched the security screens showcasing the estate. He tried to see everywhere. Junior kept his cool. *I'm not tipping my hand in this. But I need to know who he has out there coming for me.*

Junior sat in his padded chair across from Irish Pete. He downed his glass of Bushnell's and let the sting roll into his stomach. *You're too good for him. He's a guy ready to be put out to pasture.* After a while, he will start believing whatever lines you feed him. Junior held back his smirk as his eyes went to the weapons adorning Irish Pete's desk. *Are they more than decorations?* His cell chimed a text from Baron: *No word from Mac.* Junior shot back: *They find him?* Baron: *Don't know. Worried.*

Irish Pete displayed his glass to Junior. "What do you think?"

"Private label is great but my wallet doesn't like it."

"After this is through, I'll put a case in your car. I've got a few one-hundred-thirty-proof bottles on the table," he said. Irish Pete gestured to a liquor table next to the desk. It was dressed with various expensive labels.

"One-thirty proof?" Junior said. "Are you some moonshiner?"

"You go inside for a stretch, you would be surprised what you're willing to drink," he said.

"This guy who did the Boneyard," Junior said. "You know him from inside?"

Irish Pete: "Brian did the picking. Styles talked to the guy."

"I wasn't good enough for you?"

"He's gotten results, Junior."

That did nothing for Junior. *If I had a name to work with, people on the streets could help. Maybe give it to Baron's people to sort out.* Junior examined the room. It was decorated with hunting trophies, which loomed in the crackling firelight. Deer and elk heads mounted on the walls. Bald eagles and falcons hung from the ceiling. *He knows how to take someone down when they are in his sights.* All of that stuff was commonplace for any regular hunter.

But Irish Pete was not a regular hunter. He had a fancy for serious game. A stuffed Grizzly overtook the foyer with a towering menace that greeted guests. A cougar hid in the corner next to the couch. The old man also enjoyed illegal game. A stuffed silverback gorilla sat at the foot of Irish Pete's bed. There was a rug on the floor from a Sumatran tiger's hide. Irish Pete had bragged about taking each creature down by greasing a local African guide to sneak onto an international preserve. Baron sent Junior a text: *No answer from the boys*. Junior shot back: *What do you do now?* Baron: *Wait*.

"You take all of these down yourself?"

Junior knew the answer but wanted the old man to keep talking. *The more he talks, the less he suspects*. You learn about guys that way. It keeps them from getting the upper hand. *Maybe he slips and gives up the guy who is coming for you*. Irish Pete talked as if he were a different crook. *But I got him pegged. Crooks are the same. That goes for old men sitting in a converted church. In the end, there's no real difference between us*.

"Let me show you something," Irish Pete said.

The old man pushed away from the desk and grunted as he rose. He moved to a black Rhino hide hanging in the corner and brushed it aside. Behind it was a large display case. Irish Pete brought out a huge, double barrel rifle. Junior's eyes ran the two and a half foot length of the end to the trigger. *It's a goddamn hand-cannon for a comic book superhero*. His eyes gaped at the twin tubes that gleamed off the gold-plated majesty in the firelight.

"It's called a 4-Guage rifle. Used to hunt large game," he said. "I took it for a song off a descendent of Teddy Roosevelt after the housing market collapsed in Montana. This is one of the rifles boxer John L. Sullivan gave The Bull Moose before his 1909 African Safari. I used this in the motherland two winters back, where if the bribe is big enough, you can hunt game with four legs or two."

The old man went behind the Black Rhino's hide again. He produced a large rifle shell that took his entire hand due to its weight. "You got to special order these and bring down a train if you can handle the kick. My first time shooting it, I wasn't ready. I spent two weeks in a Cape Town hospital with a separated shoulder."

"Little easier when the game ain't shooting back," Junior said.

Irish Pete pointed at the Rhino hide. "That one was charging at me when I took her down. She was a weapon."

The old man put the heavy round in the breast pocket of his dress shirt. The pocket sagged against the shell's weight. Irish Pete plucked another round from the display case. *He's in his element now. He wants to show you how good he is with that thing. Man wants you to be afraid so you won't cross him.* Junior felt he tagged Irish Pete to the base of his character. *I know him better than he knows himself.*

"I got a shooting range out back," the old man said. "I can't describe how powerful this rifle is."

"You aren't worried about neighbors?"

"It's wheat fields and hills for miles. No one but us out here," he said.

He's about to make his move with no one out here but us. Junior felt uneasy. He moved his hand to his lap, feeling for his sawed off. *I'll get two shots before he can load that thing for one.* Junior wondered if he could take down a boss. *You take him down there will be consequences. That is why Sully wants you to play him, not kill him.* Irish Pete went behind his desk and dropped the remainder of his Jamison down his gullet. *He's setting you up.* The old man moved to the fireplace. He practiced his aim by pointing the unloaded rifle in the mantle's mirror. Then he set the barrel's sights on Junior. *He knows you have the stones.*

"What's the matter, Junior?"

Junior lied. "Nothing."

The old man grinned. "Wanna see something neat?"

"Sure."

The old man set the elephant rifle against the liquor table. Junior eased his hand off the sawed-off. Irish Pete grabbed one of the high proof liquor bottles off the table. He flung it into the fireplace's mouth. Flames erupted and shot a fireball back into the living room. A wave of heat blasted over Junior as it burned the oxygen in the room. Junior's eyes went to the back window. The night sky lit up as flames blew out the chimney top and died. Irish Pete winked at Junior as he picked up the elephant rifle.

"I love showing guests that," Irish Pete said. "Let's go in the back and see what we can shoot with this thing."

Junior was ready to offer an excuse to leave. *Say something personal to get me out alive.* His eyes caught the surveillance monitors behind Irish Pete's desk. A car slammed through the front metal gate. It knocked the guardians off their hinges. The vehicle charged down the drive toward the house. *He's here for me. The man's come to kill me here. I don't know how he found me. But he did.*

He clutched his sawed-off and left his chair. Irish Pete remained by the fireplace as Junior tore across the living room and avoided the stuffed Grizzly bear in the foyer. *He's here for me*. The sounds of metal meeting rock and dirt grew outside as the car approached. Junior opened the front door. Headlights blinded him. Junior shielded his eyes with his arm. He made out the vehicle's undercarriage carried the gate's frame.

I'm not scared of him. I'm ready. The car's front tire was blown. The rim grounded revolutions into the asphalt drive and shot sparks. The engine bellowed as the car crashed into the fountain base at the center of the drive. The collision impaled the radiator on concrete. Water spewed as it met the engine's heat. A wall of steam prevented Junior from seeing the driver. *He can't see me either*. Junior blasted a round into the windshield. The shot's heat caked and bent the glass. *He ain't such a bad ass.*

Junior went down the front steps. Halfway down the middle step he stopped. A Rubenesque blonde woman exited the car. *Who the hell is that?* Sweat poured down her face as she peeled out a shotgun.

Her green top and blue fabric pants showed blood from his pellet shot. *Why the hell is she here? No one said a broad was coming for me.*

"Who took my Jonas from me?"

Oh, shit. It's Gloria. She fired a shotgun blast that missed Junior's head by half a foot. He dove and crashed into the work equipment on the porch. His face stopped an inch from a board with a nail sticking out. The impact caused his sawed-off to fly from his hands and into the brush. Gloria fired another round that sent pellets over him. He scrambled to move out of her way. Junior turned to the front door and saw Irish Pete appear from inside. The old man strode forth with his elephant gun at his side.

"Is this one of your loose ends, Junior?"

The old man chuckled. He winked as Junior lay on the porch. *He doesn't think this concerns him.* Gloria shot a blast over Irish Pete's head. It forced him to crouch out of the way. *That's right, old man. Who is laughing now?* The old man glanced at the end of the blast, which chewed out a large section of a white column. *He's insulted that she shot the house rather than at him.* The old man shook his head in disbelief. He touched the scaffolding controls. The work lights ignited. They washed the drive in white light and blinded Gloria.

"That bitch," he said.

A sparkle ignited in the old man's eyes. *He's back on safari.* Gloria shot an errant shot at the front steps unable to gain a clear target. Irish Pete paid no attention to Gloria's attack. He cracked open the rifle and loaded each shell from his breast pocket. The old man pushed them in with his thumb. Another blast from Gloria blew out the front windows. Irish Pete set the rifle straight and dumped chaw into his cheek. He winked at Junior.

"Let me take care of your loose end, boy."

He centered his large rifle twenty yards from Gloria and squeezed off a round. Junior witnessed a small ball of yellow fury burst from the muzzle. The report expanded into a rolling echo of thunder that carried through the small country valley around the estate. The oscillation pressure of the rifle's blast knocked out the windows of Gloria's car and threw shards of glass into her. The gunshot's wake closed in on Junior's head. His eardrums were slammed with a sonic boom. A loud, high-pitched whistle erupted from the shot's decibel. Junior focused on the old man. He mouthed something in anger that Junior could not understand.

Junior waved apart the gunpowder plume. He fixated on the driveway and coughed as his eyes watered from the sulfur-laced shot. *I'm at war.* A figure stood in the fog. The smoke dissipated to reveal Gloria next to her car. She had no wound from the shot. Junior glanced to the car and saw that the round had torn off the roof. *He missed. I can't believe it, he missed.* The old man spat out a brown stream of tobacco juice that coated the porch.

Gloria stumbled backward confused. The blast had stunned her. But the large woman remained solid on her feet. Her eyes snapped with electricity. *She realizes she wasn't hit. Oh, shit.* Gloria's hands formed claws. *She's coming for us.* The loud whistle died in his ears. Junior heard Gloria roar as she stepped forward. *No matter what it takes, she's coming.* Gloria's eyes focused on Irish Pete. *She's less than seventeen feet from us.*

"That shot would have taken down a bull elephant," the old man said.

Yeah, but you didn't hit her. You missed her by two feet to the right. Irish Pete took aim with his rifle at Gloria. *Don't miss this time. She's eleven feet from us. Hurry, old man.* Another lightning bolt of power raged forth at the woman. The Thunder of the Gods erupted from the rifle's fury. It held enough kick that it caused the old man to take two steps back.

The front windows exploded as deviations in equilibrium were released from the muzzle. The traverse waves of the blast compressed into Junior's skull. It was accompanied by another shroud of smoke that wrapped him and walled off his vision. *It feels as if someone is standing on my chest.* He choked at the sulfur fumes for a second time. The acidic white fog was waved away. *My God, she's still standing.* The second shot exploded the remainder of the fountain behind Gloria. Concrete chunks embedded into the porch inches from Junior's head. He stared at Irish Pete and knew he was a fraud. *He's an old man with false adventures and a few goons he kills.*

"I'm out of shots," Irish Pete said.

I'll bet you are. The old man heaved the spent elephant rifle at Gloria. She batted it away. Only two steps from us. Irish Pete ran into the house's cavity to escape her wrath. Junior cowered in fear. *She's going to tear me apart for what I did to Jonas.* Gloria ran past Junior into the house. Junior stood and listened to Gloria's angry screams inside the house. Large droplets of blood trailed on the floor through the foyer. Junior entered as a crash of wood and glass were followed by Irish Pete's screams.

Junior went through the foyer. He saw the stuffed Grizzly and checked in its mouth. He found a serial number. *The old man didn't take this thing down, he bought it at auction.* Junior eyed the other mounted beasts in the living room. He was certain they had similar evidence. Irish Pete continued to scream from the back. *The old man has been conning me. Thinks I will take him serious if he feeds me enough lies.* Junior went to the oak desk and selected a Desert Eagle from the handguns.

The pistol was cocked and weighed heavy in his hand. *I should take them both out and be done with it.* Junior followed the drops of blood to the back of the house. Gloria's screams of anger filled his ears. Junior pictured himself stalking a dangerous animal on safari. He moved past the former cathedral's station of the cross. It was now a dining room with a table obliterated with broken chairs. Junior saw the broken frame of the sliding glass door to the back patio. *She threw the old man right through it.*

He maneuvered through the metal frame holding broken glass shards. Junior's eyes wandered the patio. Glass fragments covered in blood were sprayed overtop light red and gray blocks of stone. He looked at the pool where he saw Gloria lying on her chest at the shallow end. She was on top of Irish Pete with the back of his head dipping over the edge of the pool. Gloria squeezed her mitts around his throat as gore seeped out of her back and sides between embedded glass fragments. The old man clutched at her hands to pry them off. Her strength overmatched his. Gloria's teeth gnashed through her bottom lip she growled at the old crime boss.

Junior went behind Gloria before she could react. He aimed the Desert Eagle and squeezed off three rounds in her back. The shots caked her flesh but did not go through into Irish Pete. *She's not going down after all that.* He checked the gun. *How powerful is this thing?* Junior aimed higher and squeezed off another round into the back of the woman's head.

Gore bloomed from her skull. Irish Pete was blanketed in red. The woman's drive sagged as her life ended. The old man pried off her hands from his throat and spat out bits of gore. Junior laughed as Irish Pete remained pinned under Gloria's girth. *If you're going to do it, now is the time. He's pinned under her and is easy prey.* Junior kept the Desert Eagle aimed at Irish Pete. The old man noticed and stopped struggling. He eyed Junior with a tired glance.

"If you're going to do me," Irish Pete said. "Then do me already."

What good is he to you dead? You know he's a fraud. You got him regardless if you pull the trigger or not. Junior lowered the gun. He watched the old man sigh. Junior put the Desert Eagle on the patio. He helped the old man roll Gloria over. Her dead body toppled into the pool with a splash that threw a foot of water into the air. Junior eyed Gloria's body sink until she rested at the bottom. Irish Pete coughed as he sat. His neck was bruised and red from her hands. He spat into the pool.

"The boys will have to drain it to get her out," he said.

"You should stuff her in the house with all of the other game you got in there," Junior said. *Let the old man think you still fear him. Let him believe you don't know what a con he is.*

Irish Pete said, "I've been on safari with that gun and it never failed before tonight."

"She was a hard target," Junior said. *That's right, let him believe that you don't doubt his skills. To him, you act as if he is still the*

badass marksman you know he isn't.

"This is a strange night."

"You're telling me."

32 *It's World War III in there. I swear it is.* The smell of death illuminated the air inside the two-story gothic house owned by Shamus Moreland. Detective Tom Hammond had enough and went outside.

Black bags littered the front lawn. They contained human or animal corpses. The coroner was receiving them at a local high school gymnasium for examination after she had declared a mass fatality plan in effect. Tom stood on the front lawn and tried to get a sense of the place. He noted the interstate overpass with cars careening at sixty or above throughout the night. The concrete mass served as a divide between the clapboard meth dens of the valley and South Hill luxury homes. *It keeps the bad elements away from the good citizens but not tonight.*

Moreland's two story Victorian was adorned with bullet holes. Witness accounts suggested the building had an explosion of rounds. A stray bullet had travelled across the street from Moreland's gothic house. It found home in the chest of a six-year-old girl, ending her life while she slept. First responders radioed in about a Tactical van at the scene. They thought it was drug raid turned slaughterhouse. Further inspection proved the van to be stolen by a member of the Coeur d'Alene police department.

Crime scenes had common themes to Tom. An abundance of cases showed him what people were capable of doing to others. Few things shocked him. *But this is an exception, right?* Tom examined the area. Neighbors were not pooled into a cordoned off section as with most homicide cases. *They stand behind that yellow tape at most scenes and gossip about what they have heard or what they think they know.* This scene was different. Neighbors stayed inside their homes. The doors were locked and shades down.

They fear for their safety. Word had spread about Moreland's neighbor John Price. He had let his golden retriever in the back yard for a nightly constitutional. Two of Moreland's pit bulls rammed through the fence. They mauled him and the dog. *They chewed them up as if they were nothing. No one wanted to be out on the streets tonight. Mass murderers don't have the clout that Moreland's dogs have.*

Detective Dereks exited the house. His face was pale as he went to Tom. *The experience is beyond gruesome.* He could see that when he arrived. There were first responders sitting on the front porch attempting to smoke away what they saw inside. The gothic house had been a testament to the worst that humanity could train an animal to do. *And they obliged, didn't they?* Dereks drew out a pack of Lucky Strikes and Tom flipped him a flame from his lighter.

Dereks said, "Thought you didn't smoke."

"Not anymore."

Dereks lit off his flame and took a drag. He eyed Tom. "It reminds me of the Kane thing."

"Yeah, I was thinking that myself," Tom said. "Or my ex-wife."

"Did she call again?"

"Five times in the last two hours."

Dereks said, "You calling her back?"

"I don't need negative shit right now. I got enough to last me for a while," Tom said.

Somewhere, a dog howled at the fat moon in the cloudless night. The animal's cry filled the neighborhood. Everyone including Tom stiffed in fear. *We are all afraid of being attacked by the dogs still on the loose.* He imagined a bullet to the head being an easier way to die. *Getting torn apart by dogs does not sound fun.*

"Last count was six," Dereks said. "Moreland is done helping. We counted twelve cages."

"There are six dogs out here?"

Dereks said, "Doubtful. Food and water was in eight or nine of the pens. But it's hard to tell with all of the blood and shit everywhere."

"When I pulled up they were carting away survivors," Tom said. "Who have we got to talk to?"

"Moreland and this kid, Pat Quinn," Dereks said. "He slept through the entire thing. First, blue shows up and he's walking around asking questions."

Tom said, "Tick? He was in there?"

"Yeah," Dereks said. "I'm shocked he didn't jack the plasma in the living room."

Tom: "Probably didn't have time. Who else do we got?"

Dereks pointed to one of the patrol cars parked down the street. "We got Rambo Jr off the team. He's the only one to make it out alive. He said his name was Steve."

Tom's eyes wandered to the squad car. He made out Steve sitting in the back. "I need to have a chat."

He approached the squad car and noted the man wore tactical gear. Steve's face was ashen as he sobbed. Tom opened the front and sat in the passenger seat. He looked at the man behind him. Steve held a photograph of a young boy. *Did he bring his kid in there? We didn't find a child's body.* Tom got the feeling in the pit of his stomach.

"Yours?"

Steve lifted his eyes from the photograph and fought back tears. "No, he's my best friend's."

Tom rubbed his face to wipe away his exhaustion. "And your best friend was in there?"

Steve returned to the photograph and sobbed again. Tom eyed his tactical gear. It was clean minus little blood splats. He got out without a scratch. His friend is the one who took the brunt of the attack. Tom grabbed the photograph from Steve. He displayed it to him with cold eyes. That's right, listen to what I'm about to say.

Steve offered back a menacing look.

"You are going to talk. Beginning to end about what happened in here," Tom said. "No bullshit. No lawyers."

"Don't treat me like I'm one of them," Steve said. "I'm blue."

"And I don't care."

Steve appeared shocked. "I'm blue goddamn it. You don't treat us like one of them."

Tom flicked the photograph of the boy. "Tell that to him. You made his daddy go away."

"We all had our reasons for going in there," Steve said. "We were going after a fugitive who broke his parole."

"Someone breaks their parole, you call the Sheriff's Office. We didn't know you were operating out here."

Steve: "We thought we could handle it."

"Bullshit," Tom said. "You stole the van. You went into this house with guns firing. The owner says you shot him long before the dogs were a factor. What happened in there?"

Steve glared at Tom. "I'm blue."

"Keep saying that. Do it all through your interviews. Do it through trial. We'll set you up in Walla Walla or McNeil, make sure all of the boys in there know what color you represent."

Steve pointed at Tom. "You don't do that to one of us."

"You keep saying us, pal," Tom said. "But the truth is, I don't know who you are."

Steve sulked. "What do you want from me?"

Tom: "Tell me the real reason why you guys went in there."

Steve tried to speak but sobbed again. Tom displayed the photo of the boy. *I can wait all night if I have to. This kid will want to know. I will have to go to his home, tell his mother and watch her cry. But that won't be as bad as when I have to tell him. I have to have a reason that he and his friends were going inside that house.* Tom sat there and held the photograph. *I am not quitting until he talks to me.*

33 Frank opened the door to Baron Gamble's place. He saw a figure standing at the far end of the living room. The man's attention was focused outside through a bay window overlooking the airport.

Frank entered quiet guessing the man was Gamble. He noticed the expensive robe and red silk pajamas that the man wore. In Gamble's hand, a glass of Chardonnay. Sounds of classical music danced through a hidden sound system. Frank eased the door closed. He noted the extravagant furniture of a sofa, table and chairs along with an enormous kitchen. From the outside, the place was a rundown motel. Inside had undergone major renovations.

He's a corporate executive not a low-life drug dealer. Gamble's interest was paid to the large jumbo jets and private aircraft that lifted and descended on the landing strip less than five hundred yards away. The window and room rattled due to each flight's turbulence. Little blinking lights on the strip were in precision with Bach's piano.

"Did you get him, Mac?"

Frank looked at Gamble's back. The man's eyes were fixated on the air traffic. "Mac took a powder."

Gamble gave a slight turn and appeared unconcerned with Frank's intrusion. He lifted his brow then returned to watch a 737 lift off in the distance. Frank watched the man act casual drinking his wine.

He's used to this type of life. The treachery does not faze him.

"I have met men like you before," Gamble said. "Over there."

"I thought I was an American original."

"I served two tours in-country at the sandbox. The difference between the Haji and us are a brain bucket and idiot stick."

Frank said, "I wanted to be somebody in this life. But it's dawned on me that I might be that other guy people vaguely remember."

Gamble nodded and drank his wine. He set his glass onto the carpet and returned watching a plane lift off outside the window. *He's waiting for something. He knows something is coming that he cannot control.* Gamble made a slight turn to Frank.

"Grant me a last request."

"What?"

"If you are going to do it," Gamble said. "Do it while I'm watching the planes. It relaxes me."

They stood for a moment as a silence gathered between them. Frank put the empty Beretta on the table. "Too many people have died tonight."

"Including Mac?"

Frank shook his head. "He and Devon are resting."

Gamble exhaled relief. He moved to the kitchen and removed a bottle of wine from the counter. He poured two glasses of Chardonnay. *It looks good, don't it? Think of how good you have been. It's been a few hours since you've had a glow on. Why not have a taste.* Frank's eyes focused on the glass. Gamble approached as Frank sat across from the sofa. Gamble set the glasses down as he took the couch. *God, it looks good. You can tell how it's gonna make you feel by looking at it.* Frank's eyes went from Gamble to the glass.

His stomach rumbled as he licked his lips in anticipation. *You need it to get by tonight.* Feel that glow and keep on moving. Frank missed the feeling. *You gotta let that glow start coming to get by.* He focused on the glass. *And that's the shit, isn't it? You don't drink wine.* He fought the urge to touch the glass. *Go ahead. Pick up the glass and let it touch your lips. Close your eyes and feel that glow coming on. You deserve it.*

"What do we do now?" Frank said.

"Embrace the suck."

"It sounds harsh."

"How else do you deal with a situation?" Gamble said. "Beltway clerks issued FRAGOs without seeing the big picture. Fallujah's orders were for a shake and bake."

"The front lines don't have the men who make the orders," Frank said.

"No, they don't," Gamble said. "We dropped white phosphorous and fought house to house. The casualty rate was huge."

"But you got out?"

Gamble: "I was a single digit midget who received a round in the thigh to get out after a few hours. My fellow soldiers fought against another man's desperation. You cannot win against someone who has nothing to lose. And I believe there is honor in knowing when to say 'enough.'"

Frank's hand fished the rosary beads out of his pocket. *Am I desperate enough to do anything?* His fingers and thumb rubbed the beads. *The man who Gamble thinks I am is not someone I recognize.* He glanced at the wine glass. He hated it for being there. *Christine is right. I won't hear the end of it if I tell her, but she is right. I don't have much but her holding me back from being a bad guy. But I'm trying.* He pocketed the rosary and focused on the wine.

"What now?" Frank said.

"I know when to quit."

Gamble went to the kitchen. He opened a cabinet and withdrew a small black satchel. Frank's eyes remained on the wine glass. *Should I take a taste?* Gamble returned and put the satchel on Frank's lap. It startled him and drew his attention from the glass. *Is this what I've been fighting for?* He opened the satchel, unsure of the contents. Diamonds shined in the room's light. *This is what men have been killing for?* He understood why Irish Pete wanted them so bad.

Frank dug his hand into the satchel. He produced a handful of diamonds, the smaller ones fell between his fingers. *You could do a lot of things with this, Frank. That new life stares at you, waiting for you to take hold.* He thought of getting Christine and running with the diamonds. *We could try to make it out alive. Get out of this city for a fresh start. The two of us together could do some great things.* He glanced at Gamble who appeared relaxed.

"They are cursed by greed," Gamble said. "That's my theory. Tonight has enough evidence to back me. I refuse to live without honor."

Frank stood with the satchel. He respected Gamble. *The man knows when to back away from a fight.* His eyes fell to the wine glass. *He wanted it bad. Just a sip and put it down. You can walk away after that.* Frank shook off the feeling. *That isn't me anymore. I can't be that man.* Frank wanted to pour the contents of the glass onto the carpet. Instead, he looked at Gamble.

"You know, I realized something just now." Frank said. "I would not be here, and I mean this entire mess, if I had stopped drinking a few months ago."

Gamble nodded. *He agrees and you have to respect someone who recognizes their own stupidity. Don't you? Yeah, there has to be honor in that.*

The Lexus sat idling in the cold as midnight came calling. Styles Remington gripped the wheel. *This is the life you live, isn't it? The nighttime is your daylight. It's when you work the most.* Time had gotten shorter for him during the last few years. The nights were longer. *They blend together. I can't keep all of the things we have done straight.* He questioned if he should get out. *Either you get out or the old man puts you out for good.* Styles thought of Beau. *Kid didn't do anything wrong. He was loyal and the old man iced him anyway to set an example.*

34

Most goons who crossed his path had never frightened Styles. *I have taken a baseball bat to a guy's leg and watched it go sideways. I don't worry what most people think of me.* Styles thought he was respectable enough. But then, there was Detective Dan Rahn. *The cat scares me. You look at him and know he ain't messing around. He kills people for the fun of it.* The odor from the back seat was horrible. Styles wanted to hold his nose but knew there might be consequences. *With Rahn, there are always consequences.*

Rahn sat quiet in the back of the Lexus. His fedora brim was so low that Styles could not make out the man's eyes in the rearview mirror. *He's in the dark, in his element.* The man scared everyone in the old man's organization. *The devil can't always kill people himself. That's why the old man employs Rahn. He could slice a guy in two and drink an iced tea while their body gets cold.* Rahn stayed quiet in the backseat smoking his cigar and sweating an awful aroma.

The old man told Styles that Rahn served a purpose. Said he was an asshole without ambition. A guy who made the streets fear him had examples of broken bodies lying in alleyways. Styles watched Rahn's reflection in the rearview. The man's teeth danced in the small bits of light that filtered into the car. Between Rahn's lips wedged Styles' last good cigar. He had taken it when Rahn had walked up to Styles' open window. *He put a curved blade to my throat. A knife wicked as the man holding it.*

"He better show, Charlie. That's all I'm saying. He better have the stones."

"Junior was supposed to do it first," Styles said.

Rahn: "That child never follows through."

"He did the woman. The old man said he iced her without any problem."

Rahn handed Styles a cell phone. It showed pictures of Angel dead in a bathtub. "Sully did her, right in front of me."

Styles' brow curled. "I would have never figured the two of you?"

"That was the point," Rahn said. "Now I need another partner."

"You want me to turn against the old man?"

Rahn: "Read the last texts on my phone."

Styles clicked Rahn's cell. It was from Junior: *Old man wants*

Styles done. Says he needs an example for tonight.

Styles sulked as he handed the cell back to Rahn. The fat man took it and laughed. A gurgle of slop sat in Rahn's lungs that he hacked up and spat out the back window. *The old man wants me done. I'm expendable no matter how loyal I am.* He eyed the rearview. *Now I have to deal with the devil's servant to get out of hell alive.*

"What did you have in mind?"

Rahn grinned. After tonight, Styles wanted to forget the stones existed. *Everybody wants that action.* That included Sully. *And look where it got him, Rahn. It got him on a slab in the morgue.* After Rahn left his car, Styles planned to drive back to Brooklyn through the night to talk to Bad Boy and some of the ballers who he had left back in the day. I never had any run-in with them. *If I stay here, the old man has me put down.*

Rahn leaned behind Styles. He brought his curved blade against Styles' throat. The smell from the fat man was awful. Sweat and decay. Styles would have killed anyone attempting to pull what Rahn did. *But Rahn is different.* The man survived anything. *Even the dirtiest cops got blue behind him. You can't ice one of them. You do it and no amount of payoff keeps you safe.* The blue never let payoffs separate the badge. *No one blue lets one of their own go down. Not even in a fair fight.* Styles' cell rang. Rahn eased the blade from his throat. Styles displayed the cell face to Rahn. Frank was calling in.

About time, you mope.

"Be cool, Charlie," Rahn said. "It's your neck or his."

Styles answered his cell. To Frank: "About time you called."

"Sorry," Frank said. "Busy."

"Where do we meet?"

Frank: "I don't know."

"What do you mean you don't know? You got the package and you give it to me, right?"

"I don't know if you want it."

"Don't play philosophical bullshit with me. Where can we meet?" Styles said.

"Ten minutes from now at the bus station."

Styles said: "You leaving, Frank?"

"Once you have your stuff, it doesn't matter what I do."

Frank hung up on his end. Styles put away the cell and eyed Rahn's reflection in the rearview. "We meet him in ten."

Rahn nodded. He sheathed his curved knife. *The old man wants me put down.* Styles started the engine. He pulled away from the curb and went through the downtown district. About twenty blocks before this is over. He caught his own reflection in the rearview. He looked tired. You knew it was time to get out. *The old man wanting you done confirms it. Here's to your retirement, Charlie.* Styles eyed Rahn using his cell.

Rahn to his cell: "How close are you?" The fat man smiled. "Take the girl if he has her. You never know what can happen."

35

"You aren't coming with me?"

They were across the street from the bus station and held each other in the February night. Between his legs was the satchel of diamonds. Christine's eyes watered as Frank Gryzbowsky held her. *Don't do that. You know it tears my heart out seeing you do that.* He tried to act tough. *If they have me done after I make the exchange, it will be okay. But they cannot kill her.* He hugged her tighter. He knew she would not understand. *She wants you, damn it. And you have to push her away for her own good.*

"I'm cursed, Chris," Frank said. "People around me get hurt."

Christine stared at him. "You don't love me, do you?"

"Don't say that," Frank said. "You know it's not true. Don't even think that."

"Then what should I think?"

"That we have to embrace the suck."

Christine: "What the hell does that mean?"

"Gamble told me that," he said. "It fits for tonight."

"You're listening to him now?"

"One of the few people with honor I know in this world."

"What are you saying?"

Frank rubbed her cheek. "I'm no good to you."

You could stand there and explain but she won't listen. You're an old drunk and she wants you. He regretted the amount of time they had spent apart, even during those times they had been together. *You drank your time away with her.* He kissed her forehead. *It took me until tonight to realize how much I love her.* Frank shook off the feelings as much as he could.

"Last bus is in five," Frank said. "Get on it."

Christine said, "I love you."

"But that isn't enough," Frank said.

She shook her head. "What's the point of living if you never get what you want?"

He kissed her. It lasted minutes while he held her and refused to let go. *But you have to, don't you? Otherwise she is going to end up dead because of you.* He savored the normalcy of their embrace. *I always kissed figuring there would be one to follow. But now...* He wondered if he would ever touch her again. They separated both crying.

"You don't think there is any way out of this mess, do you?"

Frank said, "I don't see one. I lose everything no matter what."

She pulled out a card from her bra. "He owes me a favor."

Frank read the card: Detective Tom Hammond, Spokane Major Crimes Division. "He's a cop."

"Yeah, he's blue," Christine said. "You should trust him."

Frank pocketed the card. *I can toss it later.* He fought tears and directed her to the terminal. "You're going to miss your bus."

Christine moved from him and walked across the street without looking back. *She wants to hate me, but can't.* His eyes followed her as she entered the bus station terminal wearing his torn sport jacket with three hundred in real paper. *She loves me. Neither of us has to stay. We can find a car and drive until the sun rises in front of us. No looking back to this place without a soul. No matter what, it will work.* He shook his head. *God, Frank, you're an asshole sometimes.*

He grabbed the satchel and moved across the empty street. He went into a run as he crossed the parking lot toward the entrance. *If we had a car, we could leave this place behind.* Frank edged the entrance as a Lexus pulled up into the lot. The inside of the bus plaza was devoid of people except a security guard listening to his iPod and a young guy texting on his cell phone. A bus was idling at the far end. *We can do this together.* The bus door closed and moved on. He started to run, then saw Christine standing by the bathroom entrance. She smiled at him as he went to get on. The embrace was special. *One of those you talk about during your fiftieth together.*

"I don't listen well," she said.

Frank said, "Good thing."

They shared a smile until Frank stiffened. He felt a blade run up against his throat. The smell of a cigar and the stench of sweat greeted his nose. "Yeah, it's a good thing."

Frank turned and saw his attacker was a corpulent man in a fedora and trench coat. From his side, he saw the young man who had been in the terminal texting walk up to them. The man grabbed the satchel from Frank. "You ain't no badass, pal."

Christine tightened. "You have what you want. Let us go."

The fat man said, "I decide what goes down and when." To the young man: "Take her back with you to the old man, Junior. I want to have fun with her later."

"Let's do them now and get it over with, Rahn," Junior said. "I ain't got time for no creepy shit."

"Run along, Junior. Before I get angry, do something you regret." Junior: "What about the stones?"

"Do you want to test me, Junior? Is that what you want to do?"

Junior grabbed Christine's arm. He moved her away from the bathroom. Rahn pushed Frank into the bathroom. The sink mirrors revealed Rahn puffed at a cigar buoyed in the corner of his mouth. His brown suspenders held up a frontal mass behind a yellow-stained striped dress shirt untucked from his pants. Frank slowed as he was moved to the middle of the bathroom. Dripping water from rusted pipes greeted them.

"Careful," Rahn said. "I can rip your guts out with one stroke."

Frank eyed the reflection of Rahn's belt. It held his badge. "I thought you knew right from wrong."

"I decide what is right in this town," Rahn said.

Frank's eyes measured the blade's distance from his neck. *It is an inch or two from you. It is not enough to move against.* Frank closed his lids. *This is it, right? All she wrote on Frank Gryzbowsky?* He wanted for death. Then, he heard a toilet flush. The sound broke through the silence of the bathroom. Frank opened his lids, confused. Both Rahn and Frank watched as a woman exited a stall. She had her IPod cranked with her ear buds in. The woman went to the sink and washed her hands. She rocked to the music. The woman glanced in the bathroom mirror as she went for a paper towel. She saw the reflection of Rahn holding his blade on Frank and froze as they watched her.

Frank noticed the blade edge away from his neck as Rahn drew out a revolver. Rahn blasted the bystander in the back. Frank dropped under Rahn, who sliced the knife through empty space. Rahn screamed as Frank stood. Rahn brought the revolver to fire. Frank gripped his hands together and hammered at the fat man's chin. The attack jolted Rahn. He released the revolver, which flew into a urinal. Rahn's fedora flew off his head and Frank stomped it.

Rahn's eyes ignited as he swung the blade across Frank's chest. It sliced apart Frank's dress shirt and missed flesh. Frank kicked Rahn in the knee, which sent him into the porcelain sinks. Rahn grappled the sink for support during his fall but his weight ripped it off of the wall as he crashed. His curved knife skittered away on the floor as it left his grip. Streams of water blew out of the broken sink pipe, soaking them. Rahn stood, displaying a broken nose hanging by cartilage.

He showed a shattered grin and laughed. Rahn took his nose and set it back in place. The sound turned Frank's stomach. Rahn unleashed a primal scream and pounded his chest with his fists, then charged at Frank. Rahn's arms wrapped Frank's torso. He picked him up off his feet and pushed him backward into the bathroom stalls. The fat man barreled through two walls until he slammed Frank into the ground taking the air out of Frank's lungs.

Rahn sat on top of Frank and threw fists into his chest. Frank attempted to fend off the attack, but Rahn grabbed his left hand and bit hard on the webbing. Frank's right hand caught Rahn's face. His fingers slid toward Rahn's eyes and gouged them. The fat man screamed as the pain grew unbearable. The cop rolled off of Frank. He coughed as he moved to his feet. His left hand was bleeding and his back was sore. Frank stood frozen as his eyes caught Styles Remington standing at the bathroom entrance. He was aiming Rahn's revolver at Frank. Rahn laughed behind him as he stumbled to his knees.

"You don't understand, Gryzbowsky," Rahn said. "The bad guy wins here."

Styles moved the aim of the barrel at Rahn. He squeezed off three rounds that ended Rahn. Frank watched as the fat man landed on his side. He looked at Styles, who shrugged.

"I'm tired of being the bad guy," Styles said. "Come with me if you want her back."

Five years ago, the city was consumed with Tim

Kane. News cycles focused on a non-politician who

made his crime a celebrity. During his short life,

Kane was a top underground methamphetamine

cooker with a specialty of peanut butter crank. He revamped his

meth culinary skills by exchanging fifty percent of his take to the

Gypsy Knights in exchange for 500 crates of non-rechargeable cell

batteries they had stolen during a warehouse heist. Kane broke into a

hotel boiler room in Central District to serve as his meth kitchen. He

extracted metallic lithium and mixed in alkali metal, pouring liquid

anhydrous ammonia over a propane heater for six hours.

The explosive boil caused a blast through the hotel's heating

system. It blew through the center of the hotel, melted windows and

tossed the front doors across the street where they lopped the head

off of a Chester A. Arthur statue two blocks away. Forty-five guests,

hotel staff and pedestrians, including three small children, died in

the blast. Prior to the events of Ash Wednesday, Kane's stupidity had

been the last time the city coroner had implemented a mass fatality

plan to oversee the abundant amount of bodies ready for medical

examination.

Detective Tom Hammond remembered Kane. He had busted the

kid for meth cooking twice. Tried to give him a break once and got

fed up the second time. Kane had attended the high school that the coroner was using to implement the mass fatality plan. The place carried a gothic façade of gray stone, which welcomed Dereks and Tom as they entered. *It feels as if the place wants to devour us.*

"I went to school here," Dereks said.

"Good school?"

Dereks said, "I don't really remember."

They headed through the hall with red lockers dressing the walls. Their heels tapped in unison on the hard linoleum to the gymnasium. Tom said, "You miss it?"

"No, it was high school."

"I thought all jocks missed high school."

Dereks: "I wasn't a jock. I played in the band." Tom's cell vibrated. He glanced at it and kept walking. "She's calling you again?"

"Tenth time tonight," Tom said.

"Why don't you tell her off?"

"Then I wind up spending more money with my lawyer because she wants to fight over shit I had before she was around."

"So, you're going to let it go to your voicemail?"

Tom grinned. "Sure, because I know that pisses her off the most."

Blue tarps covered the gymnasium floor. Gurneys were littered complete with a cadaver. *It's a goddamn M*A*S*H unit.* Tom's eyes went to eight gurneys huddled together. Each held a dog carcass attended by a medical examiner. One broke apart a dead animal's rib cage with bolt cutters. They were searching for the remains to Steve Powers' crew. *Did you find what you wanted, Steve? Those dogs were your perfect match.* Tom headed to the gurneys and watched an M.E. separate a pit bull's torso. The snap of bone and muscle made him sick.

"I heard they had armor on."

"Kevlar," the M.E. said. He wiped his forehead with his arm. "Some asshole sewed it under their coats. I broke two saw blades so I'm back to basics."

His arm went deep into the dog's cavity. The squish of fluids churned as he searched inside. Various contents were brought out and deposited in the metal bowl next to the gurney. An intern washed blood and bile away. The M.E. reached in and brought out a small metal pendant necklace that he displayed. It shined clean in the light.

"St. Benedict," the M.E. said. "It didn't protect this cop from harm."

"Neither did the body armor," Tom said.

He left the M.E. and moved to the bodies of Powers' crew. *Which one of you lost the necklace?* The bowl had contained severed fingers. We're trying to put people back together again. Tom's eyes went to the department's resident M.E., Morty Van Slade. The guy was five-nine, forty-five and wore Hawaiian shirts under his apron.

He was bald with pockmarks and held a sub sandwich in cling wrap in his apron. Tom nodded at Van Slade.

"What the hell, Hammond?"

Tom smiled. "Reminds me of Kane, don't you think?"

"I thought so too," Van Slade said. "I smelled like a 9-volt for a month after that."

Van Slade put on a latex glove and examined a Tactical corpse. "Dogs and sharks are perfect killing machines, aren't they?"

"What else you got?"

Van Slade shook his head. "Aside from the one who did a Peter Pan outside that club? I got three Krispy Kremes from a chop shop fire up north. Two flattened Lincolns were out of the same place but didn't get burned," Van Slade said. He gestured to the Tactical team corpses. "And we got some bad blue here."

Tom stood by as Van Slade examined the body. The corpse had torn Kevlar cut in half next to the gurney. The dogs had ripped the man's face to shreds. His nose erased. His eyes chewed out. His right cheek obliterated, revealing a ravaged tongue. Tom glanced at Van Slade who was eating his sub sandwich overlooking the body. Van Slade offered Tom a bite but was waved off. With his free hand, the M.E. pointed out wounds to Tom.

"He must have pissed off the dogs. We found him in five of their stomachs," Van Slade said. "One of his pals has no arms. They chewed them off at the wrist and elbow."

Tom pointed to another corpse. "What about him?"

"Humpty Dumpty got it in the abdomen," Van Slade said. "We still got two more dogs to empty."

Dereks moved to Tom and gestured for him to follow. "You're going to want to see this."

They went to the other side of the gym. Dereks walked fast with Tom keeping pace. A sour smell hung in the air. It was different from death. Tom recognized the odor then saw Detective Dan Rahn's body lying on a gurney. Tom held his arm across his face to guard against the unbearable stench. His eyes watered.

"Brought him in five minutes ago," Dereks said. "Shot three times. That knife he's not supposed to carry didn't help him."

"He was on duty?"

Dereks coughed several times. Then he said, "No. But he gets honor guard the same."

Tom and Dereks left the area to breathe. The smell dissipated. Tom noticed interns delivering two body bags on gurneys. He headed back to Van Slade. The M.E. was directing the interns where to put them.

"This shit is still going down?"

Van Slade shook his head. "These two are from county. Some trucker found them trying to do a layout over on highway twenty-seven."

No. Tom stiffened as his eyes went to the bags. He felt something wrong. *It can't be.* With everything happening tonight, he had not called Hanaran. He moved to a body bag and unzipped it. Angel's corpse was lying there. Tom closed his lids. *Sorry, kid. I thought I could protect you. I failed.* Van Slade went behind Tom.

"Did you know her?"

"No," Tom said. His eyes went to the other bag. Hanaran would be in there. *I can't face him. Not tonight. I failed him and look at the result.* He and Angel will be buried in pine boxes while Dan Rahn gets an honor guard. Tom moved from Angel as Van Slade zipped her back up. He exited the gymnasium and headed to his car. *I don't know where I am going but far from here. Everything I've been taught to believe in is a lie.*

Sully Brooks could not have pulled this off alone. He would have needed help. Irish Pete and that lackey Styles Remington. Tom sat behind the wheel of his sedan and felt his ankle. The clean revolver sat there in its holster. *You've got to do something for Hanaran and Angel. They didn't deserve what they got.* Tom slammed the sedan's door and turned over the engine. He headed west toward Irish Pete's house, ready to ensure that no one could break the rules again.

Irish Pete McGrath had run the city networks for twenty-two years. In that time, he had killed several goons, cops and witnesses. But in that time, he never took a civilian hostage. It was regarded as too messy. *Some idiot three-to-fiver gets bumped and goes missing, no one cares. If a nine-to-five working stiff bleeds out, it makes the newspaper. People care about civilians. There is no class to taking a hostage.* Irish Pete considered himself a human resources wizard who could get guys together to pull jobs. *Let them worry about doing time if they get caught. Hostages were different. It never works out if you let them live because they can identify you later.*

His blood pressure rose when Junior Reed had returned to his house with a hostage that he muscled onto Pete's couch. *I was coming out of the shower, wondering where he had gone off. And he comes back with some old broad. He says this one can get your diamonds back.* Pete eyed the broad who was in her forties. *Time's been a favor to her though. Her hair is nice.* She sat quiet and let the big boys do their thing. Pete sat at his desk, wondering what to do next.

Junior had acted frazzled and nervous when returning to Pete's house. *He isn't himself as if he is unsure of his next move.* Pete glanced at Junior's cell, left on his desk. *He didn't take it to the john with him.* The kid took the thing everywhere with him. It vibrated on the desk surface. Junior dumped it on the table, pushed the woman to the couch and mumbled to himself about things as he left. The cell *buzzed*. Pete ignored it as his eyes crawled up the woman's legs. *I would take her out on the town, show her a good time.* He shook his head. *I'm too old and go to bed by eight. Then I wake up at three to relieve myself.* Pete checked his watch. It was two in the morning. *I haven't been up this late in years.*

Pete stood. Cool air touched his damp skin. He wore a red smoking robe over a pair of blue pajamas. A towel hung around his neck that he used to wipe at his face a few more times then got the wet out of his hair. It had taken him an hour of scrubbing to clean out all of Gloria's gore. *I had to go in every corner of my body to get that stuff off of me.* The cell vibrations caught his attention as it moved on Pete's desk. It rested on the edge. He hated kids and their damn phones. Junior sat here acting as if he were listening while typing on the phone. *He was sending off messages to someone else while he should be dealing with me.* Pete imagined that Junior never caught the information he should. *I am trying to explain important stuff and instead I get a Ritalin child across from me.*

Pete saw the cell vibrate again with a fresh text message. The phone was about to drop off the desk. He saved the cell before it crashed to the floor. *Phone costs more than Junior makes in a week.* Pete returned the phone to the desktop and glanced on the screen.

His touch opened the cell's text reader. Pete had no interest in the message. Until he saw the word "score" and decided to investigate. Pete put on his reading glasses and held up the phone.

The first text was from Freeway: *Where is the score?* Irish Pete stopped and wondered if it was his fence in the Garland District. Next message from Freeway: *You said this was easy.* Next message: *Old man better not find out.* Next message from D Rahn: *Waiting with Styles for man to call in.* Next message from Gamble: *Man has bag with honor. Sorry.* Pete clicked on the sent texts. One from Junior to Baron G: *The old man can't shoot. His trophies are fakes.*

Pete heard the toilet flush. He returned Junior's cell to the desk. The reading glasses were tucked into his pocket. *Junior's been double-crossing you this entire time. He worked your fence to get the stones.* Pete eyed the arrangement of handguns on his desktop. *Maybe it's time you showed him what you do to double-crossing thieves.*

"So, what's the plan, boss?"

Junior entered calm as he walked to his chair. *He shows respect to worm his way out of the situation. He thinks the hostage gets him the diamonds back and no one knows he tried to screw me.* Pete's eyes went to the woman. She stayed in her seat, scared. *This will be over soon, I promise.* Pete gestured for Junior to sit in the chair. *Sit, Junior. We got things to talk about.*

"I thought this was your plan," Pete said. "This is your hostage."

Junior's face offered confusion as he sat. "But it is your score."

"I never ordered hostages. Now there's a witness," Pete said. He saw Junior did not get it. *He doesn't have to. He's a punk. They never see all of the angles. Maybe I will show him target practice out back and aim at his chest.* He stared at Junior. Pete started to lose the last bit of respect for Junior as he saw the kid was about to pout. Pete let his right hand move over the oak desktop. His fingers brushed past the handle of the Desert Eagle.

"What should we do?"

"You tell me," Pete said. "You have the problem. The cops will come and throw you in the back of a car. You're an independent contractor. You got no connections."

"I took her to get the stones."

Pete nodded and noted Junior had failed to bring his sawed-off shotgun. *He doubts you have the willingness to kill. The kid doesn't know the real you.* When he was 15, Pete did a guy for no reason. He wanted to prove himself to the locals. *I walked up into the Otis Bar in downtown and popped him with a .45 while he was sipping a shot of Patron.* Pete got two years juvie and did another guy two months after he got released for $5,000. *I did him in a construction site. Beat him until the guy laid down in wet concrete until he suffocated.* Pete moved west to set-up his own thing. *That's why I have the edge, because everyone else out here is amateur hour.*

"You think that works?" Pete said.

"It has to."

"Why does it have to?"

"What else we gonna do?" Junior said.

Pete laughed. *The kid doesn't know what's coming. You still got that edge, don't you? Junior thinks everything is okay because you keep talking like a crazy old man.* He watched Junior yawn and stretch his arms. Pete's eyes fell to the Desert Eagle, then to the German Luger next to it. *I haven't fired that one in days. Maybe I should test it tonight. Make sure it's in top-notch condition.*

"Been a strange night," Pete said.

"Damn straight."

Pete turned to the woman. "What do you think?"

"What do I think?" she said. "I think you should let me walk."

Pete nodded. "I agree."

His eyes went to the elephant rifle laid across his desk. *It attempted to do its job tonight.* Pete selected the rifle and examined the barrel. *Reminds me of people's stories where the deeper you look the easier it is to detect the faults.* The muzzle had a crack in the right barrel that caused both shots to miss Gloria. *Junior thinks I missed because I cannot shoot. Maybe I need to show him how true my aim is.* Pete shook his head at the rifle. *It's only good as a mantle piece now.*

"You got my reward?"

Pete saw the kid cocky and brash. "What reward?"

Junior: "I found the guy holding your stones. I brought you his girl. What more do you want?"

How about the truth, kid?

"Here's your reward, kid," Pete said. He swung the rifle around and aimed it at Junior's chest. The kid's eyes blanked. *You aren't so cocky now, huh?* He squeezed the trigger as the kid's eyes shut tight as if expecting to have his life ended. The hammer snapped down with an empty click. Pete watched Junior as the kid's eyes remained shut. *He thinks he knows it all but learned something tonight.* Pete glanced at the woman. *She is tougher than Junior and has seen it all.* Junior opened his lids unsure what to expect. Pete lowered the rifle and leaned it next to the desk.

"It's unloaded," Pete said. "It can't be shot anymore."

Junior shook his head, expelled exhausted breath, forcing a smile. "You're a strange cat, Pete."

"You have got to learn about people to survive in this world."

"So what do I learn about you?" Junior said. "That you don't pay your bills?"

No, you learn not to double-cross me. Pete's eyes sank to the .60 caliber handgun on the far right of the desktop. His right hand touched the desk surface with fingers touching the gun's handle.

"When I give my word, I follow through."

"Then do it," Junior said. "Hold up your end and give me what's coming to me."

"Sure," Pete said. He yanked the .60 caliber off the desk and blasted Junior three times in the chest. There was no time for Junior to react. Flashes erupted from the barrel as each round tore through the kid and chewed out the back of the chair. Huge fabric fluff chunks floated onto the hardwood floor behind the chair. Junior slumped in his chair, dead. *I think you got the message, didn't you?* Pete stood there and soaked in the moment as the light left the kid's eyes. The fumes from the smoking gun itched Pete's nose as he focused on the woman. She was cowering on the couch, her hands over her eyes. *Now, what do we do with you?*

38

Christine Gryzbowsky sat in silence on the couch. *He's going to kill me next.* Her eyes filled with tears. She ducked her head into her arms, closed her lids and waited for him to pull the trigger. *He shot his partner as if it were nothing. Why should I deserve better treatment?* She held her breath. Flames crackled and hissed as fire ate another log in the fireplace. The house was cold even with the fire going as if it could not be warmed. She waited for the *click* of the trigger from Pete's gun.

"You want something to drink?"

She opened her lids. Pete was closer. He was pouring himself a drink from a small liquor table next to the fireplace. He made a second glass and held it out for a few seconds, then nudged it toward her. Christine took it and drained the booze in three seconds flat. The liquor burned as it went down. Christine snorted through her nose to keep from coughing. She glanced at Junior's body. Blood pooled underneath him. A giant gouge had been ripped out of his chest.

"Now, that's good stuff," Pete said.

He tossed the glass into the fireplace. The alcohol ignited and roared out a devil's bellow as the fire raged. Pete danced madness in his steps and let his robe's sleeves slack off his arms. Christine's eyes caught the illuminated trophy faces of slaughtered animals that stared back at her. Pete carried on with his lunacy. *The things he killed appear ready to attack us.* She tried to put the image out of her mind. Junior's body had little plumes of smoke running out of the gaping holes. His eyes flickered a reflection of the firelight. It remained the only living thing in his pupils. *Another prize for Pete who shows what he kills.*

"You can go home now," Pete said. "It's over."

Christine turned to Pete, surprised. *It's a trick. He wants me to try to leave so he can gun me down.* She watched the old man who appeared tired. *No, he wants to stop fighting. It's over.* Pete halted his dance and lowered his head. He went to his desk and sat behind it in an exhaustive heap. Christine noted he shook his head to ward off the grogginess of the night. The old man grabbed a pair of keys from his desk and tossed them onto the couch next to her.

"Take my car."

Her eyes caught the surveillance monitors on the wall behind him. Each camera covered the estate. A Lexus sedan went through the entrance and pulled through the drive. *Pete's got visitors.* She looked at the old man. He was rubbing his temples with his hands, exhausted. *Hurry, before he changes his mind.* She returned to the monitors. The sedan moved around the demolished car on top of the fountain remains in the middle of the drive.

"What happens now?" Christine said.

"You go home," Pete said. "That's about it."

"That's it?"

She saw Frank on the monitors. He exited the Lexus. *He came for me.* Frank tackled the steps, carrying a satchel. Pete was shaking his head, pointing at Junior and laughing. The cameras caught Frank opening the front door. The sedan's driver stayed in the car and kept it idling. *Frank's on the mission alone.*

"Forget tonight ever happened," Pete said to her.

"Can't do that, Pete," Frank said to him.

Both Christine and Pete paid attention to the foyer. Frank stood in front of a looming stuffed grizzly bear. *He looks like shit.* She was certain Pete thought the same thing. Frank stood shambled. His dress shirt was torn across the front. He hacked up a cough and spat it on the floor. Frank looked at Pete with a bandage hanging off his left brow. His face was pale, riddled with bruises and cuts. His pants soiled, destroyed from a night of bloodlust.

"Who are you?" Pete said.

"Tuttle sent me."

Frank held the satchel for display. Pete smiled and gestured for Frank to enter. He grunted as he walked, holding his side with his arm as if his entire rib cage were about to collapse. Pete rose as Frank approached as if welcoming a head of state. Frank made his way to the desk. He looked at Junior's body and grabbed the dead man's shoulder. He pushed Junior and let the corpse crash to the floor. Frank eyed Pete, then sat down in the damaged chair.

"You'll ruin your suit," Pete said.

"It's on loan," Frank said. To Christine: "You okay?"

"Define okay."

"God, that's what I love about you."

Frank gave her that smile. The one that she knew was for her alone. *That one that means he is cocky and a know it all. That grin.* She did not feel uneasy about seeing it as she had in the past. *He has this one under control. Pete doesn't even know it.* Frank and Pete stared at each other. The old man appeared to be at a loss for words. Frank tossed the satchel over the desk. Pete caught and opened the lid. His eyes lit up from the contents.

"Glad someone keeps their end of the deal," Pete said.

Pete dug into the satchel. He brought up his hand. Diamonds filtered through his fingers. Pete giggled and dropped the diamonds back into the bag. He looked at Frank who sat there with a frown on his face. Pete pointed at him, excited.

"You want something to drink?"

Frank said, "I don't do that anymore."

"Sure, you do," Pete said. "This is America. We do everything even when we say we don't."

"Then maybe I'm a socialist."

"You were at *The Sides*? No way in hell you're anything but a

Capitalist coming out of *The Sides*."

Frank: "You have an interesting point."

Pete moved a foot from the surveillance monitors and slapped the wall. A section popped out revealing a safe. A combination was performed while Pete hummed some random tune. Christine's eyes went to Frank. *He's not buying any of it. He knows what the old man is about.* Pete opened the safe and reached inside. He pulled out a stack of money, looked at it and tossed it into Frank's lap. Frank picked up the stack and examined it. He looked at Pete.

"I get street bills?" Frank said. "Don't you have something else for me?"

Pete appeared confused. "It's regular money. That's how my business operates."

"That's not what I mean."

Pete tossed another stack from the safe at Frank. It fell to the floor next to him. "That's double what you were supposed to get."

"You don't get it."

Frank stood and threw the stacks of money at Pete. They hit his chest. The old man was insulted and upset. Pete eyed the guns on his desk, but Frank pulled out a revolver. Pete held up both arms, dropping the satchel. The lid opened as it hit the floor, spilling out hundreds of gleaming stones. Some of the diamonds skittered across the floor and hit Christine's shoes. She glanced at the surveillance monitors, seeing a cheap looking sedan parked behind the Lexus. *Who else is coming to the party?* Her focus returned to Frank and Pete.

"You want the diamonds, they are yours."

Frank said, "No, I want my reward."

"I paid you."

"Styles let me in on my real reward," Frank said. "Where you shoot and dump me in Highland Quarry for my troubles."

"I don't know anything about that," Pete said.

Frank's response was to shoot six shots. Three bullets destroyed the surveillance monitors. Two burrowed into the back wall. And one went through Pete's left shoulder. The old man fell off his feet. He toppled a table full of liquor bottles. They smashed to the floor next to him. The table end crashed against Pete's head, knocking him out. Blood and high proof alcohol pooled underneath the body on the floor. Frank turned to Christine, winking.

"Like I said before Frank, you know how to make an entrance," Christine said. "And you are a lousy shot."

39 Detective Tom Hammond eased his sedan into the circle drive. He eyed the crushed fountain in the center with a car toppling it. Water, concrete and mess were everywhere. Water had been shut off underneath. *What in the hell happened here?* He had parked behind a Lexus. He noticed the reflection of Styles Remington in the door mirror. *He helped kill Angel and Hanaran. If I take him in, he walks out of court laughing at me for believing in the system.* Tom closed his lids. He attempted to pray but found no solace. *No, he doesn't get out of this. No one gets away without paying for what they have done.*

Tom smacked his hand against the glove box. The lid opened. He caught Styles' switchblade as it tumbled out. Tom pulled out a latex glove and put it on. *This is how you enforce the rules.* Tom eyed the switchblade and pressed the button. The blade *hissed* out. He spied through the windshield at Styles adjusting the Lexus' rearview mirror. *Trying to see who is back here in the car. He is wondering if it is another goon fresh off of killing Angel and Hanaran.* Tom pressed the button. The blade *hissed* back into the handle.

He exited the sedan. *Come on, you can do this. No one can trace it back to you. So do it already. Enforce the rules.* Tom slipped his right hand behind him as he edged the Lexus. His steps went silent on the drive as he noted the Lexus' door window was down. Styles had his left arm out the open window and eyed Tom approaching. *He is so certain of who he is, figuring I can't touch him. Because I am the law and between the two of us, he thinks I have to follow the rules.* Tom pressed the button and heard the hiss of the blade extend. Styles smirked at him, with eyes glinting in the cold moonlight. *He's about to tell me how stupid I am for believing in the rules.*

"Well, if it isn't Detective Tommy Boy…"

Styles never finished his sentence. Tom grabbed him and swung the blade into his neck. It sunk in, hot and deep. Styles' eyes widened as blood poured out. Tom released the switchblade and stood back as Styles rested his head against the door. *That is what happens when you break the rules.* He watched Styles for a moment. *I don't feel remorse or guilt. He deserved worse for what they did to Angel and Hanaran.*

Six successive gunshots erupted from inside the house. The gunfire lit up the inside of the house, catching Tom's attention. He moved to the front door and noted the white columns were covered in bullet holes. Someone blasted this place with a shotgun. Small drops of blood led up the steps. Tom eyed a sawed-off shotgun in the bushes next to the porch. He drew out his sidearm, entering the house. He almost fired on a looming stuffed Grizzly that greeted him in the foyer. Tom braced himself and headed into the living room.

The room was lit by firelight. Two people stood near him,

embracing. He recognized the woman. He remembered interviewing her trying to find Angel. *She called me that night and a lot of good that did for Angel.* The man fit the description at The Blacklight. They fingered him as the driver who ran Sully Brooks over with his car. Tom's eyes ventured the room. He noticed twin orangutans stuffed and mounted. *Man, Irish Pete does some hunting.* He noted the electric sparks snapping from the broken monitors on the back wall. Then he saw the body lying in front of a large desk.

"Are you Hammond?"

Tom nodded. He tried to recall the woman's name. Karen? Kelly... "It's Christine, right?"

"That's the story of Frank's life," Christine said.

"Hey, Styles could barely find it," Frank said. To Tom: "Better late than never, huh?"

Tom's eyes went from the slumped body to another lying near the fireplace. It was Irish Pete. The old man was covered in blood. A large table was smashed around him. Glass shards and unbroken vodka bottles were scattered across the floor. Tom's eyes went to the satchel lying open on its side. He stepped closer and winced at the smell of high proof liquor mixed with the odor of fresh blood. On his haunches, Tom felt Irish Pete's neck. The old man's pulse was faint. Tom heard Frank and Christine talk to each other in the background.

"You and I have gotta sit down and do this thing right. No more of what we've been doing," Frank said.

"It's about time you said that," Christine said.

"You have any ties here?"

"When do we leave?"

Frank: "Tonight?"

"You have a destination?"

"Let's go anywhere but here."

Tom lifted Irish Pete's robe. He whistled at the bullet shot to the shoulder. The old man's eyes shut tight. *He's fading fast.* Tom eyed the satchel next to him. Objects glittered and shined in the firelight. He extracted it from the mess of liquid. Tom rubbed off the waste with his fingers. *I'm holding an actual diamond. It weighted nothing but was worth everything.* He gathered the surrounding diamonds, stuffing them in the satchel. *There are enough here to forget about my life. The bills go away. The ex-wife is a distant memory. And I will never eat another microwave dinner again.*

Tom stopped for a second. He looked back at Frank and Christine who were kissing each other, not paying attention. *I've got witnesses who could rat me out for taking the bag. I can't let them leave.* Not with Styles lying dead outside. Tom's eyes dropped to his right ankle. He noted the bulge sticking out underneath his sock and trousers. The clean revolver he had for emergencies. *This is one, isn't it? Get out of your crummy life once and for all? No one's going to miss what some crook had on him.*

"You need anything else from us?"

"A few questions," Tom said. He felt them watching him.

Frank: "Can we go?"

"I need some answers."

"I am out of those," Frank said.

"Stop being difficult," Tom said. He pulled out the clean revolver from his ankle holster. Tom rose and aimed the barrel at Christine. "I hate it when people are so difficult."

Frank and Christine were not paying attention to him. They were mired in each other's eyes. They nuzzled, affectionate. *But they did it while destroying the city. They have killed people and made sure that little Tyler Baxter's dad is never coming home. Why should they get to walk?* Tom's eyes dropped to the satchel soaking in the mess of blood and booze. *Why should I play by the rules? It has done me little good so far.*

"Where would we go?" Christine said, looking into Frank's eyes.

Frank to Christine: "Anywhere we want."

"Even prison," Tom said to both.

They turned, both shocked to see his clean revolver facing them. *They thought they could break the rules and walk away same as Styles did. They would have taken the diamonds and exited the front door and lived the good life. What makes them so special? What makes them able to break rules I have to play by?* Tom stopped himself and smiled. *No, I'm not supposed to play by the rules. I'm supposed to enforce them.* Tom pulled back the revolver's hammer with his thumb. The gun's chamber *clicked* as it turned into place.

"Let us go," Frank said.

"You're a cop-killer, Frank. Detective Rahn was shit, but he was blue. No one gets away with killing blue," Tom said.

"I didn't kill him."

"You think people care what you have to say?" Tom said. "Maybe it's the truth, but I got a rent-a-cop at the station who fingers you as one of the people leaving the scene. Blue stands up for its own."

"Some principle you have there."

Tom said," We have crosses to bare. Everyone does. Turn around, on your knees, and let's get this over with."

Frank and Christine kissed. There was something lasting about the exchange. *I admire their desperation.* They separated, turned their backs to him, and went down on their knees. Both put their hands on back of their heads and straightened as if ready to die. Tom listened to the crackling sounds of the fire burn away in the fireplace as the light danced off the living room walls. Tom went to Christine and frisked her with his free hand. *She's an accessory to murder. That's justification for what I'm going to do to her.*

He frisked Frank slower than Christine. He felt a bulge in Frank's pants. He nudged his clean revolver against Frank's head as he dug deep into the pocket. He latched onto an object and pulled out a rosary. He held it for less than ten seconds before tossing it behind him. *I've put too much faith in those things. That's how I got where I am today.* Tom recalled receiving a black smudge of ash on his forehead during Wednesday morning mass. *Any absolution of my sin is gone now.*

"Let her go, Hammond."

Tom leaned to Frank and talked in his ear. "No, she stays. You brought this on her, Frank."

A shadow overcame them. Tom turned his head to see Irish Pete standing behind him. The old man hammered a vodka bottle at him. The bottle shattered against his temple. Liquor splashed into his eyes. Tom's vision blurred as the shot crashed him to the floor. Throwing his wrists out, Tom landed on his face and shattered his teeth. His left wrist bent wrong and snapped. His trigger finger squeezed shut and sent a round into the chest of a stuffed Puma.

Irish Pete pounced onto his back. The old man wrapped Frank's rosary around his throat, twisting tight. Tom gasped for air. The clean revolver was released and skittered across the floor. Tom fired elbows behind him at the old man. His eyes went to Frank and Christine as the pair escaped from the house. Tom threw an elbow into Irish Pete's wounded shoulder. The old man screamed as he fell off Tom and landed onto the pool of blood and alcohol, injuring his back. He released the rosary, which flew into the fireplace.

Tom choked as air returned. Shots of pain came from his left wrist. His temple dripped blood that covered his vision. Tom spat out fragments of porcelain while holding his throat. His eyes stung from vodka burn. Life came quick to him. Tom focused on the old man who fumbled in the wet tissue and liquor, unable to rise. Tom's eyes went to his clean revolver a few feet from him. He crawled to it and attempted to stand. His equilibrium was off. He squeezed the trigger, firing a round into the wall. Tom squinted to hone his aim at the old man. He stopped half a foot from Irish Pete with his revolver pointed at the old man's chest. Irish Pete held a 180 proof bottle of vodka with the top broken off.

"That all you got, old man?" Tom said.

The old man winked. He tossed the vodka back into the roaring fireplace. The bottle connected with the fire. The fireplace spat out a fireball that blew a massive blanket of heat around Tom. His vodka soaked clothes ignited. The heat's intensity separated Tom's skin. His ears picked up the sound of the old man laughing below him as Tom burned. The detective smiled as his legs fell out from under him. Irish Pete's expression changed as Tom dropped onto the old man. The pool of blood and booze erupted into a fountain of flame. The fire consumed the house as Tom and Irish Pete burned to death in the flames.

"Can't wait to see what happens next."

Christine turned to Frank. "Shut up, Frank."

They sat in Irish Pete's ride watching the house

40

consumed by flames. The sky had gone from dark to

light blue. Morning would be coming. Christine noted the car's clock

radio read four. In Frank's hands, a golden flask he had retrieved

from Styles' car. Nothing was left of the house except simmering ash

and a smoldering cloud of black that tumbled into the night air. Her

eyes caught a small amount of snow starting to fall.

She turned over the engine and pulled around the circle drive.

"Where do we go now, Frank?"

"Garland District," Frank said. "We have a fence named Freeway I

was told to visit."

Frank took the flask and opened the lid. Christine gave him a

curious look. "Thought you gave that up?"

"Sugar dealing at The Sides taught me something," Frank said. He

shook the flask. Fifty small diamonds dropped into his hand. They

sparkled in the light. He winked, "It taught me to look at the big

picture."

Also written by Troy Kirby:
LIQUID COURAGE
www.chaoswords.com
6 x 9
374 pages

**Library of Congress
Control Number: 2017910899**

**ISBN 0-9835184-1-6
ISBN 978-0-9835184-1-9**

**Available in paperbook and ebook/
Kindle Format on Amazon**

GAINING AN EDGE IS WORTH THE RISK…

Dean hates losing more than winning. He is willing to what it takes to not lose anymore. Including use a new underground human growth hormone called "Fireball" hitting the gyms. Anything to avoid second place at body building competitions or in his father's love.

Dean's body is changing. So is his mind.

As the supply runs low, his ex-con buddies are pushing Dean to embrace his criminal side. That includes serving as pit fighters to a Russian syndicate and drawing the ire of a madman who wants "Fireball" all to himself.

What Dean's friends haven't told him yet is that they are eying a massive payoff as a final solution. A tribal casino sitting on the edge of town. Run by a paranoid general manager who employs a mean streak security detail eager to face a challenge.

Dean and his friends are ready to play the odds to feed a nasty "Fireball" habit, armed to the teeth and ready to take down the biggest score of their lives.

www.ingramcontent.com/pod-product-compliance
Lightning Source LLC
Chambersburg PA
CBHW020227180626
46810CB00006B/2072